TASMANIA

TASMANIA

PAOLO GIORDANO

Translated from the Italian by Antony Shugaar

OTHER PRESS • NEW YORK

Originally published in Italian as *Tasmania* in 2022
by Giulio Einaudi editore s.p.a., Torino
Copyright © 2022 Giulio Einaudi editore
Translation copyright © 2024 Antony Shugaar
Published by special arrangement with Paolo Giordano in
conjunction with his duly appointed agent MalaTesta
Literary Agency and the co-agent 2 Seas Literary Agency.

This book was translated thanks to a grant awarded by the Italian
Ministry of Foreign Affairs and International Cooperation.

Production editor: Yvonne E. Cárdenas
Text designer: Jennifer Daddio / Bookmark Design & Media Inc.
This book was set in Minion and Copperplate by
Alpha Design & Composition of Pittsfield, NH

10 9 8 7 6 5 4 3 2 1

Library of Congress Cataloging-in-Publication Data
Names: Giordano, Paolo, 1982- author. | Shugaar, Antony, translator.
Title: Tasmania : a novel / Paolo Giordano ; translated from the Italian
    by Antony Shugaar.
Description: New York : Other Press, 2024.
Identifiers: LCCN 2024003180 (print) | LCCN 2024003181 (ebook) |
    ISBN 9781635425017 (paperback) | ISBN 9781635425024 (ebook)
Subjects: LCSH: Giordano, Paolo, 1982-—Fiction. | LCGFT:
    Autobiographical fiction. | Novels.
Classification: LCC PQ4907.I57 T3713 2024 (print) | LCC PQ4907.I57 (ebook)
    | DDC 853/.92—dc23/eng/20240129
LC record available at https://lccn.loc.gov/2024003180
LC ebook record available at https://lccn.loc.gov/2024003181

Publisher's Note: This is a work of fiction. Names, characters,
places, and incidents either are the product of the author's
imagination or are used fictitiously.

WOULD YOU AGREE TIMES HAVE CHANGED?

—"Clairaudients (Kill or Be Killed)," BRIGHT EYES

PART ONE

IN CASE OF APOCALYPSE

IN NOVEMBER OF 2015, I happened to be in Paris to attend the United Nations conference on the climate emergency. I say that I happened to be there, but not because I hadn't intentionally sought out that situation. Actually, environmental issues had been foremost in my mind and my reading for some time now. Let's say there had been no climate conference in the offing, I'd still have probably come up with some other excuse to get away from home—say an armed conflict, a humanitarian crisis, any preoccupation different from and larger than my own concerns. Perhaps that's the reason some of us fixate on impending disasters, why we have a proclivity for tragedies—a proclivity that we palm off as noble—and those fixations will serve to build the center of this story, I believe: our need, with every step of our lives that proves excessively complicated, to find something even more complicated, something more compelling and menacing in which we can dilute our own personal suffering. So maybe, really, nobility has nothing at all to do with it.

It was a strange time. My wife and I had tried, repeatedly, to have a child, persisting for roughly three years, subjecting ourselves to one medical intervention after another, each more humiliating than the last. Though I should say, to be as accurate as possible, it was primarily she who subjected herself to those interventions, because for me, after a certain point in the process, it was about playing the part of a pained bystander. Gonadotropin hormone injections, in vitro procedures, even three increasingly desperate trips overseas, about which we breathed not a word to a soul: in spite of all our blind determination and the substantial sum of money we poured into the plan, it hadn't worked out. The divine message conveyed by those repeated failures was clear: none of this forms part of your destiny. Since I stubbornly refused to admit it, Lorenza made up her own mind—for me as well. One night, tears already dried or entirely unshed (I'll never know which), she informed me that she was no longer willing to. That's how she put it, with that truncated expression: I'm no longer willing to. I had rolled over onto my side, turning my back to her, and let the rage steadily fill me, rage that swelled in response to a decision that struck me as unjust and one-sided.

At that time, my own little personal catastrophe loomed much larger in my mind than did its planetary counterpart, the steady accumulation of greenhouse gases in the atmosphere, the retreating glaciers and rising sea levels. In order to get out of that uncomfortable situation, I asked the *Corriere della Sera* to arrange accreditation for me at the Paris climate conference, even though the deadline for requesting credentials had already expired. I was forced to beg them, in fact, as if attending that conference were a matter of life or death for me. All I was asking was that they pay for my flight and the articles I'd write there. No need for a hotel, I'd gladly arrange to stay at a friend's place.

GIULIO WAS RENTING a one-bedroom apartment in the Fourteenth Arrondissement, on Rue de la Gaîté. Gaiety Street? I asked as I walked in the door. That doesn't sound much like you.

I know. If I were you, I wouldn't get my hopes up.

Years ago, we'd been roommates in a Turin apartment. Giulio was a university student who lived out of town, whereas I was a privileged young man who just wanted his first experience living on his own, even though my parents' home was just a half-hour bus ride away. After his degree, Giulio—unlike me—continued with physics. He had changed academic affiliations and moved from city to city countless times, though never leaving Europe, because he had an invincible political aversion for the United States. In the meantime, he'd married and divorced, he had fathered a son, and he'd finally fetched up in France, with a research fellowship at the École Polytechnique, where he was studying chaos models as applied to finance.

We ate dinner without bothering to set the table, a couple of bowlfuls of pasta piled high as if we were both still in our twenties, and I told him why I was in Paris, the official reason, anyway. Giulio rummaged through a shelf, looking for a book. Have you read this?

I said I hadn't, letting the edge of the pages ruffle past under my thumb. *Collapse*, I murmured, how perfect.

He has an interesting point of view on extinction. Here, you can borrow it.

The word *extinction* spun through my head briefly, like a label for my own personal destiny. I cleared away the dishes while Giulio quickly brought me up-to-date about Adriano, who had already turned four. I was starting to feel sleepy after that carbohydrate binge, but we'd finished all the wine, so we went downstairs in search of something else to drink.

Outside, Paris was militarized, grim. A few days ago, a group of terrorists had forced their way into a concert hall during an Eagles of Death Metal show and then proceeded to shoot into the packed audience for minutes on end. Other terrorists had attacked several bistros, and two terrorists had blown themselves up outside the Stade de France. The evening it happened, Lorenza and I were having a couple we knew over for dinner. It was Lorenza's mother who had alerted us. The first time, Lorenza had ignored the call, and the second call as well. But her mother's persistence started to seem unsettling, and Lorenza finally answered. Her mother said, "Turn on the TV," nothing more, and text messages started pinging on all our phones. We'd watched the news updates live for more than an hour, silently, and then our friends had left, summoned by the entirely irrational necessity of checking in on their kids at home. Lorenza and I had left the TV on for a long time, the red news chyron streaming by at the bottom of the screen, uninterruptedly, but by now the captions had turned into a loop. The dishes were still on the table, the food cold now, while our horror was slowly joined by something else: a private terror, ours alone, a sense of mourning without any concrete loss that had been weighing on our apartment for days now, and specifically since the night she'd told me she was no longer willing to—and I'd rolled over, facing away from her.

Giulio and I walked for a while, strolling past massage parlors with tinted glass windows, boutiques selling sex toys, and Asian food shops. Then we sat down in a nondescript boîte chosen at random, our chairs turned to face the street, and ordered a couple of beers. He went back to discussing books he'd read: textbooks on digital surveillance, the various Arab Springs, neo-populism. Giulio seemed to read books nonstop. He had a much more complex vision of reality than I did, he was much more politically engaged, and he always had been, for as long as I'd known him. At university, he had coordinated for two years running the political collective of Lecture Hall B1, down in the subbasement, the walls plastered with "No Nukes" posters and a photo of Oriana Fallaci—her name pranked to read ORINA, Italian for "urine." The only times I went down to Lecture Hall B1 was during lunch break, and only to spend time with him—as if being near him was all that it would take to raise my consciousness, make me a slightly more ethical person.

In the apartment on Rue de la Gaîté I listened to him talk as I sipped a beer. I allowed my spirit to be cleansed by his infallible expertise, by the sound of cars outside and the Brownian motion of passersby. In the brief interludes in our conversation, we both turned our eyes elsewhere, and it struck me that in those fleeting instants we were watching the same scene unfold before us: a phantom silhouette emerging from the crowd, raising both arms to the ceiling and then spraying the place with bursts of machine-gun fire. The way I felt deep down inside—sterile, as if someone had made off with my future—there was a part of me that wished that such a scene really would take place. It was an awful, idiotic fantasy, dripping with self-pity, but I indulged in it all the same, saying nothing about it to Giulio. I had never told him about our problem as a couple with having children. Giulio's and my friendship had always centered on discussing the world outside us, saying as little as possible about ourselves. Perhaps that's why it had lasted so long.

The following morning I caught the RER B, and then a bus, to reach Le Bourget, where COP 21 was being held. The security checks at the entrance were nerve-racking, but once you got inside, you could roam freely. Pavilions, small- or medium-sized auditoriums, plenary sessions, and color-coded parallel sessions. A hostess showed me to the pressroom, with a desk all my own, a cable connection, and everything else I would need. I acted as if I were used to this sort of thing, though I felt anything but.

After several days of attending panels of every description, chosen more or less randomly from the schedule, I was forced to concede that I didn't have much to write about. In the assemblies, there were discussions of the specific clauses and subsections, and sometimes even single words, that would eventually make their way into the final agreement. The speeches, in contrast, were either crushingly formal or blandly generic. The environment is a boring topic. Interminable, devoid of action and tragedy, unless you consider the slow-moving tragedies yet to arrive. On the other hand, drowning in good intentions. That's the hidden issue with the climate emergency: the atrocious boredom of it all. Witnessing the work behind crafting an international climate agreement was virtually coma-inducing. What I ought to have done was to write an eyewitness account of each and every fraction of an inch of forward progress, hailing it as a revolution, but who would bother to read it? Who indeed, if I was myself nodding off in the dimly lit conference rooms and auditoriums, my digestion heavy with the sandwiches I couldn't seem to stop devouring, lulled into slumber by the monotonous speeches of delegates, be they

Senegalese, Cuban, or even those garbed in traditional Tibetan tunics?

Five days later, I still hadn't produced a single article. My editors were starting to query me, curious to know my intentions. I'm thinking about it, I reassured them, I'm almost ready.

At dinner, I told Giulio about it. The most interesting thing I'd seen was a sort of art installation, a mini Eiffel Tower built out of stacked chairs. But it didn't strike me as enough to base an article on.

Like, mini how?

About yea tall.

No, then, that's not enough.

I'd cooked steaks for us both, steaks that I'd purchased in a vacuum pack from an organic supermarket. They were meant as a gesture of appreciation. The frying steaks filled the apartment with smoke, but when Giulio walked into the kitchen, he said nothing about the cloud of beefy fumes.

It's true, climate is a bore, he admitted.

I thought that spelled the end of the conversation. But after taking a moment to think it over, he added: You could meet with Novelli. He might tell you something different.

Who's Novelli?

A physicist, just like us.

How old?

Not yet fifty. In Rome, he taught mathematical methods of physics. He was a sweetheart all through classes, but a real stinker when it came to exams. Back then, he was a rabid anti-capitalist.

Like you?

Giulio smiled: Oh, no, worse. I ran into him again here in Paris. Now he works with climate models, something to do with clouds. If you like, I'd be glad to put you two in touch.

I must have shrugged dubiously as I pretended to mull it over, but I'd already clutched desperately at that opportunity. Anything, as long as it meant escaping another day wandering through the echoing pavilions of Le Bourget, churning pat phrases through my mind about the planet's malaise.

The last thing I was expecting, though, was to be summoned by Novelli that same evening, in a brasserie on Rue Monge. I walked over, even though it was a good two miles. The whole way there, I had my phone out in front of me, eyes glued to the screen, as I gathered all the information I could about Jacopo Novelli, PhD. Not that there was all that much on the web. He wasn't sufficiently well-known at the time (nor sufficiently controversial) to have a Wikipedia page, but he did have his own web page, crudely fashioned, the work of a self-taught WordPress dilettante. It listed his most recent papers and offered details about the complex-systems course he taught. There was also a photo gallery featuring views of cloudy skies, accompanied by brief captions classifying the type of vaporous formation: altostratus, cirrus, cumulonimbus, the nomenclature that I had refused to learn for my meteorology exam, because the class had only been worth three credits.

I didn't wait to order, Novelli told me, without a hint of embarrassment or guilt. I didn't expect you to take so long to get here.

I walked.

All the way from the Fourteenth Arrondissement?

He seemed stumped at the idea, but added nothing more. He followed my gaze as I glanced at his plate, now a plate piled high with food.

Not bad, huh? It's why I come here. Even though nobody should think of eating a hamburger this size. Because of the CO_2 emissions, of course. But also for my arteries' sake. Still, these burgers are truly irresistible. You see?

He held up the cheeseburger to show me the cross section. Each and every layer was clearly delineated. Lettuce, cheese, meat, onion. Not like the soggy messes these places usually serve. Order one for yourself.

No, thank you, though. I've already eaten.

Well, sir, too bad for you.

He sank his teeth into the cheeseburger, while I used that interlude to study him. He had the somewhat-fussy appearance of certain scientists at the height of their careers. Though as a young man he'd no doubt been a shabby dresser, like so many physics students (myself included), I guessed sartorial display must now matter a great deal to him.

Have you heard of the Kessler syndrome? he asked me. I shook my head.

Giulio tells me that you want to talk about the end of the world. Like everybody else these days, for that matter. Though, for starters, we should be clear that we're not necessarily talking about the end of the world. Maybe more like the end of human civilization. Quite another matter. Anyway, while sitting here waiting for you, I happened to think about the Kessler syndrome.

He slurped a spot of mayonnaise off his forefinger and then proceeded to pick up his cell phone and pull up a picture. What do you see there?

I don't know, UFOs? I guessed, more as a joke than anything else.

Right, UFOs, exactly, that's what all of you say. Unfortunately, there's no such thing as UFOs and this is a real photograph. These are satellites, launched in sequence by one of these new Chinese internet companies. I doubt you can conceive of the sheer quantity of metal hurtling over our heads. Practically speaking, we've already saturated the lower orbits.

He rotated his cheeseburger, savaging it again from the edge. Perhaps he was planning to leave the central, juiciest part for last.

Now, just imagine that a bolt flies loose from one of these satellites. That sort of thing must happen all the time, right? Bolts do come loose. Well, now this bolt is traveling at something approaching thirty thousand kilometers per hour, and it's become a ballistic projectile. At that velocity it can easily punch right through a steel casing. So let's just imagine that this bolt strikes another satellite, that said satellite splinters into fragments, scattering an enormous number of other metallic ballistic projectiles, which in turn strike other satellites.

A chain reaction.

That's exactly it, a chain reaction. And when all is said and done, what's going to become of this whirling maelstrom of material? No one has the slightest idea. But some portion of it could easily fall to Earth, like a sort of asteroid storm. It's called the Kessler syndrome, and you want to know the truth? It's a genuine, *actual* threat. People don't worry about it because they don't know about it. The only people who do know about it are the very same people who fire satellites into the air. Sure enough, and in fact they take the money they make doing it and use it to build atomic fallout shelters. But the people sitting at the tables in this brasserie have no idea. Right now, everybody's got their head full of Islamic State and global warming, but the truth is that there are a trillion far more distinctive and idiosyncratic threats. Drought, the poisoning of our water tables, pandemics... And then he said it! He said those exact words, right then and there!... the revolt of artificial intelligence. As well, of course, as other threats that seem to have gone out of fashion lately. Such as our good old friend nuclear winter.

For a moment, as I listened to him, he reminded me of my father. The way he used to follow my mother around the house on Sundays, tailing her like a drone: laundry room, balcony, kitchen, talking incessantly the whole time about the petroleum crisis, atmospheric pollution, light pollution. A new catastrophe every month.

I wondered whether Novelli was that kind of a husband too. Whether *I* was that kind of a husband too.

What about clouds? I asked.

Novelli grimaced. Clouds are complicated. The high ones collect humidity, so they help to heat up the planet. Whereas the low ones reflect sunlight, which helps to cool the planet down. I mean, they do good and they do harm at the same time, it's a confusing mess. There are people who think that climate change will produce a world without clouds. Clear skies, day and night, 365 days a year. I guess some people would like that. Not me.

I noticed that you collect photographs on your website.

It's a contest for my students. To see who can take pictures of the most interesting cloud. But it's open to anyone. You're welcome to contribute if you like.

I don't take pictures.

Whatever you say.

I can't reconstruct what else we said to each other that evening, among other reasons because we spent a long time together, first sitting outside that brasserie, beneath the excessive heat of those gas patio heaters, then out on the street, walking around the Jardin des Plantes. We certainly talked about the United Nations conference, about which Novelli felt only a lukewarm modicum of hope, and we also talked about the nostalgia we both felt toward a certain kind of physics, unbound by worldly concerns. And definitely, after a while, he asked me if I was interviewing him.

I don't think so, not exactly.

You can interview me if you like, he said, and I noticed that glimmer of vanity in the midst of all our talk about the end of the world.

At a certain point during our stroll, he asked me whether I had children. I immediately turned the question around back at him: Did he? Two children. The second one had come a number of years after the first one, who was already seven years old. I commented that having children might seem a little contradictory for someone who glimpsed a future like the one he envisioned. In spite of myself, I had stiffened a little. Novelli replied: How can anyone think they'll survive at all, if they don't put their faith in their children?

When we came to a halt in front of his apartment building, the conversation had died out on its own. Over the previous ten minutes we had walked without speaking. It was late enough that there was no one out on the streets. In that silence, the dread of terrorist attacks had returned. I decided to skip the metro on my way home, as little sense as that actually made. Suicide attacks demand a crowd; they're predicated on the creation of spectacular mayhem.

So what is it you do for a living, exactly? Novelli asked me, as if it was a doubt that had been buzzing around in his head the whole evening.

I'm a writer.

Giulio told me you work for a newspaper.

I do work for a newspaper, but I'm not a reporter. I'm a writer.

For some reason, that exchange dismayed me. As if I'd misunderstood the meaning of our conversation and Novelli had just trotted out his usual song and dance, from the Kessler syndrome on, flashy notions that he would have retailed in exactly the same format to any of his students.

He pulled out his keys, fumbled with them, unlocked the street door. Well, great. Good luck on your article, then. You have my number if you need anything else.

LORENZA HAD COME UP with the idea of a holiday on the island while I was in Paris, as a very contemporary form of couples therapy. According to Western wisdom, there is no kind of grief or sorrow that a week in the tropics isn't capable of soothing away entirely. Directly following a world summit on climate change, boarding a jet and flying to the Caribbean in the dead of winter might not, perhaps, have been the most ideologically consistent thing a person could do. Reckoning roughly a metric ton of carbon dioxide apiece each way, we'd be pumping something like four metric tons of CO_2 into the Earth's atmosphere just to wipe clean the sadness that was lurking in our marriage. But it was worth it. And as for my exquisite ecological conscience, well that would just have to be set aside for the moment.

People say that Guadeloupe is shaped like a butterfly. If that is true, then our resort was perched on the butterfly's right wing, at the center of a small inlet. When we arrived, they gave us two tiny rolled-up towelettes drenched in perfumed water to wipe our faces clean. There were giant tanks of water on the lobby floor, teeming with lobsters lazily twitching their antennae. Seated comfortably on white sofas, still dazed from the long trip, we listened to the countless options for rest and relaxation available to us, as well as the accepted methods of payment for same. Since we had agreed to the supplemental fee, we could now claim our oceanfront room. We were sure to like it, they told us, and sure enough, we liked it.

Once we'd unpacked, we headed down to the water to take advantage of the last beams of setting sunlight. Lorenza was wearing a brand-new beach wrap emblazoned with a geometric pattern. She left it draped over a tree trunk that seemed too perfectly placed to have been tossed up there by random ocean currents. We stepped into the water, and a manta ray sailed past us, just yards from our legs, like some omen of happiness. The waves were gentle, barely ripples on the face of the ocean. Lorenza wrapped her legs around my waist and I started moving through the shallow water in short leaps, transporting her over the gentle swell. It wasn't bad, being a couple again and nothing more, she whispered into my ear. At home, we were constantly being interrupted: interrupted by work, interrupted by Eugenio, interrupted by phone calls. She squeezed my waist with every ounce of strength in her quads, she felt younger to me, and for the first time in weeks I wavered in my sorrow, in the unstated resentment I was nursing against her. Lorenza ran a damp hand over my face, as if to put an end to my internal monologue, whatever it might be about. We kissed and then pulled apart, but even then we couldn't stop taking turns repeating what a magnificent place this butterfly-shaped island was and how happy we would be if we never had to leave it.

That perfection lasted only until that evening, when I decided to follow her around the buffet tables, inveighing against the absurdity of having three different menus, including an array of Japanese meat dishes. Was it really necessary to serve fresh strawberries on a tropical island? And San Pellegrino mineral water in plastic bottles? Could it really be that hard to find mineral water, I'm not saying *zero* food miles away, but at least not *four thousand* food miles away? Suddenly, Lorenza whipped around, plate in hand, as if torn between dropping it on the floor or shoving it into my face. She snapped: I get it, you're opposed to waste, and I respect that. But I'm opposed to unhappiness. And so.

And so: relax. That's the hotel's motto. Relax relax relax relax.

A treatment consisting of plunges into room-temperature salt water and piña coladas at four in the afternoon worked just fine. The two of us started having sex again, which was the real reason we'd traveled all this way after all. Afterward, she would lie there, on her tummy, still pantyless, reading contentedly. I was free to approach her again whenever I felt like it, or else lie there underlining the most persuasive passages in the book that Giulio had loaned me, holding desire momentarily at bay. This is what married life should look like, I told myself, this is how it always should be: bursting with this kind of sensuality. Maybe Lorenza was right, my expectations about being a father were excessive, I had fallen victim to an idealized image. There were plenty of couples who lived without children, and there was nothing to suggest that their lives were any less fulfilling or unhappier than other people's. Even in that oceanfront room, though, there still lingered a feeling of exhaustion between us, especially in our conversations. It was as if a crack was zigzagging across the center of our enjoyment. Our own private ozone hole.

In *Collapse*, Jared Diamond lays out a paradox of sorts. He explains how civilizations, which tend to progress toward greater and greater states of welfare and prosperity—we all take it for granted—sometimes actually evolve in the opposite direction, blithely laying the foundations of their own destruction. The most stunning example of this was Easter Island: it was long assumed that the island's natives had been decimated by epidemics brought by European sailors, especially syphilis and smallpox. A more recent theory, however, suggests that the population decline was actually linked to the giant statues that had been their legacy, those square-hewn, enigmatic busts that turned their backs to the ocean. To transport the monolithic colossi, in fact, the natives had required tree trunks to use as rollers, and to procure those tree trunks, they'd been obliged to deforest their island. Once the trees were gone, the whole island ecosystem went haywire, producing landslides, famines, and civil wars. In the final years, the islanders resorted to cannibalism. Cannibalism, I mean, can you imagine? I told Lorenza.

She brushed my thigh with a forefinger, her eyes never leaving the page of her book. Scissoring her legs, bent, through the air, in a pattern remarkably reminiscent of the lobsters out in the lobby, she asked: Didn't you bring any other books?

MIDWEEK, we signed up for a tour of the island's interior. We didn't really want to go, but it was one way of lessening our sense of guilt for having practically never once budged from the hotel's beach.

We left by van at nine in the morning, together with a Dutch married couple. We hiked a gentle trail, a succession of descents and rises, through the heart of the tropical forest, immersed in birdsong. At those latitudes everything looks lush and luxuriant, damp and exciting. After days in bright sunlight, the shade filled me with an unexpected sense of relief.

I found myself passionately absorbed in our guide's explanations of an invasive tree from West Africa that was aggressively supplanting the native vegetation. *Dichrostachys cinerea* was the scientific name, but in Africa they called it the Kalahari Christmas Tree. In April it produced lovely yellow and purple flowers that momentarily made you forget just how malevolent it really was. I must have overdone it with my questions, because the Dutch couple started showing unmistakable signs of impatience, and Lorenza sighed the way she sometimes does when I'm acting like a star student.

We went back to the coast. Lunch was served in a shadowy area among the mangroves. Other groups from different hotels and rival tour operators were starting to cluster there as well, and the crowds ruined the atmosphere of exclusivity that we'd been promised when planning our trip. We and the Dutch couple sat at one of the wooden tables, spreading out as much as possible to discourage anyone else from even thinking of trying to join us.

I struck up a conversation with Otto about the quality of the resort and how nerve-racking traveling had become since the Paris terror attacks. He was an engineer working in the automotive industry, but for the most part in marketing. He cared deeply about sustainability. We each drank a ti' punch, then a second and a third. Predictably, we also talked about Creole cuisine and how repetitive it eventually became.

On the way back to the hotel, I nodded off, falling so fast asleep that I didn't even wake up for the last stop. When the three of them reboarded the bus, they seemed revved up, including Lorenza. They swore it was a shame I'd missed the colonial villa. It had really been worth the visit.

ON THE NEXT-TO-LAST DAY, we rented a car to go to a beach the Dutch couple had recommended. Resort life is mostly people recommending beaches to each other. As soon we emerged from the trail through the scrub to the beach, we realized it was a nudist resort. Now what do we do? I asked. Lorenza shrugged: Well, we're here. We undressed, put our swimsuits in our bags, and spread our towels out on the sand, but just lying there naked like that seemed a little strange. So we went into the water. This was all quite fun. While we were floating about a hundred feet away from the beach, the Dutch couple joined us. They hadn't told us they'd be coming to the same beach, otherwise we'd have probably gone somewhere else. This is fantastic, isn't it? Otto commented.

Lorenza started chatting with the woman, who was pretty badly sunburned: her skin dotted with patches of red and a pale negative impression of her two-piece suit. Her legs underwater were rendered more voluminous by the refracted light.

In an attempt to get over the awkwardness with Otto, I mentioned that I'd seen how well he swam over the short distance out to us from the beach. He mentioned a swimming certificate that all Dutch children are required to earn. It involved three levels of expertise: the exam required swimming fully dressed, with shoes on, and making your way through an underwater tunnel while holding your breath.

That's because of the risk that the Netherlands might be flooded by rising sea levels, right?

Otto gave me a baffled look: Rising sea levels? No, that's not it at all. We just don't want people to drown in Amsterdam's canals.

The conversation was being conducted with all four of us fully nude, and I really couldn't free my mind of that awareness. Did you notice *them* over there? Otto asked me eventually, pointing at the beach. I noticed the dark silhouettes of young people squatting in the dim shadows of the vegetation. They were rubbing themselves rhythmically between their legs, but they were too far away for me to be able to tell if they were wearing bathing suits. What are they doing? I asked, naïvely, and Otto smiled back, as if I'd made a coy allusion rather than asking a question.

Later, we accepted their invitation to dine together. Stupidly, we dressed nicer than usual. I put on a pair of actual shoes, even though we were only going downstairs to the restaurant, to sit out on the terrace and fetch our own meals from the buffet, whose every offering we knew by heart, and order the same Chilean screw cap red wine that would appear on our bill as one of the extras when we left.

Except we did all this at Otto and Maaike's table: Otto and Maaike, our new resort friends, who lived in The Hague—that's right, The Hague, not Amsterdam, in fact, about fifteen miles outside of The Hague, in one of those typically Dutch houses that you conjure up when you think about Holland, you know the kind I mean, exactly... *of course* we'd been there, more than once, and we'd visited the Mauritshuis too—oh, *that's* not how you say it? Well, of course, we'd been dumb-struck at the sight of *View of Delft*, with that light that doesn't seem to strike the painting from without, but instead emanates from the canvas itself...

Their names weren't Otto and Maaike. I have no idea what their names were. I had no reason to commit their names to memory. I took Lorenza's hand underneath the table, and she used her thumb to caress the middle of my palm, delicately, giving me her consent.

When I woke up, several hours later, the Dutch couple had already left the room. Lorenza was sleeping, stretched out diagonally along the bed, in mute testimony to what a strange night it had been. I covered her legs with a corner of the sheet and got up. The french window was wide-open, and I stepped out onto the terrace. A needle-thin strip of pink was spreading parallel to the horizon. Above it, the sky varied from cerulean to a compact dark blue. *Someday,* I thought to myself, *this island will no longer exist, the terrace will no longer exist, and we two will no longer exist either. Lorenza and I, together, will leave no trace, like a pair of submerged atolls.*

Over the sea a circular cloud had come to rest, thick, motionless, unfathomably smooth. A gaseous flying saucer that narrowed ever so slightly toward the bottom, like a twisting spiral. I went back inside and grabbed my cell phone. I snapped a picture of the cloud and sent it to Novelli with a minimalist caption: Guadeloupe.

He wrote back immediately: Lenticular cloud. The airflow encounters an obstacle and shapes itself accordingly. Not really all that rare, but uncommon to see one in those latitudes. May I add it to the website?

A moment later, a second message arrived: If you look closely at the edges, you can just glimpse the iridescence. Those are droplets diffracting the light. Let's get together next time you're in Paris.

IN JULY, *Nature* magazine published an article about the link between clouds and climate change. Satellite pictures showed that due to global warming, clouds were gradually migrating to Earth's poles, the authors wrote. The planet's cloud cover was drifting from where it might be most useful in terms of filtering out solar rays—at the equator or the tropics—toward arctic and antarctic zones, much less helpful. This process, over time, would generate what is known as a positive feedback loop, though such a loop was actually anything but positive. The "positivity" was strictly in a mathematical sense, represented by a plus sign: +. More heat increased the pace of heating. The hotter it got, the faster it would heat up.

Back in Trieste, I began the first lesson of my course by reading aloud that article by Norris et alia. I was teaching a science journalism course, part of a master's degree in communications, and I had decided to devote the whole year to climate change. The migration of clouds seemed like an excellent starting point: as terrifying as it was poetic. This was a four-week course. I rented an Airbnb in the Cavana neighborhood. If it had been left up to me, I would never have chosen such a central and lively part of town. I would have settled for one of the hotels offering special discounts for guests working with the school, but also convenient to the 38 bus line. Instead, Lorenza persuaded me to live a little. If you're going into exile, she told me, at least choose someplace nice: unless proven otherwise, you have no crimes to expiate. But was that really true? Things had deteriorated badly between us as a couple, at first in spring and then, with a sharper, more brutal twist in summer, which we spent apart, by and large. We rarely spoke on the phone. Admitting strangers into our bed had turned out to be a reckless, dangerous act.

In Trieste, I established a new routine. When I didn't have class, I rose late, but still set an alarm for seven to activate my cell phone. That would show the world (since WhatsApp logged my latest connection) that I was no lazybones. That aside, I didn't have a lot to do, except for correcting papers. And so I walked. Hiking all the way to Miramare would take up most of the day, but there was also the Rilke Trail and the Karst Plateau, with its grim and barren wastelands. I told myself that all those miles of hiking were a necessary requirement if I wanted to come up with a good idea for the book I planned to write. I told Lorenza the same thing, and she believed it, or pretended to, anyway. Most of the time, though, I was just walking and doing nothing else, my head absolutely empty of ideas. I always wore earbuds, like a teenager. According to the history of my Spotify playlists, it appears that the year's most-listened-to song was by Majical Cloudz, a title that ended in a question mark: "Are You Alone?"

The students in my course were for the most part postdocs in the hard sciences: physics, mathematics, biotechnology. Only rarely did I stumble across a linguist or a historian, and they felt like outsiders. Everyone was there because they'd grown disenchanted at some point with the academic career path, or else were just plain tired. They'd studied too hard for too long, working on extremely challenging subjects, and now they were hoping for a rest in the gentler terrain of communications. My initial effort was to dismantle that preconception: if they thought they had explored the greatest possible depths of complexity with their work in the sciences, then in my class they would encounter a whole new brand of complexity, and it would drag them in, engaging their whole selves. It wasn't hard to intimidate them. They hadn't done any writing for at least a decade and were inhibited after a long diet of nothing but technical papers and specialized textbooks, formulas and Cartesian graphs. A blank page filled them with dread.

One of the students that year was an astrophysicist named Christian. He sat halfway back in the lecture hall, against the left wall, as if both in and out of the scene. He had an indecipherable accent, and perhaps that's what stirred my curiosity. Or it might have been the way he stared at me while I was talking about the disappearance of clouds, seemingly more wide-eyed than usual.

When it was his turn to introduce himself, he told us he'd worked for years on gravitational waves and black holes. But that field turned out not to be good for him, he said, tugging at his bangs. Midway through a project, with an article about to publish, he decided to quit astrophysics and head back to Earth. That's exactly how he put it, "head back to Earth." I asked him what he meant by saying that black holes hadn't been good for him. When he answered, he was careful not to look me in the eye: Well, Professor, do you think it's possible for something you study to get the upper hand?

IN THE CAFETERIA I went over and sat down next to Marina, who was managing the course. I asked her what she thought of Christian, and she understood instantly. He's very sensitive, she replied, better take it easy with him.

I had the impression that she was holding back some piece of crucial information. The students' files and sensitive details about their admissions interviews weren't shared with us—after all, we were teachers with short-term contracts.

I think he has some talent, I told her.

Oh, you do? And what makes you think that? You only spent two hours with them.

Instinct.

Instinct, she repeated. Then she looked up from her tray, giving me a forced smile.

In the end-of-year student evaluations from last year, there were students who'd complained that I "played favorites." There were projects, they said, that I had examined with greater attention and special interest, while there were others that I'd practically ignored. They'd written that it was always the same students who were encouraged to talk in class, and they were mostly males. Marina had forwarded the results of the questionnaire to me in a perfectly neutral email: Herewith attached please find copy of. I'd shown the final score to Lorenza (not the individual comments), and she'd hesitated briefly before saying that 7.5 didn't strike her as too bad. But I didn't want a 7.5 score, I wanted a 9 or a solid 10, I wanted special praise and the board's sincere compliments. I'd gone to Giulio in search of consolation: Does it strike you as normal that now it's the students who are grading the teachers? He'd corrected me: Student-customers. There's nothing you can do about it, that's the direction education is heading in. I'd barely had the self-control to keep from asking him *his* latest score as a professor.

Still, I hadn't been wrong about Christian. In class, he weighed in with brilliant commentary, he was always present, involved, even impassioned. One morning I read the class a passage from *Collapse*, and the next day there was a copy of the book prominently displayed on his desk.

When the time came for him to present his reporting project, he stood up and went to the front of the lecture hall. He spoke in some confusion, tugging at his bangs the whole time, and what he said couldn't really be described as an idea, strictly speaking. If anything, it was more of a stream of thoughts beneath which there seemed to lurk a concern. He talked about points of no return, a notion that was familiar to him after his years of studying black holes. When a body passes the event horizon, it vanishes, nothing more can be known about it, and everything that happens to it after that instant remains an inaccessible mystery. The body in question might be right there, on the other side of the event horizon, deformed or dismembered, or it might have been transformed into something else, maybe into pure light. Christian wondered whether there existed a similar moment in store for our planet, a boundary beyond which we would simply plummet, and after that: nothing. If so, how far away might that boundary be from now, this morning, this very instant that he was talking? Perhaps, he said, we'd already passed that boundary, but we hadn't even noticed yet. And in that case, perhaps... At that point he brusquely broke off, interrupting himself, and said: That's what I want to write about.

He seemed physically drained, as if every cell of his body were trembling. A sense of bewilderment swept the lecture hall. I reached out to his classmates, asking whether anyone had any comments on this project, and the room responded with murmurs of appreciation, though they were clearly perplexed. So I spoke up again. I told Christian that his topic was certainly intriguing, but that it also struck me as concerningly vague. It ran the risk of running off the rails. You should focus on something more concrete, where this transformation can already be seen clearly.

I wouldn't know what exactly, he retorted sternly, still without meeting my glance.

How about shifts in ecosystems?

I told him about *Dichrostachys cinerea*, the African plant that was threatening the ecosystem of Guadeloupe. But you'd need to find a situation close by, I told him, something you can observe directly, because that's what we do here, we look at reality, we provide coverage of stories.

Without realizing it, I'd walked over to him, close enough to hear his respiration in the stillness of the classroom. I was a good teacher, not someone you'd give a mediocre score to. I knew how to motivate my students, how to lead them, I had plenty of imagination, I was openhearted.

Christian said neither yes nor no, nor did he suggest he might give it some thought. He just stared at something outside the windows, as if he couldn't take his eyes off whatever it might be, an event horizon toward which we were all hurtling but that he and he alone was capable of glimpsing. He asked me if he had permission to go back to his seat.

AMONG THE REPORTING PROJECTS I recall from that school year: one particular endangered species of ditch frog, the impact of the canned meat industry on global warming, the exploration of a cavern in Slovenia that you would expect might be immune to climate change but that was instead being transformed, starkly and irreversibly.

Eventually, Christian came around, and as I'd recommended, chose a specific topic: the tree of heaven (*Ailanthus altissima*), a shrub of Asian origin that was spreading with disconcerting rapidity and crowding out our native vegetation. In the lead-in that he read aloud to the class, he described a train trip home during which he'd realized that there was tree of heaven everywhere the whole way, concealed among the plants that lined the train tracks. His text was loaded with imagery. The leaves, for instance, tossed and waved *in an attempt to communicate with him*, and at one point he described the tree of heaven as one single immense vegetable organism, a rhizome that extended just beneath the surface of the soil, girdling the entire planet.

When he finished reading, short of breath, he heard a round of applause from his classmates. I wondered whether they might consider it a show of bias, but I eventually joined in myself. Once it died down, to counterbalance that excess of enthusiasm, I started a critical evaluation of that intro, weighing in with the red pencil. When was he going to get into the particulars of the

available information? Where were his data, his information, leaving aside those subjective, sensory impres-
sions? His use of the second-person singular, moreover,
baffled me, and the punctuation seemed scattershot, at
least to judge from the way he'd read it.

Christian's expression changed as I spoke. The whole
class seemed to take umbrage, and one young woman,
Greta, acted as a lightning rod for the palpable tension
by speaking up: I liked it the way it was, Professor.
After all, didn't you tell us that we should try to write
in a personal style?

The following week, Christian didn't show up for
class. I asked his classmates if they knew the reason
why. Some of the students turned to look at Greta, or
maybe they didn't, maybe that's just something I'm
reading into my memories with twenty-twenty hind-
sight. Maybe no one turned around at all, and they all
just told me they knew nothing (lying as they did so).
But after class, one student stopped me in the hallway:
There is something, Professor. But I don't know if it's
important, and whether I ought to tell you.

So what is it?

At night, Christian always hangs out in a brewpub
called Mirò, it's a place that . . .

I know where Mirò is.

Okay, I didn't think you would.

And what does he do there?

The young man shrugged. Maybe he doesn't go
there every single night, you know, he answered, but
two of us saw him there at different times.

But you didn't talk to him?

The boy hung his head, looking sheepish. Talking to Christian isn't all that easy. I don't know if you've noticed, but he's a bit of an odd duck.

I assured him that I'd noticed nothing of the sort, implying that if anything, the strange thing was how wary they all seemed to be of him.

THAT EVENING I went to Mirò. The atmosphere was festive, like a university party. I hoped I wouldn't run into any of my master's students, because they would think I looked creepy sitting with a drink at a table all by myself. That was one reason why I chose a table off to the side, next to the waiter's station. By one in the morning I was a little tipsy and ready to leave. I couldn't say whether I was disappointed or relieved, but that's when I saw Christian come in, dressed in pajamas and flip-flops.

He was carrying his laptop. He sat down at the bar, and the bartender, a woman, leaned across to plant a kiss on each cheek. I sensed a certain familiarity between the two of them, as if that scene unfolded, unchanging, every night. The bartender served him a beer while Christian opened his laptop and started typing something. The pub wasn't a big place. I couldn't have been more than thirty feet away from him, and he had his back to me. I could see his bare heels and the strip of skin at the base of his back, where his pajama top hiked up as he crouched forward over his computer.

The computer screen was turned so I could see it, and even though I couldn't make out the individual words, it was unmistakably a page of a Word document that he was working on.

When the DJ put on a new song, suddenly shifting to a reassuring oldie from the nineties, the dance floor suddenly filled up. At that point, the only thing I could see from my vantage point was Christian's bluish heels tapping along to the music against the base of the stool. I screwed up my nerves and walked over. It took him a few seconds to realize I was standing there and to acknowledge my presence, saying Professor without the slightest sign of astonishment.

What are you writing?

Christian tilted his head toward the screen of his laptop: My piece.

Seems like a strange place to concentrate on your work.

He shrugged, and I felt that I'd lost him, so I retracted my statement: Actually, I like working with noise. It soothes my mind.

I live right upstairs. They didn't warn me about it before I signed the lease. It's the bass frequencies especially, they shake my bed. They literally make it move. Ramona and I came to an understanding. She lets me work down here, and I get free drinks. In exchange, I've stopped complaining.

He smiled at the bartender, and she stuck her tongue out at him. Ramona served me a beer too, and we drank in silence for a while. I could sense that Christian heard the call of work, but didn't dare to go back to writing with me sitting next to him.

You didn't come to class, I told him, after a while.

I'm trying to catch up.

What are you trying to catch up on?

On my piece, Professor.

You still have time. No need to get anxious about it. After all, you've made considerable progress.

There was too much packed into it. You said so yourself, Professor.

For a moment he seemed absolutely defenseless, in his cotton pajamas, printed with spaceship patterns, sitting in a brewpub where the other customers were practically elbowing past us. I wondered how many nights it had been since he'd last slept. We sat for another while in silence, until he spoke up: I'm feeling a little peckish, Professor.

Do you know where to get anything to eat at this hour?

First I'd need to get changed.

We walked out the pub door and went right back in through the door next to it. I could feel the eyes of the other students on my back as I left with a much younger man wearing pajamas. But that was an evening out in a place packed with mathematicians and physicists, people accustomed to all sorts of eccentric behavior.

Upstairs, the bass notes of the music were exploding like so many muffled roars. The bed was unmade, and looked as if it had been that way for a long time.

Any ordinary university student's room: that typical kind of disorder, no worse and no better than usual, though I could sense a strange energy just in the arrangement of the things in the place. But that, too, could be a false, recovered memory. Maybe I didn't notice a blessed thing in that apartment. Christian put on a pair of jeans and a sweatshirt over his pajama top. In an impulse of paternal benevolence that was completely out of place, I told him to dress warmly, because a cold breeze had sprung up.

He knew a food stand that would still be open, over by the train station, and we bought some oversized cans of beer. He devoured a prepackaged sandwich that looked unsafe to eat. Then we went for a walk.

Among the topics we discussed that evening: how idiotic it was to call the Higgs boson "the God particle" / the fact that we had both secretly read *The Drama of the Gifted Child: The Search for the True Self*, in the hope it might talk about us / the latest satellite mapping of background radiation / the way we'd both felt like chronic losers in high school and suffered over it for years until one fine day we no longer gave a damn / quantum chromodynamics / premature ejaculation.

Christian had no obvious or banal opinions about anything, exactly as I had worked hard to ensure when I was twenty-five myself, but while in my case it took constant effort to ensure that none of my opinions were obvious or banal, in his case it seemed more like a personality trait. I thought that, maybe, once the course was over, and the asymmetrical positions our respective roles confined us to had loosened, we might become friends. I was always in search of friends.

We walked to the end of the pier and stood there, side by side, peeing into the water. The brightly lit city stood entirely behind us, and the pier was a platform suspended over the black water as if atop a dark interstellar void. We stood wobbling gently on the pier's edge, stinking drunk, and then Christian said: I'm almost done with my investigative piece, Professor. I promise that as soon as I'm done, I'll start coming to lessons again.

A second later he added: I really care about this, Professor.

THE AUTHORITIES CAME to collect him four days later, on the night between Saturday evening and Sunday morning. It was the bartender, Ramona, who'd glanced up at the light still burning in Christian's bedroom, as she always did at the end of her shift. She'd heard what she later described as strange sounds coming from the window, and had noticed dark splatters on the windowpanes.

To strip the flesh off his arms, he'd used a fork, a detail that I'd had a hard time shaking for quite a while. But that same detail had prevented him from cutting too deep. If he'd used a knife, he would certainly have bled out, Marina told me during an emergency teachers' meeting on Monday morning. We would still need to get all the facts, but it seemed that Christian hadn't slept for several days. Plenty of people had noticed him

wandering the streets at all hours, and one of his classmates, Greta, said that he often wandered around her
house. She would watch him from her window, and
once she'd gone out into the street to confront him.
Christian hadn't shown the slightest hostility. He'd just
seemed completely out of it. He'd told her he was there
to keep her safe. Greta asked him, safe from what, and
he had replied, from the branches.

What branches? one of the teachers had asked, but
Marina just ignored her. Christian, she went on, had
stopped taking his medications without telling anyone. He'd been very persuasive with his parents. They
hadn't noticed anything either. After his emergency
hospitalization, he'd been transferred to a clinic where
he'd spent time previously. Of course, he'd be unable to
finish the course.

It was a beautiful, bright November day, and the
waters of the bay were sparkling outside the windows
of the classroom where we were meeting. The suspicion that we'd been derelict in some way hovered in the
golden morning light. But exactly what had we failed to
do? Had we failed to provide the necessary attention?
Care? Intuition?

A number of words and phrases were uttered, including paranoia, schizophrenia, and involuntary psy-
chiatric commitment. Nico, the professor of social
media, mentioned generically that it struck him that
every year the students seemed more and more fragile.

I said nothing about having gone to see Christian at
Miró just a few nights ago, and walking with him for a

substantial portion of the night, nor that I, alone among that panel of teachers, knew exactly what branches he was talking about to Greta: *Ailanthus altissima*, order of the Sapindales, family of the Simaroubaceae. Introduced into Italy for silk production around the middle of the nineteenth century. The tree of heaven, one of the most invasive species around. Could it be, Professor, that something you study could get the upper hand?

Through the transparency of the windowpane I glimpsed Christian's bedroom, I saw the branches of the tree of heaven twist their way up through the floor, shattering the floor tiles with the nodes of their branches here and there; I saw the buds open and extend, growing into pliant branches, strong reeds that punctured the mattress, growing ever stronger as the bed filled up with leaves. Now the foliage and vegetation covered walls and ceiling, the whole room had become a forest, the leaves shaking rhythmically to the beat of the music rising from Mirò downstairs, and there Christian found himself, caught in the middle, imprisoned by the branches, by the invasive species, and by his equally invasive thoughts. By now, there was no way to weed selectively, at this point the plants would have to be uprooted wholesale. And I saw him grab the first object within reach, a fork lying on the table, and use it to ward off the threat.

Could it be, Professor?

Christian snaps off the branches, in fact, he rips them out, but they're already wrapped around his wrists and ankles and neck, they're multiplying. He grips the fork, stabbing frantically, randomly. The tree of heaven branches creep into his nostrils, between the tendons of his fingers, into his sternum, up his anus, sprouting new leaves, and he goes after them, prying them out of his flesh with the tines of the fork.

Marina asked if any of us had questions. No one? Then it was time now to move on to examine proposals of how best to deal with what had happened with the class. There was a psychological outreach office at the school, and we should encourage the young people to make use of it. Even then, I continued to say nothing. I said nothing about what I'd just glimpsed in the transparency of the windowpanes, inside Christian's bedroom. We were all scientists there, scientists or at least ex-scientists, and nothing about what I had imagined was objective or verifiable. I sat in silence. I listened to the various proposals.

ONCE THE COURSE WAS OVER, I went back to Rome. Now that I'd become obsessed with invasive species, the city looked different to me, infested as it was with the star jasmines that would, come May, fill the air with their sickly sweet perfume (provenance: China), the parakeets that crowded the palm trees along the Via Nazionale (India), the palm trees themselves (Canary Islands), and the parasite that was killing them (China, again). I tried not to tell Lorenza any of this when we left the house, because I knew that was exactly what my father would have done.

On December 19 I turned thirty-four, but I remember nothing about that day. In my photos on my phone I find only two pictures matching that date, two culinary still lifes: a serving tray of raw vegetables, cut lengthwise, with a little bowl of mayonnaise at the center, and a close-up of my hand gripping a jar of preserves, with what looks to me like a defiant stance, as if telling someone: I'm busy cooking. I'm guessing we must have invited friends over for dinner, though I have no idea of how many or who, but there are certainly a lot of vegetables on the serving tray.

Most of all, though, I have no memory of having broken up the dinner party a little after eight, when a Scania tractor trailer swerved into a Christmas market in Berlin, running over dozens of people. In fact, I have no idea of how I even first heard the news, nor whether I turned on the TV to learn more about it, though that's certainly exactly what happened. Just as I must have closely followed the manhunt over the next few days for the prime suspect, Anis Amri, and the shootout in Sesto San Giovanni where he was killed, as well as the widespread indignation about the way that the most wanted terrorist in all Europe had blithely crossed the border between Germany and France, and after that into Italy.

I must also have learned, at some point along the way, that the murderous tractor trailer may have left my hometown, Turin, a few days before that, and that it was in fact in Turin that the twenty-five metric tons of steel the truck was carrying had been loaded onto it. There was a proximity never before experienced between our lives and this new form of absolute evil—that formulation may seem trite, but I can't think of any other way of describing it—an evil that was blooming here and there across the continent like a rotting corpse flower. And yet Lorenza and I continued doing everything we had always done, including birthday parties.

IT WAS AROUND THAT TIME that Giulio confessed to me that he'd been watching videos of beheadings. He found them, uncut, on Tor. They're an authentic genre all their own, he told me, with a clear and well-defined aesthetic. Take the colors, just to start: the black of the executioners and the bright orange of the prisoners' jumpsuits. If you pay attention, you'll see that they're always clean and neatly pressed, as if they'd been pulled out of the plastic packaging just seconds previous.

Those facing death sentences were well behaved. They never objected, never cried out, did nothing to sabotage the staging of their execution, as if they didn't want to ruin the quality of the video. Look carefully at how the framing changes, Giulio wrote me, observe the editing. These aren't videos made to be watched, they're videos made to be savored. Glossy production values, like a TV series.

For my first viewing, I chose the beheading of a Japanese journalist with a glassy-eyed stare. Then the execution of a British NGO worker, and after that, the video of twenty-one Egyptian Coptic Christians, led slowly, in single file, along a beach and then beheaded in unison, in a perfect geometric array.

I'd watch the videos and exchange emails with Giulio to comment on them. There were many aspects we were interested in delving into, such as, for instance, how hard it must have been to come up with such a sharp, clean slash as what the executioners posted online. Did they practice to achieve that effect? How long, and exactly *how* did they practice? Did they have mannequins or did they practice on animals, or perhaps on human corpses? And then there was the captivating question of the seven seconds. According to some experts on neurobiology, consciousness lasts no more than seven seconds after the actual moment of decapitation. That made beheading a spectacular form of execution but also particularly merciful. But how could anyone be certain? Seven seconds: that's how long it took for a person, a self, to evaporate. Another mystery that science would never be able to solve.

I realize now—as I look back at the months between the end of 2016 and the beginning of 2017 from a distance of just five years—just how hard it is to establish causal relationships between various events. Was I watching ISIS decapitation videos because I wanted to convince myself that the present day was too inhospitable to even think of bringing children into this world, or was it the other way around? But maybe the two things had nothing to do with each other at all. Maybe I was just sucked in by that new horror, as were so many others just like me. Whatever the case, in compiling this chronicle of a recent past that already seems separated by a vast gulf of distance, it's as if I were obliged to restrict myself to juxtaposing events one next to another without forcing any links between them, accepting at the very most that there might have been some correspondences. Also, without so much as attempting to draw a moral conclusion about them.

There was a study, conducted on a sample of three thousand Americans and published in *American Psychologist*, that examined the motivations driving people like Giulio and me and many millions of others to watch beheadings. In that period, according to this survey, 20 percent of those interviewed watched at least part of one and 5 percent watched all the way through. For the most part, those interviewed were Christian males and they had all started doing it, more or less just like us, with only the best intentions, so to speak. The study found a strong link between unemployment or having undergone abuse in the past. Neither thing was true of us, for me or for Giulio, at least to the best of my knowledge.

It's just possible, though, that the statistics weren't sufficiently sophisticated to pick up the incidence of outright failure to become fathers or else cases of fatherhood that had become, over the years, exceptionally traumatic or painful, as had been the case for Giulio.

For those few months we saw more of each other than usual on account of his child custody lawsuit. We were in Rome the first time he told me about it. It must have been around January 6, the Feast of the Epiphany, and I'm capable of reconstructing that date because the city had been hit by an unusual cold snap, with temperatures below freezing and stiff winds. I'd never seen the fountain on Via dei Serpenti frozen solid, and one morning we stopped to marvel at it. With his little hands, gloveless, Adriano broke loose the icy stalactites that had formed around the rim of the basin and, eventually, gave in to the irresistible temptation to lick one, while Giulio asked whether I'd be willing to help out by testifying before a judge.

Testifying about what?

About me and Adriano. About how we are when we're together. That is, to the fact that there's no mistreatment or whatnot.

Is there someone who thinks there might be?

Giulio shrugged: If you're willing to do it, you'd have to spend some time with us.

Well, it's not like I haven't already.

Sure, but your testimony would need to be documented, there'd need to be notes.

You mean, I'd have to spend time with you like some sort of investigator?

Giulio broke off a little icicle and turned it over in his hands. I hate being put under observation, he said. But I think I could stand to be observed by you.

That was by far the most intimate thing we had ever said to each other, and after it came a moment of silence. Then Giulio went on: My parents are going to come testify as well. But their point of view is considered less significant, for obvious reasons. In your case, considering what you do for a living as well, your input would be given more weight.

Okay, I said.

If you don't feel like it, I'd understand. It's a tremendous pain in the ass and—

I already told you I'd do it.

It was too cold to sit outside, so we ducked into a fast-food restaurant on Piazza della Repubblica. Adriano wanted a hot dog. Giulio said no, reminding Adriano of the upset stomach that had followed his last hot dog. Adriano started tugging on Giulio's knee so furiously that eventually he gave in.

He's getting more spoiled every day, Giulio told me, as if he owed me an apology. Then he corrected his phrasing: We're spoiling him worse and worse every day.

I was already watching them from a different point of view, as if I were evaluating them. We'd picked up our trays of food and taken a table next to the window. Adriano devoured his hot dog, defying his father repeatedly with a gleeful, triumphant grin. He might not even have wanted the hot dog itself. He was chiefly interested in winning the test of wills.

JUST HOW RELATIONS between Giulio and Cobalt had deteriorated to that point was something I both understood and couldn't fathom. His instinctive reserve had left me nothing more than a few scattered clues. As for Cobalt, at the beginning she had reached out to me, or actually she had reached out to Lorenza for lengthy phone calls of exasperated venting, but then they'd stopped talking. Taking sides was almost inevitable.

I was there when the two of them first met. Giulio and I were seniors, our second year in the master's program. We'd decided to enroll in summer school for a course in high-energy physics at CERN, where we were going to be taught by such illustrious figures as Yuval Grossman and Edward Witten. There were a hundred or so budding physicists from universities in half the countries of Europe. We wore name tags, and during our coffee breaks we ventured into discussions of things we only partly understood.

Cobalt was one of the female students wearing sweatshirts, with their hair tied back. She sat down next to us in the cafeteria and just started talking about differentiable manifolds out of the blue, as if casually including us in her lunchtime stream of consciousness. Giulio and I sat there in silence, somewhat intimidated. Wait, aren't you theoreticians? she asked when she noticed our hesitation. Theoretically, yes, Giulio had replied, and that had made her laugh. So you're a couple of theoretical theoreticians, she repeated a couple of times, as if it was the smartest wisecrack she'd heard in quite a while. She introduced herself. Her father, a chemist, had given her that whimsical name, but it had gone even worse for her brother, they'd named him Tellurium, and no, she wasn't joking, not in the slightest. Giulio had noticed the bracelet on her wrist and had guessed where it came from, so they'd struck up a conversation about travel, just the two of them.

They made a promising couple. Lorenza and I said it frequently, in the short period we all four spent time together: They're the most promising couple we know. And yet.

If Adriano hadn't been with us, in the fast-food place on Piazza della Repubblica, Giulio and I would have gone back to talking about beheadings. Instead, at a certain point, and with a certain dutiful quality to it, he asked me about my project. Maybe he wanted to even out the attention we'd been focusing up till then on him and his son. I asked him what project he was referring to. The bomb, right? he replied.

Oh, right, that one. I haven't made any progress on it. Actually, I just gave up on it.

I really liked the idea of it.

You're a physicist, of course you like it. But I can assure you that there's no one out there eagerly awaiting a new book about the atom bomb.

What do you know about who's out there eagerly awaiting what?

To keep from just sitting there with nothing to do with our hands, we'd ordered a side of french fries that we shared, taking turns dipping them in various sauces. Giulio asked if I'd mind if he mixed the sauces.

Do you know what always struck me in particular? he asked. That back at the university they never once talked with us about it. How many nuclear physics exams did we take? We studied fission, chain reactions, we knew all the calculations by heart, but no one ever mentioned the bomb. Not even Ferrone. And we all know exactly what people said about Ferrone.

What people said about Ferrone was that in the years he was doing his postdoctoral work in Moscow, he had actually met Lev Landau, and that he had become a nuclear spy. Actually, the only trace of his past in the Eastern Bloc were his phone calls to his Russian girlfriend, shamelessly much younger than him. Those phone calls interrupted every lesson, as he cried *Privet golubka!*—Hello, my little dove!

Maybe they figured that was stuff strictly for engineers, I ventured.

I don't actually think that was it, though. I believe that all physicists develop a certain instinctive reluctance to discuss that subject. As if it had nothing to do with them. And yet, if you start delving into the history of that period, in the Manhattan Project and the projects of other countries, you find all the names of the theorems we studied. Fermi, Heisenberg, Oppenheimer, Wigner. They were all involved, the good ones and the bad ones, all of them in agreement that it was right to keep going. Afterward they all justified it by saying that there was no alternative to the construction of the bomb, no alternative to arms proliferation either. But if you ask me, it was much worse than that: they were excited, or at least they were for a while. It was only once it became clear that things had genuinely turned serious, when they realized that they were building a potential end of the world right there in the laboratory, that a few of them started to pull back.

So where does this point of view take us? I asked.

I'm not sure. Maybe to the idea that even the most intelligent people on the planet—and there can be no doubt that those physicists really were—actually understand nothing about the present. As if the present could only... overwhelm them.

Giulio had handed over his phone to Adriano so we could continue our conversation in peace, but we didn't go on for much longer. I'd grown strangely sad: for myself, because for a while now it seemed to me that I did little besides abandon projects, or perhaps for him, because I had the impression that he'd found a tortuous path leading him back to a lamentation of himself, Adriano, Cobalt, and their current situation, though even I was incapable of deciphering the exact nature of it.

On my way home, I made a detour down Via Panisperna. I stopped in the little courtyard where the physics institute once stood. In that building, Enrico Fermi had realized that by bombarding certain nuclei with slow neutrons it was possible to obtain new elements. That's not exactly how the bomb got started, but it is at least partially how the bomb got started. What had once been the physics institute was now government offices, and you couldn't get inside, as I knew from the years when I was doing my earliest research. I'd catapulted myself into those rooms more than once in my imagination, I'd seen Fermi running from room to room, hugging the radioactive sources to his belly, the same ones that prompted the cellular mutations that finally gave him stomach cancer.

When I got home, I found Lorenza talking on the phone. I hovered around her until she hung up. I told her about Giulio and the favor he had asked of me: I'd have to go to Paris a few times for him. Lorenza said that it didn't seem like a good idea to let myself get involved like that.

Letting myself get involved is actually the foundation of the work I do.

And in any case, Giulio was willing to pay for my flights, if that's what she was worried about. She gave me an odd look.

Of course, I would never have actually let him pay. It was just to say that he'd do it. If needed.

Go ahead, go to Paris, she told me. Then she went back to tapping on her phone, impatient to get back to whatever I'd interrupted.

I went into the bathroom. I stayed in there for a few minutes, then came back to the living room. There I announced to her that I'd finally figured out what I wanted to write. I was going to take up the idea of the bomb again, this time I'd made up my mind. I now had the key to the book. In fact, if she didn't mind, I was going to start immediately.

MANY OF THE SURVIVORS of the atom bombs over Hiroshima and Nagasaki describe the blast as a silent event. The Japanese term for it is *pikadon*, a combination of *pika*, or light, and *don*, or roar. And yet, as John Hersey notes, almost none of the survivors recalls having heard the sound of the explosion. Everyone, however, recalls the flash of light.

The flash preceded the shock wave by a long enough span of time to allow people to observe it. For a moment the landscape was transformed with colors no one had ever seen before—many recalled white, but others talk about red, yellow, orange, and blue. In fact, in filmed records of atomic tests, the flash takes on a variety of hues, one after another, as if the film had been damaged. When the shock waves finally hit Hiroshima and

Nagasaki, it was so powerful that no one had time to understand anything.

"At 8:15 [on August 6, 1945] I saw a blinding bluish-white flash from the window," Setsuko Thurlow said in her Nobel Peace Prize acceptance speech. "I remember having the sensation of floating in the air." That recollection makes sense from a physicist's point of view. The collapse of the building beneath her feet must have been so instantaneous that it left her hanging in midair for a moment, due to sheer inertia, before dropping in her turn.

Hiroshi Sawachika, who was twenty-eight years old, wrote that after the flash he suddenly felt "weightless as if I were an astronaut." And Shuntaro Hida, in his autobiography, mentioned feeling as if he were flying. On August 6, 1945, he was out of town to examine a little girl in the village of Hesaka, roughly six kilometers from ground zero. He was about to give the girl an injection when the flash blinded him. He had gotten drunk the night before, so it's possible that he at first attributed that strange phenomenon to a hallucination. Unlike Setsuko Thurlow, Shuntaro Hida also mentions the wave of heat that hit him. He saw the roof of the primary school rise into the air and a moment later he, too, was hanging in midair, tossed by the power of the blast through two rooms and against a Buddhist altar. For the rest of his life, he would remain uncertain whether or not he had ever given the girl her injection.

———

ENRICO FERMI had seen the flash before they did—to be exact, twenty days before they did, during the Trinity test: to all intents and purposes, the first atomic explosion in history. At the time, he was forty-four years old, he'd already won the Nobel Prize, and he had fled to the United States after the passage of the Italian race laws that would have applied to his wife Laura. There he had continued his studies on uranium, slow neutrons, and radioactive decay, but now with the objective of building the most powerful weapon that had ever been conceived. On July 16, 1945, in a New Mexico desert known by the sinister name of Jornada del Muerto (Day of the Dead), the project had finally attained completion.

Actually, Fermi saw the explosion without seeing it, because at the very moment he chose to avert his gaze from the darkened glass that separated him from the desert. "I had the impression that suddenly the entire country-side was brighter than in broad daylight," he later wrote. In fact, the sun had not yet risen. It was just 5:30 a.m.

What Fermi did instead of watching is well-known: he chose to measure. He tore a sheet of paper into confetti and scattered the scraps of paper in the air when the shock wave hit. He then measured how far the wind kicked up by the bomb pushed them from his hand. With a vector calculation he'd learned in his first year at university, he estimated that the explosion of "the gadget," the bomb used for the test, amounted to roughly ten kilotons of TNT. As was so often the case with Fermi, he wasn't far off.

When he went back to peering through his darkened glass, the nuclear explosion already looked like what we're accustomed to: a gray cloud rising fast into the sky, expanding and followed by an ascending column of sand and dust. In the Jornada del Muerto desert basin, the stalk and the head of the atomic mushroom cloud were as spectacular as could be because the gamma rays made the sandy soil bounce and dance, increasing the amount of dust. It was something that scientists call the popcorn effect.

AFTER THE TRINITY TEST, many of the physicists working on the Manhattan Project doubted that the bombs were actually going to be used, and certainly not on civilian targets. These weapons were far too destructive for anything but purposes of intimidation. Robert Oppenheimer, director of the Los Alamos laboratory, estimated that dropping one of these bombs on a city would cause roughly twenty thousand deaths. That was what scientists call a back-of-the-envelope calculation, which is to say a rough estimate jotted down on whatever scrap of paper happens to come to hand. Unlike Fermi, Oppenheimer was wrong: at Hiroshima alone, the direct deaths were more than a hundred thousand. But if anyone had mentioned a number of that sort at the time, to Oppenheimer or any of his fellow physicists, none of them would have believed it.

Incredulity seems to have been a constant as we review the history of the bomb. Many of the world's most venerated scientists, including Albert Einstein and Niels Bohr, were doubtful that the atom bomb could actually be built, and in any case, not before the end of the war. But in the summer of 1945, there were not one but two bombs ready for use, with different fissile materials, based on ad hoc technologies.

That said, what scientists might or might not think mattered little or not at all. From the accounts that survive, it would appear that by that point the procedures at Los Alamos were bureaucratic, brusque, and basically military in nature. A project had been initiated, the objective of the project was to build an atomic bomb, and once the bomb was finished, the bomb needed to be dropped somewhere. We now know that the idea of a demonstrative explosion of the weapon had never been taken into serious consideration. Quite the contrary: after lavishing all that cash and brainpower on it, the first explosions would have to cause the greatest possible devastation. They needed to set the world back on its heels.

If the result was going to be truly spectacular destruction, then what was needed was a fully intact target. A committee of scientists and military men drew up a short list of Japanese cities to be taken into consideration as objectives. Initially, Hiroshima was in second place. The B-29 bombing raids had thus far left it intact, unlike Tokyo, which would have been a more obvious target if it had not already been pounded into rubble.

Kyoto, the old imperial capital, seemed like the most promising target, in terms of its cultural and symbolic value and the sheer number of wooden houses and temples that would burn splendidly, with spectacular results. But the secretary of war, Henry L. Stimson, was present at the committee's meetings, and he had gone to Kyoto for his honeymoon twenty years earlier. He still had fond memories of that trip and insisted that the city be spared.

Hiroshima was moved up from secondary target to primary target. After that came Kokura, Niigata, and Nagasaki. To make the final choice of what target to hit, they could only wait for the weather reports and make sure not to miss the first sunny day.

ON AUGUST 6, 1945, at 8:15 a.m., a B-29 dropped Little Boy on Hiroshima.

Three days later, on August 9, at 11:02 a.m., Fat Man exploded over the western section of Nagasaki.

After the flash, Setsuko Thurlow regained consciousness buried in rubble. All around her, she heard the voices of the other girls, pleading but subdued, and then the voice of a man telling her to wriggle toward a narrow opening and continue pushing to free herself.

She managed to get out, unlike her female classmates, more than three hundred of them, who were all burned alive within a few minutes. Outside of the building, in the now-nonexistent city, Setsuko Thurlow saw survivors with their skin hanging off their bones. One person was holding their eyeballs in their hands.

Skin dangling off bodies is one of the recurrent visual details in survivors' accounts. On his way home, on the evening of August 6, Hiroshi Sawachika crossed paths with a column of injured people walking along the railroad tracks. "I looked carefully and found that what seemed like string was skin peeling off their arms due to burns." He was a twenty-eight-year-old doctor, newly married, on duty at the military hospital of Ujina-cho. After regaining consciousness following the blast, he immediately began treating a wounded person, but before long a great many more had begun to fill up the wrecked hospital room. Hiroshi Sawachika describes them as spectral: they emitted strange sounds as they wept and moaned, but still they lined up in an orderly fashion, awaiting their turn. At a certain point, a woman burst in, carrying a child in her arms. She'd been blinded by the explosion, so she was unable to see that her child was dead. Mercifully, the doctor took the boy without telling her, and she had enough time left to seem to feel some "relief," before falling lifelessly to the floor.

Both doctors and nurses had been hit by the blast just as hard as the rest of the city. According to estimates published later, 91 percent of the people in the city had been exposed to the explosion. So it was wounded and dying medical personnel who were trying to care for other wounded and dying people, on the street or else in hospitals that were barely still standing, without pharmaceuticals or equipment of any kind.

For the most part, they simply dabbed Mercurochrome onto horrifying gashes.

Among these medical professionals was Yutaka Tani, who was thirty-three years old and an ear, nose, and throat specialist. He recalls that the most seriously wounded were assembled in the lobby of the Red Cross hospital, lying on tatami, "laid out like tuna in a fish market." Under their bandages, their wounds were literally crawling with maggots. It was impossible to remove all the maggots, so the air was filled with buzzing flies.

Still, all of that—namely, the burns, the suppurating cuts, the sudden blindness, the faces pocked with glass shards, the bared craniums, even the flies—all of that, horrifying though it might have been, was at least comprehensible to the surviving doctors of Hiroshima. Much less understandable was the fact that the burns were a different color than ordinary burns, white instead of red, and even more baffling were the symptoms that began to present in the hours or days that followed: patches on the skin, incessant vomiting, the dysentery that hit so many and that was initially mistaken for an epidemic outbreak. Those symptoms were all the more serious in those who had been exposed to the black rain.

In fact, after the atomic mushroom cloud rose into the air, bizarre atmospheric phenomena ensued. The most terrifying of them all was this: the sky filled with extremely dark clouds, inside which lurked dust and dirt of all kinds, much of it highly radioactive, that had seeded the water vapor, allowing it to condense. Soon, a dark, dense rain began to fall.

But because no atom bomb had ever been dropped before, and indeed none had ever exploded before, save for once in a New Mexican desert, hidden from the public gaze: in short, because atom bombs had until that day not existed at all, no one knew what it was that had exploded in the sky over Hiroshima, no one knew anything about radiation, black rain, contamination, or fallout.

Actually, a very few people *did* know. On August 8, two days after the explosion, the Japanese physicist Yoshio Nishina was brought to Hiroshima, and he had confirmed to the government that this had been a nuclear attack. How could he make that statement with such confidence? Well, he, too, had been working for years to build an atom bomb for his own country, Japan, but he now realized that he hadn't moved fast enough.

A FEW WEEKS AFTER the detonation of the two atom bombs, toward the end of August, the survivors started to lose their hair. They lost weight. Many of them started vomiting blood, which at first made doctors think of tuberculosis.

Then, in October, they recovered. Whatever this strange bomb-borne disease might have been, it seemed to be a passing affliction.

By the end of the year, however, keloids began to appear, bulging scars that were not in and of themselves especially uncommon. In the bomb survivors, however, the keloids took on unprecedented dimensions, huge and disfiguring. Three years later, cases of anemia, leukemia, and a very distinctive form of early cataracts began to appear. This was already the postwar period, the time of the Cold War and the arms race, and no one was interested in publicizing the long-term effects of atomic weapons. For the most part, survivors were tucked away, out of sight, and their conditions ignored.

Hagie Ota called her condition *itai-itai* disease, which roughly translates as ouch-ouch disease, or hurt-hurt disease. She suffered intensely and constantly her whole life. During a commemorative conference in 1978, she said: "I really feel tired all over. I feel my body is heavy, as if I were dressed in armor."

The reason she survived on August 6, 1945, was because she refused to follow instructions. Defying the regulations that called for wearing black clothing in order to be less visible in case of air raids, Hagie Ota had worn white. White, which reflects electromagnetic radiation instead of absorbing it, had partly spared her from being burned, though she only understood that many years later. Just as she had later come to realize that crossing ground zero to collect the objects she needed, and especially drinking water from there, had been reckless in the extreme.

Meanwhile, the radiation had produced a slow-motion massacre among the scientists as well. In one of the Los Alamos laboratories, in 1946, Louis Slotin was working with a subcritical mass of plutonium, surrounded by two beryllium-coated half spheres: a technology jocularly referred to as the "demon core." Instead of using wedges or shims to separate the two half spheres, as protocol required, Slotin decided to work more nonchalantly, with a screwdriver. As often happens with screwdrivers, he lost his grip, and the two beryllium masses snapped together into contact, instantly elevating the plutonium to a supercritical state and emitting a blue flash, an intense blast of gamma rays and neutrons. Just minutes later, Slotin was throwing up and nine days later he was dead.

Regular exposure to radiation caused the deaths of Irène Curie and her husband Frédéric Joliot, as well as Enrico Fermi himself. Nine years had passed since Hiroshima, and the world had already equipped itself with roughly 2,500 nuclear warheads.

As for the woman who had actually discovered radiation, Marie ~~Curie~~ Skłodowska, she hadn't lived to witness any of this. In her last days on earth, her hands were so badly burned that they'd become phosphorescent, but she refused to accept that the cause might be the sources of radium and polonium that she had handled for years without any form of protection. Studies on the interactions between ionizing radiation and biological tissues had already been published, but Marie ~~Curie~~ Skłodowska, twice a Nobel laureate, died a denialist, with the reassuring conviction that the radiation she had discovered would bring humankind nothing but good.

AFTER THE WAR ENDED, troubled by the consequences of the work they'd done (namely the slaughter
of hundreds of thousands of people and the oblitera-
tion of two cities), several Manhattan Project physicists
formed a nonprofit association that is now called the
Bulletin of the Atomic Scientists. They made it their
mission to monitor the progress of nuclear risk. In
order to do so graphically and understandably, they
invented a metaphor: the Doomsday Clock. When that
clock strikes midnight, it symbolically coincides with
the end of the world.

According to the Bulletin's scientists, things weren't
going particularly well at the turn of 2017. In that year's
report, we read: The committee "has decided to move
the minute hand of the Doomsday Clock 30 seconds

closer to catastrophe. It is now two minutes and 30 seconds to midnight."

There were various reasons: the United States and Russia were facing off on various fronts, especially Syria and Ukraine, while increasing the sophistication of their arsenals. Also, North Korea was persisting in its nuclear testing. If people weren't talking about the nuclear threat anymore, it wasn't because it had ebbed. It was only because interest in, and concern about the topic, had ebbed instead. Just to make a useful comparison: in 1990 the Doomsday Clock said that it was ten minutes to midnight, that is, to the apocalypse.

Whatever the Bulletin might have had to say, I wasn't feeling too bad about things at the beginning of 2017, and in any case that had nothing to do with any of the reasons listed in the report. From the day I made my somewhat theatrical announcement to Lorenza, I had been working on my book about the bomb with a consistency that was unusual for me, and I'd gotten roughly seventy pages or so down on paper. In the mornings I would go for long walks through Rome, following the banks of the Tiber, from the Ponte Cestio (Pons Cestius, or Cestian Bridge) to the Castel Sant'Angelo (or Mausoleum of Hadrian), the whole time mentally planning out my afternoon's spate of writing. I tried to imagine what might have been unfolding in the minds of the physicists who had worked on the bomb, what it was like for them to be frothing blends of the furor of discovery and a sneaking unease over the ultimate consequences of that discovery, as well as where their willful myopia lay, their explicit and intentional blindness, and in what proportions. I tried to guess how I would have behaved in their shoes: Would I have persisted, would I have turned and walked away, would I have been capable of glimpsing the future, and if so, would I have been able to rise to the level of that vision?

When I was taking a break from writing, I'd surf my way through Nukemap, an online simulator that allowed you to detonate nuclear warheads anywhere on earth, varying the power to quantify the expanse of destruction, the number of victims, and the range of the fallout. I would set off Little Boy, then move on to Fat Man, detonating it from the ground, then at an elevation of five hundred meters. I'd proceed to watch as the number of victims doubled.

I'd try out one bomb after another, right up to the most powerful of them all, the five-hundred-megaton Tsar Bomba. For my target, I almost always chose the roof of our house. According to Nukemap's simulation, Tsar Bomba would have left a crater four hundred meters deep in the center of Rome, while the shock wave would have shattered windows as far away as Anzio and Civitavecchia. The mushroom cloud would rise forty-three kilometers into the sky.

I was hardly alone in my pursuit: the site recorded and displayed the total number of detonations set off by its users, well over two million blasts. There must be thousands of aspiring destroyers of worlds out there.

The end of humanity as a species had become a new pastime.

As for me, I spent most of my time thinking about the bomb, instead of about the children that Lorenza and I were never going to have. I was sufficiently self-aware to understand that this was hardly a favorable trade-off, but what else could I do?

Around that time, news got out about a proposed bill in Sweden for a poorly reasoned law. The Swedish politician responsible for it was named Per-Erik Muskos. Muskos wanted to give all government employees an extra hour of lunchtime every week to devote specifically to sex. The new regulation was meant not only to promote workers' psychic and physical well-being, but also to encourage procreation, an important consideration in a country where the birth rate was currently in a power dive. This was the sort of vaguely lewd item that radio news anchors could spin out for at least fifteen minutes of airtime. In fact, I had heard it on the radio, and it had prompted me to reflect on what Lorenza and I would have done with that extra hour of free time. I doubted we'd use that hour having sex. Did that make us an anomalous couple? If so, did anomalous necessarily mean bad? Whatever the answer, I certainly hoped nobody ever thought of passing such a law in Italy.

Years ago, when we were taking our prematrimonial course, Karol had suggested we do an exercise: choose which of our five senses we'd want to keep if we knew we were suddenly going to lose all of the others. As was to be expected, nearly all of the group decided to save their sense of sight, with the exception of one young woman, who had elected to preserve her sense of smell, and three others—including me—who had preferred to keep their sense of hearing. After sharing these choices, every couple had been invited to talk it over in private. There I learned that Lorenza had taken offense. She had taken my decision personally, as if somehow I wasn't sufficiently interested in being able to look at her. Karol sat down to talk about it with us, and he had drawn all the information out of her. Then he had hugged us both, a gesture that struck me as theatrical and definitely far too intimate. In the car, Lorenza had wondered aloud, How on earth did he come up with that? All the same, that night we made love with an uncommon degree of light-hearted glee. I realized that, in some mysterious fashion, all credit went to Karol.

I would sometimes think back on it, especially when Lorenza's and my sex life together had become fragmentary and exhausting. I wondered what element on that day had unearthed an unexpected complicity between the two of us: The sequence of distancing/clarification? Or was it the laughter in the car? Or perhaps Karol's hug? If I had been able to plumb the very origin, perhaps I'd have been able to apply the same approach again, as often as I wanted.

WE'D CHOSEN the prematrimonial course, which was required, on the basis of a very simple criterion:

it had to be conducted by a progressive parish priest, and from the references that we'd been given, Karol fit the bill. After our wedding, for which he had officiated, we'd stayed in touch, and for a certain period he and I had even attended a boxing basics class together, in the San Lorenzo quarter.

Now Karol was the only outsider to know about our experience with the Dutch couple. I had been reluctant to tell him the story, I was afraid he'd think badly of me, or even worse, that it would ruin his opinion of Lorenza, whom he truly venerated. Officially, Karol was an expert on conjugal relations, but the situation we'd got ourselves into this time seemed like one that transcended that context, a much harder dilemma to grasp, a blind alley that collapsed into a singularity of warring emotions and sensations, so that each lost its recognizable configuration until it could no longer even be named.

But I was wrong to worry. When I told Karol about it, he'd let each sentence I spoke flow down into one of his vast silences, pure and free of any taint of blame. Then he'd asked me whether I felt happier or sadder with respect to that night, and I had replied in complete sincerity that I couldn't say, but I certainly felt less alive.

In February he asked me to go with him for a swim in the sea. One of the parishioners had given him a winter wet suit and he wanted to try it out. I wasn't especially eager to upset my writing routine, but in the end I gave in. The imbalance between the amount of attention he devoted to us compared to the attention he demanded of us tilted so sharply in our favor that I hardly felt it decent to turn down any invitation he might extend. At seven in the morning, I picked him up outside the church. He was waiting for me, bundled up in cap and gloves. There had been no need to set out so early, while it was still dark, but Karol's days were measured up far more rigorously than mine, punctuated relentlessly by commitments to his community, and they began long before mine did.

In the car, he offered me a piece of fruit tart that he'd wrapped up in a paper napkin. By then I'd emerged from my sleepiness and felt strangely grateful to him for obliging me to leave my bed. I almost never witnessed that hour of the morning, and it felt bracing and good, pure and clean. I told him so and he replied in a monotone, gazing out the side window: I see it every single day.

On the beach, we struggled into our wet suits. We must have looked amateurish and awkward, but luckily there was no one to see us.

Karol was daunted by the waves, which were coming in bigger and taller than the wind and surf report had promised. They didn't seem like that big of a deal to me. He gave me a tutorial on how to slip the wet suit on over my skin. Mine was borrowed, from the same person who had given the other wet suit to Karol, but the guy had assured me that it had been thoroughly washed.

When I first hit the water I felt nothing, except for my bare feet, but once I was fully immersed an icy rivulet ran down between my shoulder blades, all the way to my tailbone.

We swam perpendicular to the beach, to get out a certain distance, and then turned, horizontally, swimming parallel to the shore. I understood why the waves worried him so. Swimming against the current was much more tiring than expected, but it was even worse to try to swim parallel with the wave front, because it forced you to alter and correct your angle of attack on a continual basis. What's more, the water was murky, visibility was practically zero, and Karol was swimming faster than me. That meant I was constantly having to raise my head to see where he was now.

When we stopped to catch our breath, I was amazed to see how far we were from shore. How far do you think we've gone? I asked him.

About a mile.

I swam farther. I was zigzagging to keep an eye on you.

For a while we lay flat on our backs, our wet suits eliminating nearly all of the effort of staying on the surface. I observed Karol's abdomen, sheathed in neoprene, as it broke the surface like the back of a marine mammal. This is nice, isn't it? he asked me. Nice, yes indeed. Then he said: I have a question I'd like to ask, but it might strike you as a bit odd.

Let's see if it really is.

I wanted to ask what life is like as a couple.

I splashed water in his face and he straightened up, squinting.

There was no need to come all the way out here, I told him. You can reassure Lorenza once and for all that I'm fine. If I seem a little preoccupied, it's just because I'm focusing on my work.

On that thing you're doing about the bomb.

On that thing I'm doing about the bomb, that's right.

Karol swam a lap around me. He filled his mouth with salt water and then spat it out. He must have evaluated the escape route I had just unwittingly offered him, but then he stopped, his face turned to the sun, which was still low on the horizon, just above the flat buildings along the Roman seashore. He hugged tight the inflatable swim buoy he kept leashed to his waist. Without looking at me, he said: Actually, this has nothing to do with Lorenza. I was asking for myself.

I made an effort to remain impassive as I tried to formulate the most appropriate question to ask him. At last, I opted for the following: Man or woman?

A girl.

Karol allowed himself a fairly long pause before adding: Younger than me.

How much younger?

She's twenty-two.

A wave pushed us apart. My feet were starting to feel the chill, but there was no way that I was going to be the one to interrupt that moment. I started flexing and stretching my toes to prevent cramps.

We just text, Karol said. We talk about movies or books that we like. She's a very sensitive person. More mature than her age.

I knew nothing about his relationship with physical desire. I couldn't even say if he was a virgin. He'd entered the seminary at age twenty-one, so he'd have had time to get plenty of experience before that, but who could say? I grabbed hold of the inflatable swim buoy. In that way we were, in a certain sense, connected.

You're not saying a word, he chuckled. I've silenced you.

No. No, no. Not at all.

But I couldn't add anything to that. Karol suggested we start swimming again.

He was swimming faster now. I could feel my arms growing numb, I was starting to have trouble coordinating my breathing with my arm strokes, and I was getting the impression we were moving out too far away from the shore.

Suddenly, something appeared at the edge of my field of view. I lurched aside to avoid it. It was a large white jellyfish, with a violet border along its dome. I swam as far away as I could and started yelling Karol's name. When he finally turned to see where I was, I gestured that I wanted to get out of the water immediately.

We trudged down the beach, our wet suits dripping. We peeled them off next to the car, dried ourselves off as best we could, shivering violently all the while, and got dressed, our backs turned to each other. I only glimpsed for a moment his pale, almost hairless body, and it struck me as vulnerable despite his perfect musculature.

Then we sat down on a low wall to drink coffee from the thermos. Once again, Karol was radiating his force field of calmness. So he had taken me all the way out there that morning with a specific intention, it had all been carefully premeditated. He needed to be far away from terra firma, with me, in the absolute silence of the sea, so he could make a confession to me of something that no one else could hear. Far enough out, I thought, to ensure that those words couldn't be overheard by even the Lord Almighty.

If I were you, I'd be cautious and take it slow, I told him, without knowing why those exact words had come out of my mouth. See how it goes. Don't make any decisions.

Karol went on sipping his coffee, staring out to sea and making no gesture of a response. I'd probably been a disappointment to him. But probably his expectations of me had been excessive.

Her name is Elisa, he said.

In the car, the whole way back, he never once stopped twisting the napkin that had held the tart. Tiny shreds of paper drifted onto the car seat, and I wondered if the vacuum cleaner at the car wash would get them up.

Karol pointed to a wide space in the road and asked me to drop him there.

But it's still more than a mile away.

I'd prefer to walk. I still have time.

I pulled over, but he waited before opening his door. He grimaced, twisting his lips as if examining something, then said: I need a loan. A small loan. It seems to me that you're the only person I can ask.

Perhaps I hesitated just an instant too long. I sensed that he was examining not only every word I spoke, but every single pause. Of course, don't think twice. How much?

For the first time he smiled as he shrugged. I don't know. How much does a decent hotel cost? He laughed in his nervousness. A hotel and a dinner, maybe.

His eyes met mine and, in that lightning glance, he struck me as much younger.

Well, son, you're definitely out of practice. Two hundred euros ought to hold you. I'll send you a wire transfer if you give me your details.

Better not.

Of course, I see your point.

I pulled out my wallet and looked inside. This really was an odd scene. But I'm just not sure, I said. I've got one hundred twenty euros right here, right now. We can go find an ATM.

That's plenty. I'll make it work.

He plucked the banknotes out of my fingers and rolled them up before slipping them into his heavy jacket. I'll pay you back in a month, no longer.

He cracked the door open, but then just sat there. I'm sorry, he said under his breath.

It's just a hundred twenty euros, they're not worth anyone being sorry about.

No. I'm sorry to have disappointed you. As a priest.

When I was ten, I was my mother's secret confidant. I think I'll be able to get over this too.

This time, though, Karol stayed somber. A spiritual guide shouldn't let himself be compromised. And he certainly shouldn't borrow money.

He seemed so alone. I wished I could touch him in some way, put a hand on his thigh to make it clear that I was completely on his side, but no such contact between us was even remotely plausible.

It's pretty arrogant of you to think of yourself as my spiritual guide, you realize that, don't you?

In the end, it's almost always irony that saves male friendships. Karol took a deep breath, and that's all it took to change his expression, as if he'd not only expelled a lungful of air but also all his thoughts of a moment ago with it. He opened the car door, and with one foot already on the pavement, he added: I hardly need to tell you that I'd appreciate your keeping this confidential.

In fact, no need whatsoever.

Because all this might turn out to be nothing but a flash in the pan. In fact, it's almost certainly nothing. Just another challenge to overcome.

I watched him shrink into the distance in my rearview mirror. Before vanishing as I rounded the curve, he pulled his phone out of his heavy jacket. It was clear that he'd lied to me when he said he wanted to walk all the way to church. He just wanted some time to call her on the phone. I wondered if he would tell her about me right away, and about the money he'd finally got his hands on so they could have their romantic tryst. Everything about it was charmingly old-fashioned but also slightly laughable. But behind those obvious feelings, I found myself harboring a hint of envy, to my surprise. I could guess at the bolts of adrenaline, serotonin, and all the other electrochemical substances involved in psychic well-being flooding through Karol's brain as he hunted for the girl's number in his directory, as he waited for her to answer, as he heard her voice still muffled with sleep, and all the while walking along the side of the road, cutting through the calf-high fog that pooled around him, making him appear from this distance as if he were walking atop a low-lying cloud. He had put all that off for twenty years, saving himself for some other end, and now he could relish that euphoria directly and with back interest, like the young man he'd never been. The anticipation of the night together, the thrill of transgression: both things that seemed off the table for me, now and forever after.

I HAD TALKED TO HIM about the island, but I hadn't told him everything. Because what had happened there had been difficult to put into words, and even just trying to express it would have meant acknowledging its truth. It couldn't be done without either leonine courage or suicidal courage, and I possessed neither. The fact that I'm doing it now, nearly six years later, and to be exact, on November 3, 2021, can be explained by the fact that there's no one here but me and my computer screen, a screen that, as I proceed to tell this story, more and more resembles a mirror. When I get to the end, I might just decide to delete the whole thing.

In any case, I don't remember many details. After all, I'd had a lot to drink at that dinner with the Dutch couple, Otto and Maaike or whatever the hell their names were. Sitting across from me and Lorenza, their lips were smeared with purple wine stains from that bottle of Chilean red, exactly as both her lips and mine were stained purple, though all I can remember is *their* lips. Those darkened lips gave them a ravenous appearance, but perhaps they weren't ravenous at all, they were merely sad and in search of friendship, exactly as we were. They had a daughter who suffered from a rare disease, the kind of thing being studied by only a couple of laboratories in the world, and for which no one's ever going to find a cure. Otto and Maaike could only afford to take a week off every year on their own, and then only because their daughter was entrusted to the care of a volunteer association, and this was the week in question, so they had decided to enjoy it to the fullest.

We had learned all this during the course of the meal and afterward, when we moved out onto loungers on the terrace. From there we could see the seabed through the gaps between the flooring planks, because the terrace was on stilts over the water and the seabed was illuminated by side-angled spotlights. There were crabs and brightly colored fish and every so often a

small wriggling shark. The resort staff had assured us
that the sharks weren't dangerous. On the terrace the
other couple had listed the destinations they'd visited
in the last few years. They preferred tropical islands
because they'd experienced all the cold they needed
in The Hague. Plus, there were always affordable all-
inclusive package deals. Lorenza and I listened without
telling them much about us. We'd had a lot to drink, as
I've already pointed out, and it was becoming increasingly clear that when it came to that type of experimen-
tation, we two were the beginners there. We started
talking about the hotel, benefits and shortcomings.
Otto and Maaike were envious of our ocean room. Of
course, they'd considered getting one, but the extra fee
had been daunting. Still, they'd love to see what one
looked like. They wondered if they were very different,
really, when it came to the furnishings and the décor.

It just seemed natural to offer to take them to see
it right then and there, and it was Lorenza who made
the invitation, not me, I'm almost positive of it, just as
I'm almost positive that when she said it she was looking at me, not them, which made no sense in theory,
except for the fact that it was a way for her to confirm
and verify what had, until then, been at the very most
a temptation, a vague possibility fluttering in the air
around us.

All four of us walked down the extremely long
pier that led to our room, and as we walked I thought
about the little sharks beneath us and the wooden pil-
ings driven into the sandy seabed that were no doubt

coated with razor-sharp mollusk shells. When we got to the room, we pretended that we really had brought them there for a guided tour: here's the minifridge, this is where we watch the sunrise, if we wake up early enough, that is, there's even a little patio, and no doubt, taking a plunge first thing, straight out of bed, is the best. I caught myself standing there, in front of the wide-open window, spouting that stream of banalities to Maaike, who had started staring at me with an odd intensity, and it was her gaze that suggested I turn around. Behind us, Otto had his face pressed against my wife's neck. He was sucking on Lorenza's flesh and she was staring wide-eyed in my direction, her expression betraying just a hint of sadness. I didn't feel anything specific. Which is to say: nothing that I could file away with precision, nothing that would prompt this given reaction rather than some other. I felt aghast and thrilled and scared all at once, a set of feelings that approached in terms of intensity certain out-of-control emotions you might experience around age thirteen but then never, never again.

Now Maaike was standing next to me, caressing my arm politely, as if calming my nerves while she watched the same scene unfold before her. As before, Lorenza was doing nothing, or what she was doing, I thought to myself, was not putting up any resistance. She let herself be pushed onto the bed by Otto, where he undressed her and went on kissing her in a way that struck me as somehow furious. Then Maaike pulled away from me and went over to assist her husband.

Lorenza lifted her hand and, without smiling, said to me: Come here.

I lay down next to her and for a fairly long while we both lay there, inert, letting the Dutch couple do as they saw fit, after all, they had the requisite experience, they knew everything, whereas we knew nothing. We were just bound together in a melancholy that had never seemed so immense and bottomless as it did, right then, in that moment. We could only let ourselves be kissed and caressed, and there was even a certain gentle sweetness in the way they did it, a gentleness veined with brutality.

Lorenza and I exchanged a few brief phrases in Italian, in low voices. The fact that the Dutch couple couldn't understand them made them extraordinarily intimate. We said are you really sure about this and I love you, and then I told her I was sorry and Lorenza said don't worry about it. I hoped that there wouldn't be actual intercourse at the end, at least not between her and Otto, but if it happened I wouldn't do anything to prevent it.

Now Maaike devoted herself to my genitals, exploring all around and behind them, with a special earnest dedication. At a certain point it was as if I had thought to myself, *Okay, this is the moment when you surrender, this is the moment after which you can control nothing*, but it's only as if I'd thought that, because in reality I'd already burrowed down into a place where no thoughts were happening at all, where all that existed was the body and its actions and blind instinct. Lorenza was far away. It was that distance and that blind instinct, I think, that made me lean over Otto. I rolled over onto my side and I stretched out over him. I kept my eyes closed while I did it, but I sensed his surprise and, more distantly, I sensed Maaike's surprise as well as Lorenza's. The room froze still for a moment, maybe because I had violated the preordained geometry, until Otto's hand (if it was his, I think that it was his) came to rest on the nape of my neck, exerting no pressure, without encouraging or discouraging anything, only—I thought from that solitary recess of the soul into which I had tumbled—forgiving me for everything.

IN THE MORNING, Lorenza and I said nothing about it. We said nothing about it that afternoon, or for that matter the following evening. We went down to the hotel's beach separately. It was a very long day, during which we spent more time than necessary packing our bags. At dinner, we waved goodbye to the Dutch couple from afar. It was everybody's last evening there, so it was completely understandable that we wouldn't sit at their table again. Lorenza pilfered an avocado and a mango from the buffet and slipped them into her suitcase. I told her they would get cold in the airplane's hold and would probably be ruined, and that it might very well be considered illegal to transport fruit aboard an intercontinental flight, but she paid me no mind. I don't remember, once we were back in Rome, ever tasting either the avocado or mango. Perhaps, after all, she just kept them both for herself.

BY MARCH I'd reached the point of no return with the book. I decided to reward myself with a trip to visit Giulio in Paris, because if nothing else, the court date was drawing near.

By a margin of mere hours, I dodged a terror attack at Orly, a minor incident no one even remembers anymore. A lone terrorist had stolen a Citroën and driven it to the airport; once there, he attacked a female soldier, successfully wresting away her assault rifle, but was successfully shot and killed before he could do anything worse. Attacks like this one barely even made the news anymore, but showing up at the wrong time might mean finding an airport paralyzed by police activity or, even worse, seeing your flight canceled entirely.

Giulio came to meet me at the Denfert bus stop, then we walked together back to Rue de la Gaîté. A fine drizzle was falling, diagonally, and it sprinkled the lenses of his glasses, though he hardly seemed to notice. He asked me if I'd ever visited the catacombs and I told him I hadn't. So we made plans to do so together... one day, but certainly not that weekend, because he was going to have Adriano. After all, that was the reason I was there in the first place.

When are we going to go get him? I asked. I realized how inadequate that use of the first-person plural really was, but Giulio overlooked it: Tomorrow morning.

Adriano wasn't going to be spending the night. Cobalt preferred not to have him sleep away from home, because she claimed that afterward he was off-kilter for days on end. Away from home would be to stay at your place?

Exactly.

If he wanted to, Giulio could have appealed that sort of decision in court, lash back, point by point, and never give up an inch of ground, but as he told me, in a divorce like theirs, he needed to pick his battles carefully. He couldn't afford a military escalation, he said. And by now you ought to be an expert on that sort of thing.

I ignored that reference to the book, in part because it had the ring of mockery. Giulio often had an indecipherable way of talking about my work, as if he didn't really take it seriously. It was as if, all in all, he considered it the product of blind luck that I'd wound up doing what I did for a living. I asked him which battle he'd picked this time.

Enrolling Adriano in an Italian school.

Cobalt doesn't agree with that?

No, she wants him in a Parisian school. To help him fit into his surroundings better. At least that's the official version. But I think it's mainly to help Adriano get along better with his new stepfather.

She's with somebody?

With Luc. And has been for two years. A bit of a right-winger. And definitely wealthy.

Giulio's main worry, in the case that Adriano *did* attend a French school, was that he would no longer be able to help with his homework, that he would be cut out of his education entirely, after he'd already been cut out of much of the boy's everyday life. Giulio's French was barely workable, just survival level, and at the university he worked with Italians, Russians, and Germans. Everyone talked English all day long, and outside of the university his life was basic, just the bare necessities.

So, anyway, what all that means is that tomorrow evening we'll be free men. And we're invited to a party.

Will this be a nerd party?

Not too much of one, at least I hope. At Novelli's house.

It had been more than a year since I'd first met Novelli. With the exception of the surreal exchange from Guadeloupe, we'd written each other roughly a dozen or so messages, nearly all of them mere notes of courtesy. Best wishes for the holidays, that sort of thing. One time he sent me a link to one of his publications, but the message was a forward, so I'd taken it for granted that it had probably also gone out to a considerable percentage of the names in his directory.

He's become something of a media star, Giulio told me. He was asked to appear a couple of times on France Inter to talk about climate, and apparently he showed unexpected flashes of talent. A number of listeners wrote in and asked the station to invite him back. Or at least so he now claims. In any case, he must have gone over well. Throw in the Italian accent, which the French seem to go wild over, for some twisted predilection all their own. The fact is, he's become a regular guest, and these days he's a commentator on just about anything he wants to be. Truth be told, I've only listened to half of one of his appearances, on a podcast. But I told him you were coming to town and he's happy to have you at his birthday party. If you don't have anything else planned, that is.

We should find a gift to bring.

Giulio shot me a glance. It just hadn't occurred to me. I'm afraid that my level of social ineptitude has reached rock bottom.

Tickets for a show? I suggested. Wine?

Cheese, as creamy as possible. He's crazy about it.

When we got to the piazza, we veered off in the direction of the supermarket. Bringing a gift of a cellophane-wrapped store-bought cheese hardly seemed like the height of good manners, and I thought what Lorenza would have had to say about it. That said, the etiquette among physicists was different than in the rest of the

world. It called for extreme frugality and lack of ceremony, and I'd lost my familiarity with it.

We took advantage of the opportunity to buy a bottle of wine just for us, some chocolate, and a couple of
bags of potato chips. We walked up to the cash register
with an array of groceries that screamed out *bachelors*.
Just seeing it all heaped up on the cash register con-
veyor belt gave me a bolt of energy, a surge of vitality, as
if I'd suddenly turned young again. I insisted on paying, since I was the houseguest, but Giulio refused to
hear of it. You're here to help me, he said in a suddenly
harsh tone of voice, and I complied to keep him from
feeling bad about it.

LATER, IN THE BATHROOM at his apartment,
I noticed scratches on the door handle. When I asked
him what those were, Giulio just continued arranging
the cushions on the sofa that he was making up into my
jury-rigged bed for the night.

They're from a few weeks ago, he said, after a pause.
Adriano shut himself in.

Damn.

To be more exact, he locked himself in, with a key.
He was furious at me, though I still don't know what
about, exactly. The usual issues with the iPad, I'm
guessing. He told me that he wouldn't come out of the
bathroom until I had called his mother. At first I just
ignored him. But then, after two, then three hours had
gone by, he was still in there.

Three hours?

He even stopped answering me. If I pressed my ear against the door, all I could hear was this scratching, and then even that stopped. I don't know why, but I started to get worried.

I told him that *I* sure knew why, and the reason seemed pretty obvious. Giulio, as usual, tried to minimize: Nothing bad could have happened to him. You've seen that bathroom, there's nothing in there but the toilet. Still, after a while I really freaked out. I started jerking and hammering on the door, but I just couldn't get it open. Kicking it down was out of the question. It would have hit him in the face. I called and called him, but he wouldn't answer. Plus, it was almost time for me to take him back to Cobalt. If I didn't show up on time, I'd never have heard the end of it.

We were both standing. Giulio in front of the window, at an angle, seemed to be talking to the cushion that I'd tossed to the floor.

In the end, I went downstairs to a neighbor's apartment and borrowed his tool kit. I came back up and disassembled the lock. When I opened the door, he was fast asleep in there. He was sitting on the toilet seat. I don't know how long he'd been sleeping. But he'd definitely been scratching at the doorknob with a nail before that. Don't ask me what he was doing with a nail in his pocket, because I really have no idea.

He tossed a sheet on the sofa without tucking it in.

Anyway, lately he's been pretty calm. Should we go get something to eat?

We went down to the Lebanese place and got drunk. In that more forgiving atmosphere, I allowed him to renew his interest in my book. I no longer sensed the undercurrent of mockery, or if I did, I no longer much cared. As was to be expected, even though I'd been working full-time on the project for two months now, Giulio knew lots of things about the subject that I'd never heard of. On one of his solo trips, he'd been to Karabash, a small town in the Urals, not far from Chelyabinsk. There, for decades, Russia had secretly conducted its atomic program. Theoretically, anyway, the city was off-limits, and the whole area was heavily guarded and patrolled. In fact, though, Giulio had made his way in without any great difficulty, with the help of a guy he'd found online who organized "horror tours." He'd brought a Geiger counter with him, and near what was generally referred to as the lake of death, the needle had jumped from the microsievert range up into millisieverts. It was a fairly, uh, I don't know, *attractive* place, he said.

Attractive?

You could sense a sort of dark power. Not exactly malevolent. It came from the radiation or from the history of the place. Anyway, I didn't stay there long, or at least I don't think I did. I hope not long enough to cause some kind of weird mutation. He laughed. We hadn't had Adriano yet, and I really wasn't planning to have children at all. I hope I didn't unintentionally harm him.

———

THE NEXT MORNING, I waited in the apartment while Giulio went downstairs to the building's courtyard to get Adriano. It was raining harder than the day before, and I was afraid that this was going to turn out to be a very long day. I walked over to the window to watch the handover. I had a certain indirect experience with this sort of thing, from when Lorenza was doing the same thing with Eugenio. Once I'd found myself sitting in a car, hidden around the corner from the handover site, waiting for the two of them to reappear together. After they got in the car, there was always a fairly long period of silence while Lorenza and I gave Eugenio the time he needed to get acclimated to the other half of his life.

Giulio's apartment was on the third floor, so it was a fairly short straight shot to the courtyard below. I watched Adriano throw himself at his father and grab his legs, while Cobalt was hidden beneath a red umbrella. She handed a bag to Giulio, who took it from her while clearly keeping his distance. Then Giulio must have said something that drove Cobalt into a rage, but all I could hear was her response, because she was speaking at a much higher volume: We've already booked the train tickets!

I cautiously cracked open the window, just enough to let the sound through.

Every time we have to plan our vacations, Cobalt was saying, every single time, you find a way of gumming up the works.

Now I could hear him too: Gum up the works. You always choose such interesting turns of phrase. Gum up the works.

That's when Cobalt really lost it: Are we going to have a language usage lesson, Giulio? Today, again? Let's go, I'm ready!

He told Adriano to stand under the umbrella, but the boy walked a few steps away and started scratching the edge of the gate with a branch. While he did it, he seemed raptly absorbed in what he was doing, even though it was clear that every sense in his body was focused on his parents' conversation. Giulio suggested Adriano go upstairs, saying he'd be up right after him, but again, Adriano failed to obey him.

And then he turned back to Cobalt and said: Let me remind you that spring vacation belongs to me.

I decided that he'd changed his mind and now considered it advantageous for the boy to hear what was being said. He was very chilly, whereas by that point, Cobalt was clearly very agitated. Oh, really? she said. Oh, really?

The agreement we signed calls for an even split of vacation time. Unless you've forgotten that. Now, taking into consideration that—

Oh, Giulio, just fuck off!

At that point, Adriano looked up at his mother. I could imagine that he was accustomed to that sort of tension, but I had no idea whether he was used to open and direct insults.

Giulio said: Oh, very nice, in that typically mocking tone of voice he used. Then he pulled Adriano to his side, and hand in hand they walked in through the main door. Cobalt said goodbye to her son, calling him *chouchou*. But she didn't turn to go right away. She just stood there, motionless, and she might have been staring at the main entrance door, now shut, but that was just a guess because her open umbrella continued to hide her from my sight. She lit a cigarette, and a few seconds later, she must have felt my eyes on her from on high, or else she was expecting to see Adriano at the window. Whatever the reason, she looked up and at that moment our eyes locked. Cobalt didn't look surprised, she didn't smile, she didn't so much as wave her hand. She simply registered my presence. Then she turned and left the courtyard.

FOR MANY YEARS, the nomadic life of research fellowship recipients had seemed ideal for Giulio and Cobalt. The cities they went to were always too expensive for the stipends they received, but it never seemed to be a problem. They lived in bare-walled, scantily furnished apartments, which they never even bothered trying to decorate. After all, they never planned to stay more than two years. They ate whenever possible in the university cafeteria and saved every penny for travel. Any chance they got, they'd buy tickets for the most absurd places in Africa, or Papua New Guinea. Once I went to visit them in Copenhagen, and I'm not exaggerating when I say that, at the front door, tossed casually into the heap of objects on the side table along with the house keys, there were two packets of Malarone anti-malaria medication.

When Cobalt realized she was pregnant, Giulio had already purchased tickets for a trip to Cambodia. They left when she was midway through her seventh month. Both his parents and hers were furious at them, but they weren't the kind of couple who paid much attention to their parents' wishes (not back then, at least, but then things changed and they each went through a sort of retrocession, allowing themselves to be reabsorbed by their nucleus of origin).

Once they arrived in Phnom Penh, they rented a car and slept in hostels and anywhere else they happened to fetch up, occasionally in the homes of locals. They knew no other way of traveling. Cobalt did make sure that the vegetables they ate had been properly cooked. Despite her precautions, she caught a parasitic worm. By that point they'd already visited Angkor Wat, so they decided to head north, into Laos, into forested regions that were less heavily touristed. One morning, Cobalt woke up with a blazing fever and serial vomiting. Perhaps in part because of their fear and panic, in their search for a hospital they got completely lost, winding up on a dirt road amid wild vegetation, a road that seemed to go on forever, plunging ever-deeper into the wilderness. In the little villages they passed through—actually, not even villages, just collections of mud-and-corrugated-aluminum shanties built around a stretch of dirt roadway—there was never anyone who could offer directions. The only advice was: Keep going, keep going. Darkness had fallen. After driving for ten hours, they finally arrived in a little city, where they managed to find an emergency clinic and a pharmacy. By that point, Cobalt was in the throes of delirium.

They told us about Cambodia after Cobalt had given birth, back in Rome, when Lorenza and I went to visit them with a bouquet of flowers and a terry-cloth towel for the baby. They didn't seem particularly upset. In fact, they joked about it, with the subtext that this hair-raising in-utero adventure would surely turn Adriano into a globe-trotting explorer.

GIULIO HAD MADE DETAILED PLANS for the weekend. In the past, I had more than once noticed this frenzied need of his to plan out his time with Adriano, as if afraid he might unexpectedly find himself alone with the boy, with nothing in particular to say or do—as if that void might produce a bewildering and intolerable moment of confusion for them both. I wondered how much my presence and judgmental gaze weighed on them, that strange, entirely masculine, tripartite con-figuration, so avuncular and unnatural. Perhaps when I wrote up my account, I would be obliged to mention Giulio's performance anxiety, though quite possibly any such annotation would only reflect badly on him.

I had brought a gift for Adriano, that game where you have to pull the rectangular wooden blocks out of the tower without letting it collapse. It seemed like a sufficiently ecological game to meet with Giulio's approval, and so it was—to a fault. In fact, Adriano already had one, in his other home. Giulio upbraided him for saying so, even though it was a perfectly innocent thing for a kid to say. Adriano was mortified, and in the first few matches we played he brought a level of aggression to every turn he took, until I feared he might knock down the tower at any moment with a swipe of his hand. Giulio couldn't seem to stop apologizing to me, but after three or four matches in a row—matches we made sure he won—Adriano dropped his bad mood.

We got crepes in a place on Rue d'Odessa, a restaurant furnished in Breton style, with dark wood everywhere, where Giulio and I devoted our entire and total attention to his pointless sideshows. I was already starting to feel quite weary. If that were my child, I thought to myself, I'd have established some boundaries.

Giulio had made plans for that afternoon: a show at the Fondation Cartier, "The Great Animal Orchestra." The artist, Bernie Krause, had traveled the world and recorded the soundscape of various ecosystems: in Zimbabwe, Canada, and the heart of Amazonia. "Biophony" was the word he'd coined to describe his experiment. There was no mistaking the fact that the project contained an implicit criticism of human activity, and that among the countless ways that we are destroying nature, we're also doing so acoustically. Krause had visited the same places years apart, documenting the disappearance from his new tapes of the cries and sounds of dozens of species of insects, reptiles, and amphibians.

For a while I walked along through the show with Giulio and Adriano, but I found their presence to be a distraction and so let them go on ahead. I sent Lorenza an audio message with the sounds of Sequoia National Park. We had been there years ago, and there isn't really much worth recalling about that trip except for the fact that, when evening came and we returned to our rental car, we discovered that the battery had been drained because I'd left the headlights on. The parking lot had emptied before we knew it, and there we were, in the midst of that unsettling landscape. Finally, after complete darkness had descended, an Asian American park ranger came and went and then, finally, vanished entirely. Eventually we resigned ourselves to the prospect of spending a terrifying night inside our now-powerless automobile. Then suddenly, out of nowhere, a giant truck showed up, spangled with red lights; it was delivering a shiny car identical to the one we were in, suspended diagonally on the cargo deck. Though we were exhausted, I had driven until dawn in the direction of the coast, with Lorenza fast asleep on the seat beside me and the rising sun in my rearview mirror. I let my relief that the two of us were still alive sweep over me, along with the silence and perfection of that instant.

Lorenza replied to my audio message with a question mark. She had a point: she could hardly be expected to track back to that shared memory from the mere sound of Bernie Krause's recordings of bird-calls and creaking tree trunks. Still, I took umbrage, as if she were intentionally being insensitive. I couldn't think of another moment in our lives when we'd been so far apart from each other, and not just physically: in the very flow of our everyday thoughts. I went down to the lower floor of the gallery, where Krause had devoted a hall to the Pacific Ocean. The room was as dark as an oceanic abyss. Giulio was sitting on the carpeting with his legs stretched out in front of him; Adriano was lying with his head on his father's thighs. He's asleep, Giulio whispered to me. That doesn't usually happen.

I knelt down beside them, and there we sat, before the vast, broad, dark screen upon which white lines kept appearing and disappearing, an electrocardiogram of the sea. For at least half an hour we listened to the sounds of lapping water, seagulls, sea lions, and finally the secret language of cetaceans, with their incredibly high-pitched sounds, until those frequencies, too, had become so familiar that I almost felt as if I could understand them.

NOVELLI'S APARTMENT was on the top floor of a Haussmann-style building. He came down to greet us at the door. I saw his body appear gradually, from feet to head, through the elevator's glass door. As I was pulling the door open, I heard him say: Come on, let's go, get in, get in.

Shaking my hand, he announced that he'd read a few things I'd written in the meantime, including that piece about the island of Sylt, concerning which he had a few criticisms to offer. How long will you be staying in Paris? he asked me. I'm heading back to Italy tomorrow, I replied. Too bad, we could have had lunch together.

If we'd realized that this was a proper dinner party, Giulio and I wouldn't have been so lackadaisical about timing. Our seats were the only ones still empty, except for a third. I sensed impatience in the air, even though everyone else made polite introductions. There must have been a dozen people all told.

The conversation almost immediately broke up into a myriad of uncomfortable dialogues between neighbors: where are you from, what do you do, Italian food as against French food—discussions worthy of international panels, where it was impossible to say exactly what language should be spoken. Only Novelli's wife, Carolina, seemed not to care in the slightest. She just confidently spoke Italian to everyone. As for him, he was beaming. He distributed his attention and consideration impartially to one and all, even though his tic of continually tugging at his shirt collar betrayed a certain unease. What should we do? he asked, after a little while. Should we wait for him a little while longer, or just uncork the champagne now?

The table voted unanimously to uncork, and I looked at Giulio, who shot back an expression as if to say I have no idea whom you're talking about. Novelli poured champagne for everyone, just a shade too carefully.

I chatted for a while with my neighbor on the left, a Finnish professor at Paris Diderot University. That conversation was less than delightful. In general, the evening was struggling to get into gear. None of us knew the others well enough, and there seemed to be a general sensation that the guest list had been thrown together without much discernment. At times, unintentionally, everyone fell silent at the same instant, and for a few seconds the only sound was the clinking of silverware. Novelli had brought our cheese to the table without placing it on a dish, and he kept it beside him. He broke off a chunk with his fingers and, talking as he chewed, declared: All right, then, it's time for some riddles.

He challenged us to list the seven independent island-states of the Indian Ocean. At that point, the atmosphere warmed up, in part because by then we'd all had enough to drink. Maldives, Madagascar, Seychelles, Mauritius, Sri Lanka: the first five popped out immediately. But then, when everyone else had run out of ideas, I was the one who nailed the sixth one: the Comoros. We still needed the seventh one.

Of course, it was a question with a trick at the heart of it. After everyone had broken down and begged him, Novelli announced that the seventh island-state was Bahrain, because the Persian Gulf was geographically part of the Indian Ocean. There was a storm of objections. Someone took advantage of the uproar to turn up the music, a small group started dancing, and we all left the table, as if set free. Novelli's daughter burst into the living room in her pajamas and demanded that her father dance a few turns on the floor with her. This is a home full of life, I thought to myself.

The empty seat, meanwhile, remained empty. When the doorbell rang, Novelli let slip an exasperated "at last." Carolina went with him to the door to welcome the guest, but when they opened the door it turned out to be a neighbor enraged by the noise. Carolina lit into him in Italian, with great vehemence, while Novelli, facing his guests, offered a mute but mocking impersonation of the man that proved irresistible. Nonetheless, after shutting the door, he stepped over to the stereo and turned down the volume.

I bummed a cigarette and went out onto the cramped little balcony. In the distance, you could see both the delicate stalk of the Eiffel Tower and the Tour Montparnasse, with blinking aviation lights on top. One of the guests was standing there with her back against the slate wall, gazing out with indifference at the panorama. I hadn't exchanged a word with her at dinner because she'd been sitting at the far end of the table. She was the first to speak, complimenting me for having nailed the Comoros.

Actually, it was just a wild guess.

I don't believe you. I bet you were one of those kids who learned all the capitals by heart and then begged the grown-ups to quiz you.

That strikes me as a good description of most of the people here this evening, I pointed out.

Just think, I've even been to the Comoros. The place is full of jihadists.

She lit my cigarette and started another one herself, even though she'd just crushed out the one she'd been smoking before. She wasn't a friend of Novelli's, nor even of his wife. She'd only just met them that night. Like me, she'd been dragged there by a friend, in her case a woman. I asked her what she was doing in Paris and she replied: One of the stages on the Kamikaze Tour.

She listed the cities she'd visited in the past several months, among them Tunis, Brussels, Berlin, and Moscow. She reported on terrorism as a stringer for a news agency, even though her core business, as she put it, was refugee camps. Just think of a shithole, and I've got it stamped on my passport, guaranteed.

She told me her name, and even though I did my best to hide it, it must have been obvious that it meant nothing to me. Curzia shrugged: My girlfriend is a *real* correspondent, she's great. I mean, aside from and on top of the fact that they pay her triple what they pay me and they throw in an incredible place to live in the Marais.

I'm sure you're an ace yourself.

That's utter nonsense!

They send you out on assignment. If you weren't good at it, they'd stop sending you.

They send me out on assignment because I'm willing to go. And I'm willing to work for cheap.

We were both done with our cigarettes, but neither of us showed any sign of moving from the balcony. Curzia pulled out some grass. As she was rolling the joint, I asked her where she'd managed to find it. After all, she'd told me that she'd only just arrived in Paris a few hours ago. You have no idea of the people I hang out with, she replied.

For a moment I pictured the banlieues, the outskirts of Paris teeming with Arab immigrants, huge public housing blocks, sentinels on the roof, and so on, those frightening neighborhoods you can glimpse when you ride through them on the RER, places I'd only ever seen in movies. I told her about the time back when I was in high school when, with some of the girls from my class, we walked six miles from one town in Liguria to another, in search of someone who would sell us some hash, and how we returned to our campsite, empty-handed and completely broken-spirited. I think I'm a little too bourgeois, I said.

Curzia took a circumspect look around the apartment: The guy who didn't show up works for the French broadcasting network. My friend tells me that Novelli wants to make the leap to TV. But it didn't go well for him tonight. Do you follow him on Twitter? He trots out these riddles there too. He's a pretty funny guy.

Then I'll follow him.

It's not like you're obliged.

She said it brusquely, as if her mood had suddenly darkened. After a moment of awkward silence, we went back to talking about her. I asked her what the most horrifying story she'd reported on as a correspondent was, and she came up with a bloodcurdling tale of mutilations inflicted with machete blows. I was about to tell her about the beheading videos, but then for some reason it struck me as childish and I kept it to myself. Curzia said that in spite of herself she'd become quite the weapons expert. She was pretty sure that if she were in a garage somewhere with everything necessary for the task, she'd be able to put together a piece of medium-powered ordnance and make it explode properly. I'm not exactly the kind of girl you want to hook up with at a party, she summed up.

That allusion triggered an awkward moment, for me at least. In part to maneuver around it, I asked her whether she'd ever given serious thought to the possibility of a terrorist group getting its hands on weapons of mass destruction.

Which terrorist group? she asked in a pained voice.

Oh, I don't know. Al-Qaeda or ISIS.

Al-Qaeda and ISIS have nothing to do with that. Neither does Al-Shabaab or Boko Haram.

Okay, I said, in a tactical retreat.

And what kind of weapons of mass destruction? Like, say, bacteriological weapons?

Like, say, nuclear warheads.

Curzia took a greedy drag on the joint, narrowing her eyes, thereby acting as if she really knew the subject at hand.

If any of the terror organizations seriously wanted to, they'd be able to obtain them. Pakistan has had a nuclear program for at least ten years now. And they're not exactly a bunch of moderates there. But atomic weapons are mostly just a pain in the ass. If you have them but you don't use them, you've lost your credibility. But then, if you do use them, well...you'd better be ready to face the music. Why are you so interested in that question?

No real reason. Just something I'm writing.

Aren't you the mystery man!

She handed me the joint again, holding it vertically, but I didn't want any more. She flicked it out over the edge of the balcony. The absolute predictability of both the party and our conversation on the balcony suddenly seemed to have tired her out. Looking out at the horizon line, she said: What a fucking bullshit city. Then she moved past me, flattening her body against the doorjamb and excusing herself as she squeezed by.

CAROLINA TURNED OFF THE LIGHTS and the cake arrived. Novelli pronounced a short address of cordial gratitude in French. He was a little tipsy too.

Curzia, who was wearing a very long chenille robe, was hard to lose sight of. Through the glitter of the sprinkles on the cake I noticed her whisper something into her girlfriend's ear. I guessed it might be a comment about Novelli, who really was funny as he posed with his wife for the numerous cell phone cameras trained on him. She pushed her way through the crowd, passing by me, and said out of the side of her mouth: I'm leaving, you want to come? I muttered something about Giulio, which she interrupted midway through: Well then, so long, bourgeois boy.

Heading home, about an hour later, I felt vaguely guilty about something. Maybe toward the god of opportunities that I shouldn't have let slip, a god I was especially adept at disappointing. I knew that the grass mixed with all that alcohol was going to leave me with a hangover, and not only one of physical discomfort, but also a lousy mood in general. I expected to be in terrible shape tomorrow morning, and I had come there with one specific mission, to help Giulio with his son. That surge of contrition toward Giulio was pretty paradoxical, seeing that it was Giulio who'd brought me to the party and that now we were returning to his apartment together. But then, Giulio had stayed sober.

And in fact, the following morning I didn't bother to get up when Adriano arrived. From my berth on the sofa I heard them move around the apartment, treading silently. Every so often Adriano would say something in a loud voice, with the clear intention of waking me up, but Giulio immediately hushed him, and they'd go back to their whispering. They were there no longer than was strictly necessary, after which I heard the door swing open and then click shut. By then I was awake, but I lay in bed a little longer before getting up, taking a shower, and having something to eat.

By the time I joined them at the park, it was almost noon. Giulio came to greet me, emerging from the fenced-in play area, and asked how everything was going. I hope we didn't wake you up. We were as quiet as could be.

You didn't wake me up.

Are you sure?

His excessive concern irritated me. I was tempted to grab him by the shoulders and shake him, shout into his face: *Why the fuck are you such a wimp? Would you quit serial-apologizing for everything? Can't you see that she's going to skin you alive if you keep it up?*

Don't worry, I said.

Three girls were facing off in a game of physical coordination. They were taking turns climbing up onto a chair and trying to lower it slowly to the ground by putting one foot on the seat back and then tipping it over and carefully letting it drop down in a leveraged fall. None of them could quite manage it, and they went sprawling, laughing endlessly as they did. I ardently desired their carefree thoughtlessness, even though I couldn't quite see what was keeping me from it. I had no responsibilities, no one I had to set an example for, and my life was offering to let me be a perennial adolescent. Indeed, it was denying me any real alternative. If I'd decided to go play at chair-tipping with those three young women, no one would have been able to say a word to me about it. So why was I determined to be all buttoned-up? Why was I so similar to Giulio, who'd jumped straight into a world of trouble and was now hip-deep in it? What was the point of becoming a grown-up once and for all, but still envying the young?

When I was fifteen, I'd met a girl while on a sort of study vacation. She was older than me, and over the course of a couple of weeks in England, she'd turned me from the child I was into an adolescent. To all intents and purposes, she'd done it merely by changing the music in my headphones from an embarrassing heavy metal to certain darker and more up-to-date playlists. At the end of that summer, I had gone to see her in La Spezia. On the basis of those two days, I based twenty years of dreams, which in all likelihood actually altered the real-life unfolding of events.

Whatever the case, from her house, C. took me on her scooter to Lerici. I'd never been on a motor scooter before, so she'd had to explain every detail to me: how to get on, how to hold tight, how to keep from overbalancing on curves; what's more, I'd never been to Lerici before, and strange though it may seem, I'd only ever been to the beach a few times in my life, even at that relatively advanced age.

We'd climbed out onto the rocks and from there into the dark-blue water, and there we'd floated side by side. I would later write a very short poem about that moment, the only poem I've written in my whole life, with a self-explanatory title: "Lerici, August 29." I was terrified of getting a sunburn, because I'd forgotten to apply suntan lotion. In that period I was sure that I sunburned easily, but C.'s mother first, and later C. herself, had made fun of me. No one could get a sunburn, even if they tried, in late August in Liguria.

We'd gone back to her house, and after lunch I lay down on her bed, while C. copied a cassette tape for me. I was in a semiwaking state, "Witches' Rave" was playing and I felt overheated. I wasn't all that certain I hadn't gotten sunburnt, because my shoulders were glowing with heat. Two steps away, C. was fooling around with the tape deck, and all I needed to do was reach across the bed and run my fingers through her hair to get her to turn around and consider forgetting about the cassette tapes and come over to me on the bed, maybe even lie down next to me on what was, after all, her own bed. I'd imagined it, and imagined doing it, watched my own arm reach out and all the rest, but instead I'd let myself sink down into that secret sweetness, without daring to do a thing. Before the end of that song, I'd had a wet dream, though a weird waking one, and the only one in my life that took place in broad daylight.

THE JELLYFISH that I'd barely missed while swimming with Karol, I later learned on the internet, is commonly known as the barrel jellyfish; its proper, scientific name is more of a mouthful: *Rhizostoma pulmo*. It can develop to an imposing size, comparable to the dimensions of a fully grown human being, but upon contact it causes nothing worse than temporary rashes. In the seas around Europe, the barrel jellyfish is quite plentiful, and perhaps it will become even more common in the future. What little evidence we have lacks solid foundations, because there is a shortage of historical surveys; still, many marine biologists agree with the hypothesis that one of the many effects of climate change is likely to be the overproduction of jellyfish.

The barrel jellyfish comes to mind as a simple analogy, if I try to reconstruct my own condition in the spring and, later, summer of 2017. It's something to do with passivity, with the way jellyfish have of allowing themselves to be transported by currents, while putting up only the slightest degree of resistance.

FOR INSTANCE, it's quite possible that if there hadn't been a terror attack just a few hours after my return to Rome, and if more than just a few hours had passed since my encounter with Curzia on the balcony, it might never have occurred to me to search for her on Twitter to see if she'd gone to London. In that eventually, I wouldn't have decided to follow her on Twitter (having made sure where she was). Then she would have been unable to follow me back less than a minute later. It would then never have occurred to me to DM her to find out if everything was all right with her. Also, I wouldn't have next retreated to the bathroom, closing the door to continue an exchange of text messages about a subject that was in no way intimate and personal, and yet, in a way, really was. After all, there was an exciting and exclusive aftertaste to the shared urgency of such a bloody event. Finally, I wouldn't have taken care to delete all my text messages, one after the other, before emerging from the bathroom.

Khalid Masood, age fifty-two, had suddenly swerved off the traffic lane on Westminster Bridge and started driving down the sidewalk in a Japanese car he'd rented just a few hours earlier from the Enterprise office. Forensic examinations would later establish that the car had been racing along at roughly seventy-five miles per hour, slamming into people and hurtling them into the air, knocking a woman over the railing and down into the icy Thames before crashing into the security gates protecting Parliament. Masood must have been in quite a frenzy by that point, because once his vehicle was no longer drivable, he tried to escape on foot and stabbed an unarmed policeman to death, before being shot to death in his turn. The attack lasted a total of eighty-two seconds.

In the days that followed, Curzia wrote me about Masood. She tracked his movements all over England, but when she was done with that investigation, Masood's deeper motivations, if there were any, remained a mystery to her. No clear connections had emerged with any of the leading terror groups, nor with the Islamic State. Masood had taught English in Saudi Arabia and had been raised by a stepfather whose surname he used at times and at others didn't. What nook or corner of his life concealed the impulse that had driven him to commit indiscriminate mass murder? There was no way to know.

Stockholm, Saint Petersburg, then Paris again and London as well: the abundance of terror attacks that year consolidated my correspondence with Curzia, even though, looking back, I have the impression it would likely have continued in any case. Soon enough our correspondence began to expand to other topics and migrated over to WhatsApp. Our chats never appeared in the sidebar, because I'd delete them as soon as I was done texting. In her messages Curzia was just as capable of being cutting and dry as I'd perceived so clearly during our only conversation in real life, on Novelli's balcony—a quality that for some reason she lost entirely in the articles she wrote, where she almost always came off as impersonal. We talked often about how a certain kind of journalism—the kind she did, made up of constant ping-ponging from one city to another, skimping on meals to be able to pocket at least some sliver of her per diem—made little or no sense in the current age of social media. It might make no sense to someone like you, a fat-cat member of the nouvelle bourgeoisie, Curzia would write me, but I assure you that it makes perfect sense to me, because I've busted my ass to build that career and anyway I've got rent to meet in a house I almost never sleep in. She'd call me an "armchair journalist" when she was in a good mood, and an "interloper" when she wasn't. I did my best to respond tit for tat, calling her a "press officer for ISIS" and a "promising young tax write-off." She'd tell me to go fuck myself, and then wish me sweet dreams.

A few hours later, when I woke up, I found a photo she'd sent me, a carelessly photographed detail of the hotel room she'd wound up in: the hand shower in the bathroom, an ominous stain on the wall-to-wall carpeting, a dried-up condom someone had dropped under the bed. Curzia never took pictures of herself, but she made sure that some part of her could always be seen, as if by mistake: the nail polish on her big toe, a pair of fingers gripping something.

We both believed, by that point, that we were fully anesthetized to terror, and we were hardly alone in that. The hashtag #PrayFor was waning in impact on a daily basis. The previous two years had featured a continuous undertone of #PrayForThisOrThat, but by now this was the world we were living in, what were we supposed to pray for or against? All we could do was accept it.

But the terror attack at the Manchester Arena in May was different. A bombing at a concert of young girls and boys, many of them so young they were accompanied by their mothers. A pop-inflected bloodbath.

Curzia remained in Manchester for nearly a week. On the evening of the third day she had a nervous breakdown. She sat helplessly paralyzed in front of her computer screen, incapable of writing, for hours. She'd spent that afternoon around the Manchester Arena, then outside of hospitals, where she tried to track down relatives of the victims, asking them questions that—she explained to me in a deranged barrage of text messages—seemed meaningless to her, indeed outrageously offensive. What were they supposed to say, anyway, huh? What the *fuck* was there to say?

From the newsroom, they wanted her to ask the relatives of the victims about the bunny ears, the bunny ears that Ariana Grande had worn with her mask onstage, and which now, turned into a badge of mourning, had become the emblem of the massacre on social media. People have been murdered, and we're talking about bunny ears? I mean, can you believe it?

She'd lost any and all sense of irony. She'd been seized with an all-encompassing surge of nausea, but she couldn't seem to vomit. At nine in the morning they'd started pelting her with a hail of phone calls from the newsroom. She lied, swearing that she'd almost finished, even if she hadn't written so much as a sentence yet. She threw back three single-serving minibottles from the room fridge to soothe her nerves, but she still couldn't collect her thoughts. In that state of confusion, she phoned me, and I hurried into the bedroom to answer. She was in the throes of a full-blown panic attack. I'm not going to get another assignment from them as long as I live, she kept saying, over and over.

I told her I thought she should call the managing editor and just explain things to him, straight and sincere, tell him she wouldn't be able to file her story that day. Maybe the pressure has just been too much, it could happen to anyone.

What the fuck do you think he cares? All he sees in me is a space I can fill on tomorrow's page!

I listened to her rough, panicky breathing for a little while, interrupted every so often by the same few words: What am I going to do, eh? What am I going to do? I looked at the door of Lorenza's and my bedroom, as if something might arrive from there at any moment. In my stupid caution, I'd made sure to leave the lights off.

I asked Curzia to tell me where she'd been over the course of that day, to list the places as well as the people she'd talked to there. She reeled off a tangled, confused report, but we managed to identify two or three significant moments. I told her to transcribe those moments exactly as she had shared them with me and send the piece. But she wanted me to read it first, she was no longer sure about anything, not even her spelling. So I waited in the bedroom for another twenty minutes or so, in that guilty penumbra, with a growing sense of concern about how on earth I was going to justify my behavior to Lorenza.

Curzia sent me her piece and I read it carefully. She wrote me that she felt better now, that she was going to go grab a bite to eat, she didn't even know when the last time was that she'd eaten—then she added that I had just saved her life. I deleted the messages before going back to the other room.

HERE HE IS, Eugenio said when he saw me. Let's ask him.

They were sitting in front of the computer, Lorenza leaning slightly forward as if she were hunting something attentively on the screen. She didn't turn around, she said nothing. I walked over and Eugenio pointed at a line on a form: We need to upload this form, but the computer doesn't want to take it.

I doubt the computer really has any preferences in the matter, I replied.

To soften the acidity of my response, I put my hand on his shoulder. Eugenio didn't dodge the pressure, if anything he pressed back slightly, adding a bit of counterpressure of his own. For weeks, Lorenza had been dealing with the bureaucratic hoops required to send him to the United States for his fourth year of high school. Bureaucracy exasperated her in general, but this set of challenges was unprecedented in its complexity. Most of it meant filling out forms to relieve the host organization of any legal responsibility for him, but letters of introduction in English were also required, along with insurance policies, report cards, transcripts, and seemingly endless questionnaires about Eugenio's dietary, athletic, cultural, and social preferences, as well as his linguistic and interpersonal abilities. Each and every page had to be downloaded, printed, filled out, signed, scanned, and finally uploaded again through the portal, which involved ten consecutive steps with increasing levels of difficulty, like the levels of a video game.

Lately this is how we'd been spending our evenings, with the two of them at the desk, irritated but in alliance against the computer, while I steered clear. But that evening Eugenio said: Mamma, come on, let him try, so Lorenza stood up and I sat down in her place.

Being close to Eugenio had become strange. By now he had an adult body and a specific odor, which I no longer thought matched his smell as a little boy. I could tell he had smoked a cigarette and then chewed a mint. He did it every evening, after dinner, on the little terrace just off his bedroom. It was a sort of personal ritual and we pretended not to notice. Many of the concessions we made with him came out of the fact that Eugenio was, all other factors aside, the child of a divorced couple, so he could claim some right to an extra dose of tolerance. At that moment, however, I thought it was a good idea to remind him that he'd signed a contract with the organization—a contract in which he had agreed not to smoke during his stay in the United States.

Otherwise they'll send me back home, I know, he said in a flat tone of voice.

I couldn't seem to decipher his feelings about his year abroad, but if I had to guess I would have said neither aversion nor enthusiasm, but rather a docile form of compliance with a desire that was Lorenza's more than his.

The contract also stipulates that getting laid is forbidden, I said in a bid to create a bond of masculine complicity. You're going to have a year of exasperating necking and heavy petting ahead of you.

He flashed a faint smile at his screen. He was embarrassed to have me talking to him about sex, especially when I did it in such coarse terms. His love life was shrouded in mystery. He seemed to feel no need to share any of it, even with me, even though I constituted a figure midway between a parent, a big brother, and an accidental flatmate.

First you have to convert the file, I said.

Why?

Look at the list of extensions. The file you're trying to upload isn't in any of those formats.

We finished that step and moved on to the next one. Eugenio threw himself against his backrest. Shit, another form to fill out!

We can fill it out together, if you want, I suggested. I knew that my willingness to help was nothing more than a form of reparation for what I'd been doing in Lorenza's bedroom until just a few minutes ago, but Eugenio didn't realize that and seemed relieved.

Describe yourself with three positive adjectives and three negative ones.

I hate that kind of question.

And you're right. But come on, just think of three adjectives.

Loner. Obsessive.

And the third adjective?

He hesitated, then added: Bit of a snob.

Excellent. So now we have the negative ones.

Actually, those were the positive ones.

I looked at him and realized he wasn't kidding. All right then, let's see if I can come up with three: imaginative, ironic. I couldn't think of a third one, I kept circling back to stubborn, but I wasn't sure where to place that among the qualities. Well? Eugenio prodded me.

Perspicacious.

What the hell: perspicacious?! Do you seriously think I'm perspicacious?

Yeah, I think you are.

He shrugged his shoulders slightly, as if to concede that opinion of him of which he so disapproved. I sensed Lorenza's very discreet presence behind us. Sure enough, there she was with a dish in one hand.

All right then, I'll put down perspicacious. If you can think of something better, then we can circle back and make the correction.

But Eugenio was absent now, staring into the computer screen with indifference. What do you think? he asked. Will the American family really put limits on my internet usage?

IN BIOLOGY, the practice of caring for other creatures' offspring is known as alloparenting. That would make me a sort of "allofather" to Eugenio, after all these years, which isn't much of a definition, but at least it's neutral. It contains none of the contempt implicit in "stepfather." According to ethologists, alloparental care isn't very common among animals because it offers no benefits in evolutionary terms. It can only be found among lionesses, in certain species of chimpanzees, and long-finned pilot whales, which sometimes take the young of other members of their species and shepherd them from place to place in the oceans. More commonly, animals tend to rip other creatures' young limb from limb.

When I first got together with Lorenza, I knew nothing about Eugenio's existence. Strange as it may seem, she still hadn't mentioned him the evening she showed up at my home with a complete meal packed up in Tupperware containers, because *she wanted to cook for me.* And she still hadn't mentioned him later, that same night, as justification for leaping out of bed in apparent haste, getting dressed, and leaving, instead of spending the night with me, as might have seemed only natural. I have wondered more than once whether her omission at the time meant that there was a seed of deceit at the roots of our relationship. But I know that there was no intentional strategy on Lorenza's part. Back then, she existed in two different states: one in which she was Eugenio's mother and the other in which she was dating me, and there were no possible connections between the two states, because any potential border crossing between the two would have meant losing all hope for our relationship, which was already in sufficient peril in and of itself.

For that matter, I myself existed in a twofold state. Handling our age difference was already a significant effort. I was twenty-six, while Lorenza was in her midthirties, and whenever I talked about her with my friends at the time, including Giulio, I sensed how strangely they reacted, and I felt strange in my turn. I found myself reckoning up all sorts of different numbers: by the time I'm thirty, she'll be closing in on forty, when I'm forty-five, she'll be fifty-four, and so on and so forth. Then I'd watch forty-five-year-old men and fifty-four-year-old women and I'd come to the conclusion that there was no way this could work out. Even if we were able to preserve our exceptional rapport, our bodies weren't going to spare us. As adults, we would become grotesques. It was as if, when I met Lorenza, I'd slammed headfirst in the most relentless of all commandments for a young male: Thou shalt have no woman older than thee.

We'd been dating for at least a month when she texted me suggesting we meet in a certain café. She wanted to introduce me to an important person. That adjective—important—was all it took to set my mind to rummaging through all the clues scattered through the previous weeks and assemble them into a meaning. So, the following day, as I approached the table where she and Eugenio were already seated, I can't say that I was genuinely surprised.

Eugenio was arranging the deck of cards of a game called Magic: The Gathering, and when I sat down he just kept it up, unperturbed. He hadn't bothered to look at me, though I could clearly see how vigilant he was. He had pointed to one of the monstrous creatures on the cards and explained what powers it possessed, its life points, its techniques of defense and attack. Then he'd taken me through the same process with a second card, and then with a third and a fourth. If Lorenza tried to break in, he'd raise his voice ever so slightly and continue talking as if nothing had happened. I feigned a passionate interest in the monsters, but to scramble his approach I would point at them in random order. Eugenio refused to allow himself to be distracted. He'd take a sidelong glance at the other cards

I pointed to and tell me, Hold on, we haven't gotten to them yet. When I asked if he'd give me one, he hesitated before shaking his head slowly and solemnly: no. At that point, Lorenza weighed in brusquely. For the rest of our time together, Eugenio uttered not another word. He kept his eyes focused on the card holder, as if we'd ruined the game for him. As if we grown-ups had devastated even that last remaining world of fantasy.

From that day forward, I had been given permission to visit their home, albeit with plenty of provisos. If our intention was for me to spend the night, then Lorenza and I would act out a bit of theater: after we finished our dinner or watching our movie, I'd say goodbye and leave. For the next half hour I'd wander around their residential neighborhood, walking around the same block over and over, awaiting the all clear so I could go upstairs. The next morning, I'd remain motionless in bed, with the bedroom door securely closed, listening to the sounds of breakfast, the water running in the bathroom sink, all of the various preparations for the coming school day. Sometimes Eugenio would talk to his mother about me, and I'd feel like an immaterial being, a specter trapped inside the walls of the apartment. We had no specific plan about when the right time would come to tell him the truth, and probably we didn't even want to tell him at all. We'd have preferred to just let it slip into his mind through habit. It seemed to us that that would be less painful for him. Or else that it would be less painful for us.

But then, one night I opened my eyes and in the darkened room found myself face-to-face with Eugenio. His breathing was labored, possibly because of a nightmare. We calmed him down and put him back to bed, and the next morning I stayed in the bedroom like always. I had no idea how his short-term memory operated, whether Eugenio could truly believe that finding me in his mother's bed had just been part of a dream. In any case, he said nothing about it.

A few months after that minor incident, I was about to leave for a trip. I stepped into his bedroom to say goodbye. Eugenio gave me one of his unenthusiastic pecks on the cheek, before going back to his Magic card game. As he did, though, he picked up one of the cards from the floor, as if he'd just made that decision then and there, and told me I could keep it. It was the card of the Beanstalk Giant, a hairy humanoid with abnormal feet. The caption was cryptic: Beanstalk Giant's power and toughness are each equal to the number of lands you control. I asked him whether the giant was powerful, and he replied, Pretty much, yeah. When I thanked him, he made a point of telling me that the card he'd given me was a duplicate, an extra.

I kept the Beanstalk Giant with me for ten years, in an inside slot of my wallet, until one day, while I was eating outdoors at a restaurant on the Esquiline Hill, a thief riding a scooter snatched my phone and my wallet from right under my nose. I had carelessly set them at the edge of my table. After freezing my ATM card and activating a new one, after buying a SIM card with the same phone number as before, and going through the exhausting process of renewing all the one-time code generators on my new smartphone, it suddenly dawned on me that the Beanstalk Giant was the one and only irretrievable loss. If I could have asked that thief for just one mercy, it would have been to give me that card back. More than once, I'd been on the verge of telling the story to Eugenio, but he didn't even know that I had kept the card all this time. Most likely, he didn't remember that the card even existed. He would have considered it pathetic.

TO CELEBRATE his departure for the United States, I bought him a pair of tickets to a Radiohead concert in Florence, with an extra ticket for anyone he cared to invite. I knew deep down that Radiohead was a tribute to my own seventeenth birthday more than his own, but Eugenio had listened to them often enough, whether or not he wanted to, and then there was the ever-laudable goal of solidifying the relationship that neither of us had chosen, at least not exactly, and to consolidate that goal by *doing things together*. What's more, I had been unable to find anyone else to go to the show with me.

In the end, he invited a classmate from school called Sara. In the car, the two of them barely interacted. I thought that if I'd been in his place, seventeen years old in a car with my stepfather and a girl, I'd have felt I was responsible for her, and I'd have been hyperalert the whole time. Whereas Eugenio and Sara seemed not to feel the slightest pressure to behave in any particular way. They spoke from time to time and took turns isolating themselves with their earbuds.

I was a little out of practice at attending music festivals, so I'd insisted on leaving far too early, with the unexpected result that we were almost the first people there, walking along between crowd barriers in the hot sun at one o'clock in the afternoon. It was scorching hot. Eugenio and Sara stretched out, blithely indifferent, on the yellowed grass. I felt my apprehension surge at the thought of the hours stretching out ahead of us, and I considered leaving, taking them to see the center of Florence, at least the church of Santa Croce and the baptistry. But the walk there from the parking area and the succession of security checks we'd had to pass through had been exhausting, so I gave up that idea.

Eugenio and Sara headed off toward the food stands. Inside the arena, there was a circular economic system in operation, one based on the purchase of tokens. Only after converting cash into tokens could you buy food, beverages, and merch. I had no idea what the reason for that might be, whether it was one of Radiohead's brainstorms or whether the tokens were just a way of getting people to spend more money, but to make sure I was duly generous toward Eugenio and his friend, I purchased a truly outlandish quantity of tokens. In fact, even now, many years later, tokens keep turning up in my car, under the floor mats, wedged in at the sides of the seats. Plastic coins, ancient and unusable, relics that testify to a time in the recent past, not all that distant and yet completely finished.

When the crowd started to fill the arena, we stood up. People were packing in, mostly in front of us. I observed with a hint of satisfaction that Eugenio seemed contented. More than that: he was excited, and so was Sara. They'd never been to a concert this size.

The opening band hadn't started playing yet when I turned around to look behind me, toward the expanse of crowd that stretched as far as the eye could see, where there had once been an empty stadium. Now, behind us, there was a carpet of heads. I didn't so much imagine as actually *saw* a bomb explode. I realized that where we were now, there would be no way to escape. We would be hemmed in, trampled underfoot, crushed against the hurricane fences. I told Eugenio that we should probably move back, get closer to the mixing console, or anyway, get out of the mob, and he stared at me in disbelief: We waited all this time just so we could be this close to the stage! He told me that I was welcome to move back if I wanted to, we could meet up at the end of the concert.

By now James Blake was up on stage, and the audience had surged forward. I couldn't leave, I couldn't abandon them to this mob. The music started up, and the bodies all around us started to move and sway. I found myself taking the impact of those surging waves, suddenly stiff, unable to pick out the details of the song, focusing instead on a different noise, a dull roar that seemed to rise up from my entrails, which if I had to describe it I would have called the sound of anguish. I was surrounded by the concert's euphoria, and at the same time by the panorama of silence and devastation that the concert could turn into in the blink of an eye, as if the scrim separating current reality and another alternative scenario had suddenly thinned to a terrifying degree.

My sense of alienation lasted at most for a few minutes, or maybe less: a handful of seconds, and then it vanished. But it had happened, and it left a hangover for the rest of the concert, and even afterward, in the dark, rolling along on the darkened highway, with Eugenio and Sara fast asleep in the back, like children. It was really very sad as to what was going on throughout the world with terror.

"IT IS REALLY VERY SAD as to what's going on throughout the world with terror": that's not something I ever said. It was Donald Trump who spoke those words at the beginning of that same month. A few hours before he made his speech, a gunman had entered a casino in Manila with an assault rifle and a container of gasoline. He started shooting wildly, then he poured gasoline all over the gambling tables, the seats in front of the slot machines, and the carpeting, and set fire to it all. The devastation was so bad that in the frantic hours following the attack, the authorities announced that there had been a number of attackers at Resorts World Manila. In fact, however, in the end it turned out the gunman was a loner: Jessie Javier Carlos. The body count of his victims rose to thirty-eight, caused mainly by the panicky stampede and smoke asphyxiation. Carlos himself was one of the dead. In the last picture of him while still alive, he's sitting on a flight of stairs in the building, face uncovered, one floor up from the fire. He's wearing a black watch cap and looks dazed, as if he's resting.

It was June 2 in Manila when the attack unfolded, but back in the United States it was still June 1 when Donald Trump mentioned the slaughter in Manila, at the beginning of his Rose Garden press conference. If we compare the dates, then, we have this impression of a strange reversal of time, as if Trump were talking about something that hadn't happened yet. Actually, of course, it was just a matter of the international date line, the time and date difference between Manila and Washington, D.C. Solemnly, but paying mere lip service to the deaths, Trump said that he was sad about what was going on around the world with terror. Then he moved on to the next topic.

After all, he wasn't there to talk about terror attacks and the Philippines; he was there to announce the decision to pull the United States out of the Paris COP 21 climate accord that had been signed by his predecessor, Barack Obama. Trump's hostility to environmental policies was hardly a surprise, but the announcement itself certainly came as a shock. Trump placed a special emphasis on the word *withdraw*: "The United States will withdraw from the Paris Climate Accord." Following those words there was a burst of applause from the audience. The president added a few vague comments about the possibility of negotiating a new accord, and then uttered a short, even more brutal, phrase: "So we're getting out."

They called me from the newsroom to get a comment, seeing that I'd attended COP 21 as a correspondent. I knew that if I wrote a piece about it, I'd be unable to keep from being overwhelmed by a wave of pessimism. Without the United States, there was no way to limit global warming. Not just because the U.S. was responsible for one-fifth of the world's total emissions, but because Trump's speech proved something that anyone who paid any attention to the climate crisis knew full well but kept tucked away in the bottom of their heart: the great collective effort to reduce humanity's impact on the planet was actually a lost cause. Any individual nation's commitment could be whisked away at a moment's notice, and in fact that's what had just happened.

But it didn't strike me as a good idea to give credence to those fantasies of failure in an article. Instead, I suggested to the deputy editor of the *Corriere della Sera* that I do an interview. I knew a person, an Italian climatologist who was pretty popular in France, who would certainly have a much more interesting point of view than I did.

The interview with Novelli appeared in the newspaper the following morning and began with a terse drop quote: "Data don't lie. Sometimes people do. But data don't, they are what they are. Period. Provide me with accurate measurements and I can tell you the truth about the world."

The accusation of lying was clearly directed at Donald Trump and anybody who might have applauded him at that press conference, but there was no mistaking the fact that Novelli meant to include in the accusation of lying a much larger group, indeed, an entire portion of humankind. During the course of our conversation, he made repeated references to populist movements, with their anti-science ideas. Those movements had been gaining in credibility in Europe, and especially in Italy. He was so explicit in his statements that when it came time to edit the interview, I found myself softening the tone of his polemic and actually cutting out entire sentences. That said, I only had fifty column lines available to me, whereas our conversation on Skype had lasted more than an hour.

I study clouds, Novelli told me, how they form, how they migrate, and how they affect climate. Well, now, do you know that here in Italy we've had fourteen parliamentary inquiries into chemtrails? Fourteen. That means that on fourteen separate occasions, a member of our national parliament has risen in the chamber to discuss the hypothesis that regularly scheduled airliners are releasing mysterious substances into the atmosphere, substances that are supposed to be capable of taking control of our minds.

And instead?

And instead what?

Just what are those stripes in the sky we see when planes go overhead?

Ordinary contrails. Nothing but condensation. Warm air that cools rapidly. There's no mystery about it. [And don't ask me questions that you already know the answers to.]

The words in square brackets are the ones I didn't use in my article, but they're still there in the transcript that I've kept.

I don't know if you've read this article in *Esquire*, Novelli said, a study on the psychological condition of climate experts. Like yours truly. Basically, it turns out that we're one of the categories of scientists most likely to suffer depression and various other mood disorders. Like, tell me something I don't know. Pre-traumatic stress disorder is what psychologists call it. Or else Cassandra Syndrome. That's what we feel every time we see a graph appear on our monitor, and in that graph we can glimpse the future. And it's what happens to us when we try to get that information out into the world at large, for our fellow citizens, the free press, and important decision-makers. If you'd like me to give you a fitting description of the times we live in, I can't think of anything better: this is a pre-traumatic era.

And how are things going today?

Today's been a rotten day. A day worth marking on the calendar with a dark circle. Dark, but not black. There are blacker days than today. Because today, at least, there's a general sense of shared grief that cushions the solitude.

Novelli showed me the data from the previous year, the data that to his mind didn't lie. The most unsettling statistics had to do with the seas and oceans, even though nobody ever thought about them. But that's exactly where climate change could be seen in the starkest terms. The waters of the Gulf of Alaska had warmed up so sharply that there'd been an extraordinary bloom of toxic algae. Did you happen to hear about it, by any chance? No, of course you didn't.

In the meantime, California has recorded a total of over seven thousand wildfires, with the loss of twenty-six million trees and an estimated monetary cost of half a billion dollars. In China, in the Wuhan region, an absolutely disproportionate quantity of rain has fallen, even considering the fluctuations due to the El Niño seasonal current (after I finished the interview, I looked up the exact location of Wuhan in the Maps app, and I checked to make sure I was spelling it correctly. It seems ridiculous, looking back on it now, and yet that's what happened).

There are the data, Novelli said. Then there are people, with all the lies that they tell.

Behind him, I could glimpse the apartment where I'd attended the party. I asked him what kind of a world we should get used to, and he replied with some impatience: A world like the one I just described. Where on one hand you have people dying of thirst and on the other, people who are drowning. Do you have any familiarity with the concept of gradualism?

Not very familiar, I'm afraid.

We all have gradualist minds: If things have always gone a certain way in the past, why should that stop now? Humanity has been living on the same planet for two hundred thousand years. Does it seem plausible that it should all decide to collapse during my lifetime? It seems improbable, after all. Even scientists tend to think that way. In fact, the great catastrophes, such as the extinction of the dinosaurs, have always struggled to gain acceptance and be taken seriously. But it turns out that we actually are living in an era when everything is changing. And drastically so. It's happening to us, all of us, now. The phenomena that we'll be witnessing in the coming years are going to be increasingly extreme. The sooner we accept that fact, the better it will be for everybody.

I said to him, Elon Musk has withdrawn from a series of initiatives he had agreed to work on, in protest against Trump's decision. Novelli grimaced into the webcam. Let's forget about the various Elon Musks. Elon Musks don't really count. They're not going to suffer, not really. They're already preparing for when the catastrophe hits. They're readying bunkers and spaceships, they're collecting weapons and buying land where they'll be able to move and live in safety.

Where would you purchase land, for instance? For survival purposes, that is.

I would never do anything of the sort.

No, I mean if you absolutely had to. In case of apocalypse.

Novelli stopped to think for a few seconds, then went on: In Tasmania. It's far enough south to escape any excessive temperatures. It has considerable freshwater reserves, it has a democratic government, and there are no predators of humans. It's not too small, but it's still an island, so it's easier to defend. And believe me, people are going to have to defend themselves.

Yes, he added, with growing conviction, if I absolutely had to pick a place for purposes of survival, I'd choose Tasmania.

The next day, after the article appeared, he called me to complain about the headline: *Trump's America Condemns Us*. He felt it was defeatist and put too much emphasis on the United States. He refused to believe me when I told him that I'd had nothing to do with it. In a somewhat contradictory countermove, he tossed out an inference that I'd softened certain statements of his. But then, having let off a bit of steam, which struck me as nothing so much as an excuse to share a few comments on how the piece had turned out, he relaxed and even admitted that, all things considered, the interview wasn't bad at all. The picture of him, which took up a fair portion of the page, had satisfied him in particular.

It was during the course of that phone call that we finally graduated from the formal *lei* of Italian to the informal *tu*, the rough equivalent of being on a first-name basis. And it was from that day forward that our long-distance interactions intensified, until we were talking quite frequently. Emails, text messages, and with a certain regularity, phone calls, because Novelli liked talking on the phone. He would call me at all hours, and often for no clear reason, without even bothering to pretend that he did have one. In fact, he would frequently declare openly that he just felt like chatting for a while.

I think that I wanted to be friends with him from the very beginning, from the first time we met on Rue Monge. And I also believe that Novelli, too, behind that off-putting attitude, was looking for company. Otherwise, I wouldn't know how to explain the extremely rapid progression of our relationship.

What I liked best about him was his intelligence in the broadest sense, or better still, the severity of the method he applied to the use of his intelligence. But it wasn't just that. I liked him for some reason that went beyond the exchange of ideas, beyond our shared roots in physics and our shared concern about global warming. His physical essence had a lot to do with it. The corporeal component of our perceptions is generally underestimated in male friendships, but it has actually played a fundamental role in many of my own. Novelli was no exception: his rotund face; his dark, gleaming eyes; his midsection, not fat and yet substantial, which was highlighted by the skintight shirts he insisted on wearing. The specialty he worked on was clouds, but he seemed to have both feet planted firmly on the ground, much more than I did. That always gave me a sense of concreteness at a time when, evidently enough, I must have felt a need for it.

But our closeness had also been encouraged by other circumstances: that same spring, Lorenza and I had suddenly found ourselves alone. Alma and Fabrizio, the only mutual friends who had remained close with us over the years—we were with them on the evening of the Bataclan, and we'd been with them countless other evenings that merge and juxtapose in my memory—had suddenly vanished from our lives, leaving behind them a sensation of disbelief and disappointment.

I can try to summarize, in the sparest and most minimal terms, exactly what had happened, but I'm very much conscious that such a summary is necessarily a rough approximation. After all, that break with our friends led to countless conjectures and exhausting conversations between me and Lorenza. Many of those conversations took place late at night, and they all turned out to be fruitless, or worse: conversations that no doubt altered the very truth of what actually happened.

A couple of years previously, Lorenza had received an inheritance from her godmother, the woman who had held her at her baptism. It was hardly an astronomical sum, but it was enough to make us wonder what the wisest thing might be to do with it. In the end, she had entrusted the money to Fabrizio, who worked for a bank. As a decision, it was entirely natural; and in fact the night that she told me about it, I'd had no objection to the idea. In fact, I didn't even particularly bother to read the investment plan that he had sent her, because there was nothing I could think of to add. I had nothing to offer, really.

The money had just sat there in the bank for several months, theoretically accumulating interest, and if we received any reports from the bank in the mail,

I'd never noticed them: actually, though, I don't think any ever came. In a certain sense, Lorenza had decided to ignore that money, until preparations for Eugenio's year abroad made it necessary to withdraw part of the total sum. That's when she'd asked Alma to mention to Fabrizio that we were planning to withdraw part of our investment.

After assuring Lorenza that she would talk to him about it, Alma stopped responding. In all the years we'd known them, nothing of the sort had ever happened. She would send laconic messages to Lorenza, apologizing and making excuses. Apparently, she was just very busy. Then even those messages stopped coming. Lorenza would write to her several times a day, increasingly confused, until she finally asked me to write Fabrizio to find out what was going on. He replied to me, saying that, yes, actually, it was about Alma's health: even if he'd never actually uttered the word cancer, I'd come away pretty certain that that was it.

I remember Lorenza sitting in the kitchen as if it were happening this second—she was as shocked at the fact that Alma had said nothing to her as she was by the news itself. It had never occurred to her to revert to the matter of the money we'd invested. For now, she'd ask her father for a loan, even though that was the last thing she wanted to do.

A few days later I had to travel for work, and I don't even remember where to. While I was gone, Alma had posted a picture on Facebook. Lorenza happened to see it: Alma was out somewhere for dinner, and she looked to be in excellent health. Lorenza tried to get in touch with her to ask for an explanation, and once again Alma had failed to reply. In fact, now Lorenza couldn't even seem to write her on WhatsApp or contact her on social media, as if Alma had blocked her (which turned out to be the case).

The suspicion that had been floating subliminally in both our minds had finally taken concrete form. One morning Lorenza went to the bank in person. She'd had to wait a long time before Fabrizio agreed to see her. She told me afterward that she could see him in his cubicle, terribly busy with who knows what, but not so busy he could go on ignoring her after half an hour, an hour, an hour and a half. That whole time, he'd only once given her a faint and embarrassed smile. When Lorenza finally took a seat across from him, he could only offer her confirmation of what she already knew, and a clear reckoning of just how bad it turned out to be. The meeting had been very brief. Fabrizio had printed out a graph for her showing the performance of the fund over the last few months, and at the end of that historical accounting, the current value of her investment, practically zeroed out. Later, when we sat down and went over it carefully, we saw a great number of transactions that Fabrizio had ordered: we'd never been informed about any of them, and they really made no sense whatsoever. But he'd been working with our authorization—the document that she had signed.

Lorenza had transferred the few thousand surviving euros onto Eugenio's prepaid money card, as if she didn't want to run the risk of leaving the cash in that account for even a minute longer. Then she had focused on trying to get in touch with Alma. One afternoon, she staked out her apartment building. Exactly what happened during the ensuing encounter is something she never shared with me. In the days that followed, though, she'd been silent in a way I'd never seen before. She was constantly losing things; she cut and wounded herself in stupid ways.

ONE OF THE COROLLARIES of Alma and Fabrizio's disappearance from our lives was that we found ourselves without plans for the summer. Otherwise, we'd probably never have taken into consideration the idea of spending the holidays with Novelli and his family, whom Lorenza didn't know in the slightest. But it turned out that they were renting a time-share villa in Sardinia, that the villa had direct access to the water and an extra double room available. So why not? Novelli wrote me. Yeah, why not? I suggested to Lorenza. They didn't even want us to put in money. She agreed almost immediately. When I pointed out that it had been almost absurdly easy to talk her into it, this had been her answer: Let's be honest, lately we haven't much felt like spending time together, you and I.

The little villa in Sardinia was part of a larger residential complex that you reached by following a private road, complete with a guard who scrutinized you closely before raising the access barrier arm. According to Novelli, it dated back to the golden age of nonper-mitted construction, when Italy was a paradise of lat-itudinarian development and builders did exactly as they pleased, including throwing up garish eyesores right on the beach. So much the better for us, he con-cluded, gazing out with ill-concealed satisfaction at the expanse of water, arms clasped behind his back and thumbs wedged into the elastic of his shorts.

The house was nothing much to speak of. It had alu-minum window and door frames and undistinguished furnishings. It didn't even have air-conditioning. The owners claimed that was out of respect for the origi-nal structure, but Novelli said it was sheer chintziness. The exterior, however, was magnificent, and we spent most of our time outside anyway. A gravel path wound its way through a garden full of succulents, dominated by an enormous, fleshy agave that had already shot its towering flower skyward. By following that path, you could walk down to a little bay. It was quite a challenge to reach that beach by following the coastline, and only the occasional intrepid young couple managed to do it. And so for the most part we had the place to ourselves. The seabed—which in the time we were there I surveyed closely with a scuba mask and Novelli's guidance—was abundantly populated by octopuses, anemones, and sea urchins—and even by intact, purplish coral struc-tures, standing at least a couple of handbreadths tall.

Every morning I was the first one up and about. I'd head down to the beach on my own. The sea was calm, and I always had ambitions to swim out into open water, but for the most part I just floated lazily, close to shore. By the time I got back to the house, Novelli's children were wandering around, a little lost, in search of food, grabbing packs of cookies from the pantry and leaving them around the place in the most unexpected locations. Sometimes I'd go back to bed with Lorenza, who was awake by then but seemed hesitant to leave our room. The sheets were always dusted with a sprinkling of sand, especially where our feet had been, and we were both relieved to see that it would be impossible to think of making love, with the other rooms so cheek by jowl to ours.

Aren't you enjoying yourself? I kept asking her, obsessively.

It's a nice place.

But you're not enjoying yourself. And yet we spent our holidays with Alma and Fabrizio for years and years.

And just what is that supposed to mean?

Oh, nothing. But you might try to make more of an effort.

Did you make an effort with Alma and Fabrizio?

They were your friends more than mine.

I didn't know that's how you felt about it. I wish you'd told me.

Every day, Novelli and I would make calls to report yachts coming too close to shore, even though the coast guard never showed up. In the late morning, we'd go together to San Teodoro to buy groceries, picking up vegetables and local ricotta-based sweets that no one ever ate. Then we'd stand in line at the fish store. As a Ligurian, Novelli knew what he was talking about when it came to seafood. He'd discuss the different varieties. He'd bargain, sometimes with an excessive zeal and determination, as if trying to teach me how. My basic approach had been learned in supermarkets. As we left, he'd say: You see? You can forget about that sort of thing in France.

He had an ambivalent attitude toward Italy. He alternated a sense of superiority, ostentatiously thrilled that he lived in a scintillating, cosmopolitan city like Paris, with almost childish manifestations of nostalgia. Carolina, on the other hand, was very explicit in her intolerance of France and everything French. She would trot out caustic imitations of the Parisians, with all their *oh là là* and *ah bon* and *voilà* and *hop!* She described them dismissively as class bigots and lazy bums. One evening, while we were dining on the terrace, Lorenza snapped. Those are just stereotypes, she opined. Oh, let me assure you, that's what they're like, Carolina retorted. And I can assure you that it isn't true, Lorenza shot back.

The exchange went on for a while on that level, and it would only have degenerated if Novelli hadn't come up with one of his typical puns, changing the subject just in the nick of time.

NOVELLI AND I had developed the habit of taking one last nighttime plunge when everyone else was already inside and fast asleep. In comparison with the now-cool air, the water seemed comfortably tepid, and I floated there, soaking, for long stretches. Amid that lulling calm, we had some of our most focused conversations. Truth be told, I mostly just listened. Novelli was more of a source of answers than questions, and I was the reverse. The night we narrowly avoided getting into a real quarrel there was a fire to the south of the bay; it sketched out a red wound in the dark silhouette of the promontory.

I think Carolina has had it up to here with Paris, Novelli said, his face darkening. She has it in for the French, but the truth is that she just hasn't found anything to do there. She's fixated on it by this point.

Fixated on what?

He ran his wet hands through his hair to smooth it down. With the idea of working. We don't need her salary. We're not rolling in gold or anything, but we're getting by just fine.

Would you feel fulfilled without working?

What does that have to do with anything? It's not a symmetrical situation. And she's always been fine with it in the past. Carolina has never had a calling, shall we say, of any real intensity.

He stated it with a harshness that surprised me, then and there. Then he added: In any case, next winter we're moving back to Italy. It's been decided.

There was going to be a competition for a tenured position in Genoa, his home city. It was limited to outside faculty, but basically it was just being staged so they could hire him. And why wouldn't they want me? he added. With the river of grants I can steer their way!

For a while, we floated there, watching the glare of the fire down the coast. The Canadair water bombers kept diving and soaring, back and forth incessantly, dumping tanksful of salt water.

If it wasn't such a tragedy, Novelli said, you'd have to admit that it makes for an incredible spectacle.

BY THE SECOND WEEK, Lorenza was living separately from the rest of us. She'd read for hours on the beach, in a secluded corner, or else she'd just stay in our room. At meals, when it was inevitable for us all to be together, she rarely spoke. The elements of incompatibility between her and Carolina had become increasingly accentuated. I noticed that it no longer came naturally to me to stick up for her, even if she was mostly in the right. For instance, there was no question that Carolina's rude impetuosity was enough to put anybody off, and it was also true that Novelli almost always monopolized the conversation: and if he wasn't especially interested in what I might have to say, he was completely indifferent to Lorenza's opinions. Still, there was really no need for her to react like that.

I'm behaving very well, she told me one night in our room, when I tried to discuss the problem yet again. I gestured for her to lower her voice and she said the same thing again, a little more quietly: I'm behaving very well, as if making it clear that there was really nothing more to be said on the subject.

But on the next-to-last day, we rented a boat, a speedboat that could comfortably hold six and which Novelli could pilot because he had a boating license. We sailed around Tavolara Island and then stopped and anchored for a while in a large inlet where the water was a Caribbean blue. Novelli pried open loose oysters with a little knife, even though that was against the law. He squeezed a lemon over it for Lorenza, who sucked it out of his hand. The mood had changed.

We ate raw shrimp and drank white wine aboard the speedboat, while the children swam around us wearing scuba masks. When we returned it was almost nightfall and we were euphoric. We opened more wine and sat on the terrace until late, because no one had the strength to get up and walk to the light switch. I suggested going down to the beach. It was our last night there, and the air was still, not a breath of wind. Lorenza was uncertain about it, but everything was going so nicely, she didn't want to ruin the party. She said let me go get my swimsuit, but we stopped her: we'd lose our momentum.

We staggered off, lighting our way with the flashlights from our phones. I doubt there was a moon out, or anyway what I remember is complete darkness, because when I turned my beam from the beach out to the water, for just a fleeting instant, what revealed itself to me was the figure of Carolina, nude, standing knee deep in the waves. Lorenza must have seen her too: must have seen the only slightly darker triangle of her pudendum, and perhaps she sensed what I, too, had sensed, namely that Carolina was waiting for us. I don't know if that's what stopped her, but the fact is, she said: I'm not going in.

Novelli was already heading for his wife, I could hear the water slapping around his ankles as he went and I could glimpse his white ass cheeks, like balloons bobbing on strings. By now, we were there, not going into the water would have been rude. Please, I begged her. You go, Lorenza answered with a sudden weariness in her voice. Please, I whispered again, stepping closer, and it was in that moment that she said the words that would haunt me endlessly after that: I feel so sorry for you.

Sorry about what?

I'm just so sorry for you, she said again. But don't worry, you still have time. You can go. I mean it, you *should* go. Take advantage.

I couldn't manage to tell her, No, I had no intention of doing anything of the sort. Novelli and Carolina were waiting for us, and I was probably more worried about that fact. Give me the phone, Lorenza said, I'll hold on to it for you. She turned the flashlight toward one side of the beach, where it wasn't illuminating anyone, just an inanimate jutting rock spur.

I undressed. Carolina shouted for us to hurry up, she must have swum out a certain distance by now. I swam a few strokes to catch up with them.

What about Lorenza? Novelli asked once we were in the water.

She's cold.

Too bad! But he really didn't seem to care much. Carolina said: Look straight up, it's incredible! But I turned to look toward shore, where I could only guess at Lorenza's shape, because in the meantime she'd turned off the flashlight. Or else, I thought to myself, she was already gone, she'd walked up the trail all by herself, up, up, to the house.

IN MY PHONE I have the pictures of the days we spent in Sardinia: the four of us together on the terrace / Carolina laughing at something, her leg pulled up on the chair, a cigarette wedged between her fingers / Novelli paddling away with Lorenza in the two-person sea kayak (a sting of completely irrational jealousy when they vanished beyond the shoals and didn't show up again for another half hour) / children aiming water guns / Lorenza again, lying on the bow of the speedboat. In the pictures, everything looks happier than I remember it.

I can scroll through the summer of 2017 like that in less than a minute, just by moving my thumb and without understanding a thing about it: a screenshot of an online horoscope warning me and all the other Sagittariuses against a week in which we were likely to lack "intellectual confidence" / a video of a man, taken from behind, as he stands atop a bungee-jumping platform: he's already harnessed, he gives the thumbs-up to whoever's filming, then leaps into the void with a shout. After a few jerks in the frame, he can be seen dangling yards and yards below, above a rushing stream. It was Karol who sent it to me, and he was the one who jumped / a succession of articles about the August 17 terror attack in Barcelona / a photo of a ceiling lamp that Lorenza must have liked, or else I must have liked, but which we'd never buy / a sleeping man, and I have no idea who he is / another sleeping man (who sent me all those pictures of sleeping men, and why? Or could it be that I was sending them to someone else? The gallery gives no context, just the dates) / dishes in a restaurant in Puglia / another screenshot of news reports, with, in succession, the report of the death of a Venetian couple who had made a risotto with poisonous flowers and an in-depth piece on certain oral tumors, possibly due to oral sex.

There's a slideshow, complete with soundtrack, documenting Eugenio's departure for the United States. The iPhone serves it up to me periodically. I wish it wouldn't, that my iPhone would be a little more considerate with my memories, but I always wind up watching it. In one shot, Eugenio is standing next to his suitcase and he's flashing a V-for-victory sign, but you can tell he's at a loss. In another picture, he's hugging Lorenza and she's crying. And in yet another, he has his back to us, and he's already made his way through security.

The iPhone chose as a soundtrack "Born to Be Wild," which might have seemed perfect for those pictures, but once again proves that the algorithm understood nothing about that morning at Fiumicino, understood nothing about the awkwardness in the airport lobby when we were all there, me, Lorenza, Eugenio's father, and his girlfriend; understood nothing about me as I noticed the order in which Eugenio said goodbye to us, nor the sadness that washed over me as I saw him finally vanish into the line for security, a sadness I hadn't expected at all, a sadness I couldn't say whether was for him or for me.

I move on, now we're in September: a resort in Ko Lanta where Lorenza and I only thought about going / Novelli's daughter reading *Wonder* on the metro / Eugenio in his new American life / a satirical cartoon featuring Donald Trump and Kim Jong Un, after North Korea detonated a hundred-kiloton H-bomb. I'm sure I must have talked to Curzia about it, as we both wondered whether nuclear escalation was a real likelihood, and then we decided that it was mostly my own fear, because by now I had a genuine obsession with atomic bombs.

A TICKET FOR THE CENTRE POMPIDOU and a French film poster indicate that in October I went back to Paris. The time had come for me to deliver my testimony about Giulio and Adriano. In the preceding months I had taken extensive notes about them, including a list of terms, abstract words like caregiving, fun, and understanding. But I didn't want the result to be a collection of ceremonious phrases. I wanted the document to be incisive, so I had finally made up my mind to focus on one particular episode.

One day, in the neighborhood around the galleries of Saint-Germain, we had stopped in front of an African mask shop, and Giulio had described to Adriano the origin and magical properties of each mask. He'd displayed an expertise so unmistakable that even the shopkeeper had noticed it through the plate glass window. He had invited us all in, and had then taken over the lesson, providing a trove of information. The masks were exorbitantly priced, and in fact they were luxury accessories for Parisian homes, furnishing the myth of a primitive Africa, but to us that mattered little or nothing. The important thing to us was that Adriano remained calm and collected the whole time, without displaying any of his usual signs of impatience, none of the outbursts of temper that had led the teachers at the preschool to summon Giulio to a meeting only a few days earlier because of a particularly worrisome classroom disturbance caused by Adriano's attention deficits and hyperactivity. In the shop, Giulio had shot me a fleeting glance that was eminently eloquent: as if to say, You see? You see the way he really is? So why are they doing this to me? In the end, Adriano had been so patient and attentive that the shopkeeper had given the boy a piece of carved wood. It probably wasn't especially valuable, but in the hours that followed, Adriano had held on to it, gripping it tightly as if it were the most precious object he'd ever possessed.

I held out the sheets of paper to Giulio's lawyer, apologizing to her in advance for the poor translation into French. They would surely be able to fix it up. As long as they kept the meaning, I would have nothing against that.

Very touching, she said after reading it. Truth be told, though, she had already prepared a rough draft of my deposition. There had actually been no reason for me to bother going all the way to Paris. I could perfectly well have sent her a scan of the document with my signature by email. But as long as I was there: she picked up the phone and dialed an internal extension, calling her assistant into the room and asking if she'd be so good as to print it out. During the minutes we sat waiting, Giulio and his lawyer chatted between themselves. They had a rapport that surprised me, and it was clear that Giulio trusted her implicitly.

The new text was very spare, terse. Basically it stated that, having known and spent time with them for years, I could safely declare that Giulio was a person of great personal merit and that his interactions with his son, to my own knowledge and witness, had always been correct. I signed it, wondering how anyone could think of choosing an adjective like that, "correct," to describe the relationship between a father and a son.

Once we'd left the law office, Giulio and I walked along together, but there was a strange atmosphere in the air. Having completed the mission that had united us over the past few months, it seemed that we no longer had much to say to each other. I was also a little disappointed. I had imagined that I would play a more decisive role in that situation, that I'd be a protagonist in a life that had nothing to do with my own.

Giulio informed me about the new developments in the lawsuit with a sense of exhaustion, as if he felt the obligation to do so because I'd taken yet another plane and really had nothing to show for my trouble. He had lost the battle over Adriano's school. Adriano had started attending French elementary school, in seventh grade. There was nothing about that solution that Giulio liked: not the method, not the teachers, not the elite social milieu.

I really don't understand what his mother has gotten into her head, he said. They weren't going to be able to provide Adriano with a lifestyle even remotely comparable to that of his classmates. Unless full custody was entrusted to Luc, of course.

And yet Cobalt's line of reasoning had persuaded the judge: from that school, Adriano would be able to gain access to some of the finest high schools in Paris, and from there he'd be given an assured route to the *grandes écoles* and a prosperous future.

A very clear strategy of the dominant classes, Giulio said. The social escalator is reserved for you, right at the very start, when you're six years old. There's a lockstep march through school, no one else can butt in line. This guarantees the crystallization of privileges.

Needless to say, he had read up on the subject. He'd perused a vast body of documentation. He'd read textbooks, setting his own situation in the context of a number of abstract economic mechanisms. Politics had returned to his life in an unexpected manner, but if his political activity in his twenties had been dynamic and determined, now politics was something that was being visited upon him. And if in his twenties politics meant protest marches and an almost excessive volume of human interactions, now it had become the loneliest activity imaginable.

While Giulio was studying new manifestations of social injustice, Cobalt had come up with a surprising volume of material against him. That material began with a report from the teachers at the preschool, who had reported on the hostile and largely unhelpful attitudes that Adriano's father (Giulio) had displayed toward them. There was also an expert report produced by her lawyers, the work of a child psychotherapist, according to whom the boy, after his longest stays with his father, regularly displayed somatic manifestations of discomfort: rashes, constipation. Things he's suffered from his whole life long, Giulio told me privately.

Among other things, he had given no authorization for the child to be subjected to any examinations of that kind. His lawyer had raised an official complaint and the judge had taken it under consideration. Perhaps, in the end, Cobalt's initiative would backfire on her.

Forgive me if I've asked you to come all this way for no good reason, he said.

We were on the bridge, in front of the Arab World Institute, and it was going to be another ten minutes before we'd be parting ways. It's not a problem.

No, seriously, I apologize.

Since he had nothing else to add, I simply said: Okay. Then we said goodbye. Maybe we'd see each other again before I left, but neither of us was very convinced of it.

I HAD DECIDED to stay at Novelli's place. The official reason was that Novelli had a spare room he could offer, more comfortable than Giulio's sofa, and what's more, a place where I could focus on my work. Actually, of course, as Giulio realized perfectly well, my affections had tilted in Novelli's direction, especially after the holidays we had spent together. Giulio remained impassive as I told him the news. There was no room for jealousy among grown-ups, which is what we were. But to find ourselves in that new configuration was something different, uncomfortable in some sense, as if there were a betrayal at the bottom of it all. Before we went into the lawyer's office, he asked me in a carefree tone of voice that, of course, actually pointed in an anything-but-carefree direction: So, are you more comfortable at Novelli's place?

Yes, I was more comfortable there. At least I felt I was contained in the warmth of a family: if I had been straight with him, that's what I would have said. And I'd have added that there was no reason to get upset about the idea or take it too personally. My quest for that kind of warmth was a weakness I was all too familiar with. It dated back to my earliest memories, though I have no idea where it came from. Even back in elementary school, I would spend as much time as possible at the home of my Vietnamese neighbor, whose name translated as Slow-Moving Cloud. Her mother did jigsaw puzzles with thousands of pieces that took up the whole floor, and in the evening we would sit in the kitchen and eat lychees in syrup.

A few hours after saying goodbye for the evening, Giulio forwarded an email that had in its turn been forwarded to him by his lawyer. From the subject line, I knew that it was a document related to his custody case, but I couldn't bring myself to read it. I was at Novelli's place and we'd just picked up some carryout pizzas from an Italian restaurant: italiano *italiano*, the children liked to say over and over: *Italian* Italian, which is why the crust was so good. It didn't strike me as anything special, but that didn't matter. All that I cared about was the soft light in that apartment on the top floor, the uneaten pizza crusts in the takeaway boxes, and the children with their bare feet perched on the sofa upholstery or else waving in the air. Tomorrow I'd be flying back to Rome, and I wanted to relish that domestic peace without interference.

But that's not the way it went. While Carolina was getting the littlest one to sleep in the other room, we put on a movie and I had just started to nod off when we heard a series of explosions. Carolina came back out into the living room. The blood had drained from her face immediately. Novelli and I grabbed our phones, while the first reports were popping up on Twitter. Apparently those blasts had come from the area around the Eiffel Tower, so they were pretty far away. Still, we went out on the balcony and stood there, listening intently. Below us, the street was empty.

After a while, his daughter joined up. We heard what sounded like a burst of gunfire. Are those shots or bombs? she asked. It sounds a lot like submachine gun fire, Novelli replied.

She told me that at her school, they did monthly drills. The headmaster would sound the alarm by blowing a horn (an actual oxhorn, like in the Middle Ages, though who could say why), their teacher would close the windows, draw the curtains, and turn out the lights. Meanwhile, some of the students would block the classroom door by piling chairs up against it. All the students had to crouch under their desks, turn off their cell phones—not just turn their sound off, but actually power them down, because at the Bataclan, when everyone was already playing dead, the terrorists had fired down from the balcony into the auditorium seating below, aiming at the bodies on the floor wherever a phone lit up. Then we all have to remain perfectly silent and still and wait, Novelli's daughter said. Wait for what? I asked. *For someone with an AK-47 to burst through the door,* I thought to myself. For the horn to sound a second time, she said. She told me that during their first drills, her classmates would cry and so would she, but by now they were just used to it. During the last drill, she'd actually fallen asleep.

I wrote Curzia to ask if she knew anything about the attack, and that's how I found out that she was in France, a coincidence that I found vaguely menacing. She wasn't in Paris, though. She'd just arrived in Calais, where she was reporting on what was known as the migrant jungle camp, one year after it had been cleared. She didn't know anything about the attack, and like us, was trying to figure it out from Twitter. I could sense Novelli glancing at my fingers, and before he could say anything, I offered a justification: I'm just asking her about it for my newspaper. Maybe I should go get closer to where it's happening.

Eventually, we came inside from the balcony and sat back down to finish the movie. A few hours later we found out there'd been no attack. It had just been fireworks, and it was even a permitted display: from the set of a series that the Wachowski sisters were filming, a Netflix production.

THE NEXT DAY, there had been a bit of uproar. The authorities had warned the residents of the immediate neighborhood through a messaging system, but the fireworks had been audible over a much wider area, possibly due to atmospheric conditions.

On his radio show appearance, Novelli had mocked the situation sarcastically. Then he had spoken in more serious terms of how reality and mere imagination mingle in our lives in truly odd ways. I was eating breakfast, listening to him, watching him walk around with his cell phone pressed to his ear as he gesticulated with his free hand, and once again I was astonished at his sheer talent, his expressive facility.

After my interview, he had timidly extended his range of subjects to include Italy, and his name had started to appear on the list of experts to talk to in case of earthquakes, mudslides, avalanches, unusual cloudbursts, or volcanic eruptions. No doubt, the fact that he'd been mentioned in the deck as a Nobel laureate didn't hurt—and even though that was an exaggeration, it wasn't exactly false. Ten years before that, when the IPCC (Intergovernmental Panel on Climate Change) had received the prize together with Al Gore, Novelli was one of the few Italians on the panel. The fact that there were dozens of other scientists on the panel with him was basically just a detail.

I needed to head back to Rome. Novelli walked me to the bus stop. The sky was covered with just one cloud, white and compact: an altostratus, as I had learned in my time with him. That type of sky really bothered the cataract in my left eye. I started trying out my usual tests, squinting my eyes alternately, a tic that Eugenio had borrowed from me.

Novelli told me about the work that he was going to have done to fix the family home in Genoa. He wanted to get started as soon as possible. By now Carolina had really reached levels of paranoia about living in Paris.

I'd noticed it too. She no longer took the metro. She didn't want to go to the movies, to restaurants: anywhere, basically. And she was starting to infect the children with her anxiety. She wouldn't let them go to birthday parties if they were outdoors. There was no reasoning with her about it.

After we had already reached the bus stop, he added: Ah, I almost forgot. It seems that we're going to become colleagues.

The way he said it made it clear that he hadn't almost forgotten at all. Quite the contrary, he'd been planning that announcement the whole time.

They've asked me to write for the ***. A column about the environment. Crazy, right? I don't really have all that much time to spare, actually, what with my research and the classes I'm teaching. But I didn't think it seemed right to say no. Otherwise I'd be leaving the field wide-open to all these self-proclaimed scientific popularizers. And climate denialism, you know. If there's one thing this country needs, it's a minimum level of scientific rigor.

I pointed out to him that ***, as a newspaper, struck me as decidedly too partisan, and hardly in line with his convictions.

Every newspaper that exists is partisan, he replied. I mean, what? Doesn't the paper you write for take sides? Plus, let's be frank, there are no longer any *real* political differences. There's only being in favor of the truth or against it.

In the meantime the bus had pulled up to the sidewalk. I realized that Novelli would have wanted more time now to talk this over, but he'd miscalculated the time available by waiting until the last minute to maximize the surprise of his news.

Maybe you can give me some writing advice, he said, even though I knew he'd never really ask me for it. We brushed cheeks in farewell, and I boarded the bus.

As the bus pulled away I turned to look back. Through the window I could see him where I'd left him, lost in thought, his hands in his pockets. I'd forced myself to remain impassive just a moment earlier, but a faint sense of friction, based on nothing, really, must have been perceptible to us both, because a minute later I received a text from him saying goodbye once again and telling me he hoped to see me back in Paris again soon. It hadn't been necessary. In fact, that sort of open expression of feelings wasn't like us at all. I texted back, saying I hoped so too, and adding my congratulations for that new gig of his.

Later, while I was waiting to board at the gate, I opened Giulio's email. There was no opening text at all, just the thread of successive forwards and a PDF attachment. It was a memo that Cobalt had delivered to her lawyer. The text was in French, but I could still make out from the syntax that it had originally been written in the first-person singular, and therefore by Cobalt herself, only to be subsequently modified into a more neutral third-person singular, where she was identified as Mme V.

Cobalt recounted the years when she'd lived with Giulio in Geneva, together with Adriano, a newborn infant. They'd moved there because she had been awarded a fellowship at CERN. The stipend was generous but still insufficient to make ends meet, given the Swiss cost of living. Giulio had failed to find a position of his own. All the same, he seemed unwilling to give up any of their previous lifestyle, especially the travel. At a certain point in the memo, she described Giulio as *irréaliste* with respect to their financial situation at the time.

I scrolled through the pages, all the way to the end, and an English term in italics caught my eye: *gaslighting*. I looked up the word. In psychology it means an effort to confuse a victim's memories through a process of programmatic manipulation, eventually making the victim doubt their own recollections. It's a technique that can be observed in many situations of domestic violence, and it's frequently employed by sociopaths. It can also be utilized by certain repressive regimes. It can be so pervasive, it can so confuse the victim's mind, that it can induce them to commit suicide.

I stopped reading. I'd started to feel a surge of nausea. The passengers for the flight were already standing in line, I needed to join the queue, but I remained seated. Boarding had begun, and the line snaked forward, one passenger after another.

The last passenger to board was a young man traveling alone, wearing a down jacket that was too heavy for the weather in Rome. They called my name, once, twice, three times. Outside the plate glass windows, I saw the aircraft pull away from the jet bridge and trundle off toward the airstrip. Only then did I stand up. I made my way back past the sequence of security checks and out of the terminal.

PART TWO

CLOUDS

ON AUGUST 9, 1945, the heavy bomber *Bock-scar* took off in the dark of night from Tinian, a tiny island in the Marianas Archipelago that had only been captured by the American army one year earlier. The B-29 Superfortress's destination—that is, the target on which it intended to drop the atomic weapon hanging in its bomb bay—was the city of Kokura, the location of a military arsenal.

After flying over a long expanse of the Pacific Ocean, first black and then lit by a brightening dawn, and after waiting futilely for the arrival of another heavy bomber assigned to film the mission, *Bockscar* flew to Kokura, arriving there at exactly 10:44 a.m. It found the city under heavy cloud cover, however. It was a strange cloud, very dark, possibly of natural origin or else due to the smoke from other bombing raids that the wind had pushed there. Whatever its source, it covered the target, hiding it from the view of the aircraft's commander, Major Charles Sweeney.

The B-29 continued circling the city aimlessly for a while longer, waiting for the sky to clear, but the cloud showed no sign of dispersing. Lest the plane become a target for Japanese fighters, especially while carrying an atom bomb, the crew decided to give up on Kokura. Around eleven, *Bockscar* turned south, heading for another city on the island of Kyushu, the next city on the target list. Its name was a combination of two words describing its morphological structure: *naga*, or long, and *saki*, or promontory. The long promontory: Nagasaki.

Terumi Tanaka was only to learn all these details many years later. In the summer of 1945 he was only thirteen years old and was attending the first year of junior high school (in Japan, school starts in April). While the older students were working full-time making weapons and armaments, Terumi and his classmates contributed to the war effort every other day: one morning at school, the next morning at work. Their job involved fabricating spears from bamboo shoots, digging pits on the beach to trap enemy tanks, and gathering kudzu, a perennial vine that was harvested for its starch to use as a biofuel, instead of increasingly scarce gasoline.

If at first American bombing runs had focused exclusively on strategic objectives, by now civilians were considered combatants, and therefore targets. In early August, Nagasaki was one of the few cities that remained intact, along with Hiroshima, Kokura, and a few others, but the air raid siren could be heard frequently there as well. When that happened, Terumi sought refuge in the forest. That summer, therefore, his life unfolded in a limited radius: home, school, beach, and forest.

Actually, there had been a couple of bombardments just a few days earlier, on July 29 and again on August 1. A total of seventy-two planes had hit the city, in groups of six, and each raid had lasted for three hours. But the bombs had fallen for the most part on the industrial district, to the west, while Terumi lived in Nakagawa-machi, in the central valley. One day, during lessons, the air raid siren had gone off. Terumi and his classmates had run into the woods and up the hill. From there they'd been able to get a clear view of the enemy planes as they bombed the factories. They'd relaxed at that sight and watched the bombing raid until the planes flew away. "There was a strange peace," Terumi Tanaka told me when I interviewed him, nearly eighty years after that summer.

Then came August 6. Little Boy, the first atom bomb used in warfare, had been dropped on Hiroshima. Terumi learned about it the following day, from the radio or perhaps from the newspaper, even though he hadn't heard about any "atom bomb," because arms of that sort simply weren't a concept yet. The terminology employed, at that point, was simply a "new kind" of bomb, and the damage it had inflicted was still being evaluated. Word spread that people should dress in white, not because of the radiation (no one even knew what radiation was), but because the new bomb "emitted intense heat."

And so Terumi's life in Nagasaki proceeded normally from August 6 to 9: home, school, beach, and forest. Alternating duties meant that the ninth was a school day. Around eight o'clock that morning, however, the air raid siren went off. There were two types of siren: one that warned of grave peril, the *kūshū-keihō* (when it went off, it meant you were not to move from your location), and another, known as *keikai-keihō*— which meant only that the citizenry should exercise caution. That morning the *kūshū* didn't last long, but the *keikai* went on and on. Terumi decided it would all be over soon enough, so he figured he should leave home and head for school. "But it was very hot out so I stripped down. I sat there on my tatami for a while, reading."

As he sat there, feeling lazy, he noticed the sound of the airplane. By now he'd developed an ear for it, and he knew how to recognize a B-29, because a B-29 had four engines and therefore a louder roar. Terumi went over to the window and tried to get a glimpse of the heavy bomber in the sky. That day, there was cloud cover over Nagasaki too; not a compact layer like over Kokura, just scattered clouds here and there. The B-29 must be hiding behind one of those.

Terumi turned to look at the spot where he'd been lying until just a moment ago. The room was small, six tatami in all, at most he might have taken a couple of steps. At that point the flash arrived. "Some people described it as a glow that arrived from a specific direction, but it was different for me." The light didn't come from any direction in particular: "It was instantaneously everywhere." A kind of light that was "different from any other," Terumi added suddenly.

His room was on the second floor of the house, and the flash had frightened him. Terumi therefore hurried down the stairs. As he was running downstairs, he saw the light change many times: from white to blue, then to yellow, red, and finally a very intense red. The sequence might have been different, but he could still remember the colors with great precision. On the ground floor, there were other tatami, and Terumi lay down on his belly, covering his ears and eyes with his hands, as he'd been taught to do in the drills at school. From that position, before the blast wave hit him and a moment before passing out, he had an instant to think about the meaning of that red, so intense: something very large and very close to him was in flames.

His mother and his two younger sisters, ages six and ten, were also in the house with him. Terumi hadn't seen them. The house they lived in was one of Nagasaki's traditional dwellings, with an *engawa*, a sort of raised patio, a kind of stilt structure, and they had all three thrown themselves out of the building, instinctively fleeing in the direction away from the epicenter.

When Terumi regained consciousness, his mother was calling him. He couldn't see her, and she couldn't see him, because the explosion had thrown a door on top of him. This door consisted of a wooden frame in which six frosted-glass panes were set. "Miraculously the glass panes hadn't shattered. Many of our neighbors were injured precisely by sharp fragments of wood and shards of glass."

He managed to get free of the door. The house was a mess but still standing. All four of them were still alive. Their mother decided to take her children to the shelter, which was about a hundred yards away. As they left their home, Terumi saw for the first time the wreckage surrounding him. "Each family thought their own house had sustained a direct hit by the bomb. But they were wrong, all of them were hit equally hard."

The shelter, a sort of bunker, rapidly filled up with people. "At first, every family had had their own shelter, but they weren't really safe. So the neighborhood had built a shelter into the hill, behind the Shinto temple. I remember it as being enormous, but when I returned to that place ten years ago, I realized that it couldn't have been that big." It was basically a hole dug horizontally into the dirt, with water leaking in everywhere.

"You'd need to understand how Nagasaki was built," Tanaka-san told me. "The city wraps around a bay and is split into three valleys. The western valley is the industrial zone. I lived in the central valley, which is a residential area, as is the eastern valley. The prefecture and government buildings were located where all three of the valleys meet. The B-29 was supposed to drop its bomb there, on the most important and highly populated area. But there was a cloud directly overhead."

And so Major Sweeney chose the western valley, which had already been bombed before. There were mostly factories there, but also Nagasaki's Christian community. That's where Terumi's two aunts lived: Rui, his mother's sister, and Koto, his father's sister.

After the explosion, for a fairly long time, those who lived in the central valley had no idea of the level of destruction on the other side of the hill. Nor could they have imagined it, given the fact that nothing like this had ever happened before. From the color of the sky, though, it was easy enough to guess that that part of the city was on fire. "The sun was red in the middle of the blackness." In spite of her son's entreaties, Terumi's mother thought it was too dangerous to go there.

Around four in the afternoon, the prefecture building caught fire. Terumi headed in that direction, worried that the flames might reach his neighborhood, but the wind shifted just in time. On his way back to his home, he walked by his old elementary school, the school he had attended until just a few months before. When he looked inside, he saw the main classroom was full of wounded people. "There must have been at least a hundred people. People must have brought them there by car." There were no doctors, no nurses, just three women tending to all the wounded as best they could. "Many of them were burned, and yet they were shivering from the cold. They were dying before my eyes." When they died, they were picked up by their ankles and wrists and carried out into the courtyard. There a trench had been dug to cremate them.

At home, Terumi neatened up the house a little, but he and his family went back to the shelter to sleep. They felt safer there. During the night, one of the missing girls returned home, the daughter of the landlords who had rented the Tanaka family their home. She was a student, and that morning she had been working at one of the factories. In the shelter, everyone was overjoyed, especially because the girl showed no signs of any evident injury. "She would be dead before the end of the war on account of radiation exposure, after days of raging fever."

ON AUGUST 12, three days after the explosion, Terumi's mother finally agreed to go with him to the western valley to search for her sister and sister-in-law. They decided to cut through the woods and climb over the hill: the path was roughly two-and-a-half-miles long. When they got up to the pass, the western valley opened out before them: incinerated, flattened. "There was nothing left." All that still stood were the skeletal steel structures of the factories.

His maternal aunt, Rui, lived in a somewhat isolated house. Terumi thought that the fire might not have spread that far, but when he looked in that direction, he saw nothing.

On their way down the side of the hill, they passed dead people or people in their death throes, abandoned for days without assistance. "At the sight of the first corpses, we were frightened, but there were so many of them that from a certain point on, we stopped feeling anything at all. We simply stopped talking."

They didn't talk when they reached Aunt Rui's house either. She hadn't been burned: "She had been crushed." Rui's body was lying there, and it was about to be cremated. But her father was still alive, "so badly burned you could see his arm bones."

When he said that, Tanaka-san made the first movement visible on the webcam, running one hand over his forearm, describing the entire length of his grandfather's exposed arm bone. Then his arm disappeared again below the frame of the shot.

His grandfather was still sufficiently conscious to realize they were there. He was begging for water. Terumi wet a handkerchief and extended it to his lips. "But his lips had practically melted."

Other relatives had arrived before them. They had put together a jury-rigged cremation ceremony, stacking firewood on a sheet of corrugated metal. Terumi wanted to watch, but his mother had objected. While the rest of the family was arranging Rui's corpse for cremation, they continued in their search for Aunt Koto.

TANAKA-SAN'S FACE FROZE on the monitor. A moment later, he disconnected. Ryosuke and I waited for ten minutes or so, then Ryosuke tried to phone him, and followed up with an email, but there came no reply. Probably he was tired, Ryosuke said. That seemed likely: Tanaka-san had spoken for nearly three hours, without ever getting up or asking for a break. He just took a small sip from a cup from time to time. He was almost ninety years old.

He wrote back the following day, with an apology: the Wi-Fi connection had stopped working. He gave me another appointment a few weeks later. Once the three of us were all online, he was ready to start back up from the exact point he'd left off at. But maybe I wasn't ready. It seemed a little too impersonal, so I asked him about the object I saw hanging on the wall behind him: it was a sort of many-colored cloak, all of the hues very intense, purple, green, dark blue. Tanaka-san reached up and brought a corner of it close to the webcam. He showed me that every piece of it was an origami of a small, stylized bird, specifically a crane. In all, there were a thousand origami cranes, all threaded together. According to folk tradition, anyone who completed a *senbazuru*, a cloak of a thousand origami cranes, could make a wish and have it come true. I didn't dare to ask what wish he had made.

IT TOOK ALMOST TWO HOURS to burn his aunt Rui's body. In the meantime, Terumi and his mother had reached the home of his aunt Koto. It was only six hundred yards away, and it normally took just fifteen minutes to get from one house to the other. This time it took them at least an hour, because all the buildings were burned, collapsed, razed to the ground. They had

to edge between scattered rubble and stone foundations of the now-vanished wooden houses, working
their way around them or else climbing over them.

Aunt Koto's house was barely a quarter mile from
ground zero, which meant that it was well within Fat
Man's radius of total destruction. Inside that radius,
even the corpses were indistinguishable, so badly
charred it wasn't even possible to guess their sex. But
that day, *ground zero* had no meaning for Terumi, any
more than *radius of total destruction* or *Fat Man*, because none of those things existed yet.

Terumi and his mother examined the corpses one
at a time. At last they reached the ruins of a house that
looked like his aunt's: they checked all the corpses
around it. Often, when they turned the corpses over,
they would crumble, disintegrating in their hands. In
the end, though, they managed to find Aunt Koto and
her nephew, Makoto: on a couple of shreds of cloth, at
the bottom of the legs, they had recognized the pattern
of one of his aunt's kimonos. It wasn't the actual fabric
(the fire had burned it), it was an impression of the pattern impressed on the flesh. As for Makoto, his corpse
was possible to identify because he was so much taller
than average.

Makoto had arrived in Nagasaki a week earlier for
a food holiday. He was studying mathematics at the
University of Tokyo, which had spared him from being
drafted into the army. But in the big cities, food was
so scarce that from time to time, students were sent
home to their families to get some nutrition. Makoto

had been scheduled to head back to Tokyo on August 9, that is, that same morning.

Terumi and his mother knew that they wouldn't be able to carry those corpses by themselves, so they decided to head back to Rui's house, where the rest of their relatives were. Though the house had been crushed, it was still one of the most intact structures around, so a great many of the burn victims had gathered around it. Their wounds were all black. "Black with flies," he said. It had been three days since the blast, and in the August heat, the smell of suppurating flesh was attracting flies. "As you got closer, the flies scattered, and then you could see that the cuts and injuries beneath them were full of maggots." Since there were no doctors, the relatives used chopsticks to extract the maggots from the flesh.

Normally in Japan, human remains were collected in a *kotsutsubo*, a funerary urn, but for Aunt Rui they used an ordinary kitchen vase that had survived intact. When the cremation was complete, Terumi saw that his aunt's bones on the corrugated metal still described the shape of her body, and he burst into tears. That was the one and only time he wept. When they moved on to the subsequent phase of the ritual, which called for each relative present to use chopsticks to fill the vase with the deceased's remains, he had once again become calm and silent.

They decided to return home before dark, taking a different route. This time, instead of climbing over the mountain, they would walk around it from the south.

On the central road, which ran down to the port, a passageway had been excavated through the rubble, running roughly along the trolley tracks. Terumi and his mother followed that path. Then, for a certain distance, they followed the river's edge. Under a bridge, in a small man-made lake, Terumi saw thirty or so corpses floating. "They were badly swollen and their mouths were wide-open."

But what really struck him was the sight of a little boy, or it might have been a little girl. Next to the river there was an open space left by a house that had burned, and behind it was a stone wall running diagonally: the little boy, or little girl, had been "glued" to the wall, arms and legs spread-eagled, as if crushed there by the pressure of the blast wave. Terumi and his mother continued through the rubble for another two and a half miles, in utter silence, surrounded by a very strange smell, until they reached Nakagawa-machi.

I SEARCHED FOR NAKAGAWA-MACHI on Apple Maps and shared it on the screen. When the map appeared, Tanaka-san leaned forward, toward his monitor. "That's it," he said, "that's the place." He led me toward the exact location of the Shinto temple. Behind it was a hillock, and behind the hillock the bunker had been dug.

Together, we reconstructed on the screen the route that he had covered with his mother, the way there and the way back, and we assigned the correct names to the stages in the trip. The mountain was called Konpira, the river was the Urakami, his aunt Koto's neighborhood was Okamachi, and that's not where the bomb was supposed to explode: the target had been farther south, in Hamamachi.

If it had not been for the clouds, Terumi and his mother and his classmates would all have been little more than half a mile from ground zero, well within the radius of radiation, where the chances of survival were minimal. Then everything would have turned out so differently. Terumi wouldn't have been sitting across from me, telling me his story, and his mother, Tanaka Moto, would not have lived to age 102, caring for herself with traditional medicine, salted plums, and sake.

If it hadn't been for the clouds, things would have gone the opposite way: after the blast, it would have been Aunts Rui and Koto climbing over Mount Konpira to search for them, turning over corpses one by one in search of a scrap of kimono tattooed onto the skin, finally identifying them, mother and son, and arranging their funeral pyres as best they could with the scraps they could scavenge, surrounded by the worst devastation humankind had ever witnessed.

NOVELLI AND I talked frequently about the importance of clouds in the history of the bomb, just as we talked about the importance of clouds for him, and the importance of clouds in general. I remember one time in particular: it was the middle of the night and we had continued drinking after Carolina and the children had gone to sleep. We were just sprawled, one on each sofa, and Novelli seemed strangely vulnerable. Usually, he played the part of the disenchanted cynic: he swore that the only thing that mattered to him about science anymore was to get automatic raises and avoid teaching freshmen. I knew, though, that deep down that's not how he felt. I knew that like any other scientist he preserved a romantic attitude toward his chosen profession. I knew that he dreamed of one day putting his own name on something, an equation or maybe even a constant of nature. If you could give your name to anything at all, I asked him that night, what would you choose?

Nothing at all. Nothing.

No, just for fun, I insisted. What would it be?

Novelli heaved a sigh, then he admitted that there was one thing, actually, but not an equation, not a constant. Then what was it?

If he could choose, he would pick something more... impermanent.

Like a cloud?

That's right, like a cloud. Exactly. After all there were Kelvin-Helmholtz clouds, spectacular and rare, clouds that sketched rollers in the sky, waves of sharp-peaked vapor. So why not "Novelli clouds"? The competition his students were taking part in was part of that objective. Perhaps, sooner or later, one of them would photograph a truly special formation. Then, he would study the cloud's origin, and he would give it his own name.

At that point, he slid down off the sofa and knelt on the carpet. He placed the screen of his phone scant inches from my nose: Look, here, look.

He thumbed through a gallery of clouds, some of them so strange that they resembled the effects achieved with computer graphics. Mammatus clouds, shelf clouds: Weren't they incredible? Humankind had been looking up at the same skies for thousands of years, and yet new configurations were still being discovered and classified. The World Meteorological

Organization had just added a new one to the cloud atlas: These, they're called asperitas clouds.

I could smell his hot breath, rife with vodka, directly in my nostrils, but it didn't bother me.

You know what the most extraordinary thing is? That asperitas clouds, too, are made of water vapor. All clouds are nothing but water vapor. Surrounding conditions may change, air pressure, temperature, wind currents. But there are so many combinations that the variety that can be created is potentially infinite.

He went to his browser and typed something in. A video started up, showing in time-lapse photography a gaseous front, light blue and compact, advancing over the surface of a lake. The cloud was shaped like a tube and was suspended in an unnatural fashion in the middle of the sky, so unnatural that I asked him whether it had been photoshopped. Novelli shook his head and said, It's a roll cloud. When a mass of hot air slides quickly over a compact mass of cold air, it happens sometimes that in the area where they intersect the clouds are literally rolled up. He mimed that process by running his fingers over his other hand's flat palm. They can extend for hundreds of kilometers. They move along without losing their shape. This cloud was filmed on Lake Michigan, but they're very rare. Unpredictable.

We went back to watching the cloud as it moved through the sky, and I noticed that it looked potentially stormy. Novelli assured me that it wasn't, that for the most part roll clouds were harmless. It should inspire you, he added.

Inspire me to do what?

You could write a book about it. I could help you.

Let me guess: you could be the main character.

Oh, that would be up to you.

We could call it *The Man of the Clouds* in that case.

I like it, Novelli said. *The Man of the Clouds*: that sounds nice.

Though neither of us realized it, we were at the height of our friendship, and together we were looking at pictures of clouds on the phone. For a few hours I actually gave his proposal serious consideration: a four-handed book on clouds. It would be nice, for a change, to share a project with someone else. To share a project with him.

A few weeks later, "The Man of the Clouds" debuted as the title of his column, in the weekly supplement to ***. Novelli never asked my permission to use that phrase, and I acted as if nothing had happened. After all, I wasn't even sure that a late-night conversation between a couple of drunken men actually gave me grounds to claim copyright.

IN NOVEMBER 2017, I went back to Trieste to teach my course. After months of monothematic reading on the atom bomb, my head was packed with the lives of nuclear physicists, so I decided to focus the lessons on that type of storytelling. As an introduction, I confessed to my students that I'd had an adolescent soft spot, that I'd gone to see *A Beautiful Mind* all alone, on the day it first appeared in movie theaters. I wanted to watch it with unbroken concentration. I told them how, after seeing it, I'd fantasized endlessly about filling windowpanes with nonsensical formulas, just like John Nash. Then I went on to talk about scientific biopics in more general terms: there was always a moment in the narrative when the protagonist, after battling against widespread skepticism, was greeted with a roar of applause. Had they ever noticed this detail? Alan

Turing, Thomas Edison, Stephen Hawking: that cathartic applause had showered down on each of them, at least in the cinematic version of their lives.

At that point one of the students, a young woman, raised her hand and asked whether I might have thought of including any women in my pantheon of great scientists.

A shiver of satisfaction ran through the classroom, as if many of the students might have asked that very same question, silently, in their heads.

I admitted that I hadn't really considered the matter in those terms.

She tilted her head and smiled, implicitly denouncing my naïveté: Really, Professor?

Don't get me wrong: I admire female scientists to exactly the same degree.

To exactly the same degree.

Of course.

And who do you admire in particular, for instance?

In my mind, I ran through a list of names, a pretty short one, truth be told, and then spoke: Well, Marie Curie, for starters.

The young woman touched her forehead, a gesture that gave a sense of exasperation to the words she next spoke: Maria Skłodowska, you mean. Nowadays, perhaps, we can at least have the decency of using her maiden name.

Maria Skłodowska, if you prefer.

It's not me that prefers it, Professor. It's just the right thing to do.

She had a very skinny face and dark hair, worn in a bob, with short, straight bangs, a style that had become so popular in recent years. She was definitely from the physics department. Do you mind if I ask your name? I said.

Fernanda Rucco.

Fernanda. Pleasure to meet you.

I was pacing back and forth, as I usually did, and for a fairly long while I must have remained silent. I wasn't thinking about any particular strategy. It was more that I was measuring that unexpected moment of discomfort inside myself, wondering whether I really deserved it. The words from a few minutes ago echoed in my ears: Really, Professor? The class waited, attentively.

Fernanda, I like your willingness to wade into the argument. That's exactly the kind of confrontation I'm looking to establish in this class. So let me accept your challenge and give it some thought. Of course, it goes without saying that women have been underrepresented in the history of science. All you have to do is count the number of female Nobel laureates in—

That won't take long, she broke in. In physics, in the past hundred and twenty years, three women scientists have won the Nobel.

A smile escaped me: I would have bet money that you're studying physics.

But Fernanda ignored that attempted moment of benevolence. What I said was by no means a challenge, Professor. It was just a correction.

———

LATER, IN THE CAFETERIA, I told Marina how
Fernanda had made me feel completely inadequate, as
if I'd been thinking about everything the wrong way
all my life. She remained neutral, perhaps reserving
the right to evaluate that possibility in due time. Then
she admitted that she'd experienced a similar moment
of tension at the beginning of her course: she'd made
reference to Richard Feynman's autobiography, I knew
the one she meant, of course? Of course I knew the
one she meant, it was required reading for any aspiring physicist at the university level. *So, what about it?* I
thought to myself.

So Feynman was a sexist and a serial molester. I
happened to notice.

I happened to notice too, Marina said. But I don't
think we noticed quite enough. And that's the point.
We hadn't taken it seriously enough. To these kids,
that's unacceptable. I went back and reread parts of
the book, and Fernanda has a point: Feynman calls the
girls who don't want to go to bed with him whores, he
also calls them disgusting, and he does it in more than
one place. What's more, he considers women unsuit-
able to study scientific subjects.

I never cared much for him. Feynman, I mean.

But you probably never cared much for him for the
wrong reasons.

And that was the truth: the reason I didn't like him
was that he was a braggart, because he made physics

seem easy, when it had never been at all easy for me, and because he played the bongos. But I had barely noticed his sexism when I read the book in school.

I went outside with her so she could smoke a cigarette. Coming back to Feynman, I said, if I were you, I wouldn't feel too bad about it.

That I hadn't noticed it at all?

Even sensitivity needs to be put into context. When we were at the university, everything was different.

Marina exhaled a plume of smoke: That seems pretty easy for you to say.

Maybe so. But it all seems a bit overblown to me.

When we went back inside, instead of continuing with her to the elevator, I turned and headed for the library. That evening I called room service for a grilled ham-and-cheese sandwich and I reworked the lesson plan. I added a short story by Alice Munro about the Russian mathematician Sophia Kovalevsky, even though I found it boring, and then I reread from start to finish Marie Curie's autobiography. The first page made it clear that Fernanda was right: "My family is Polish and my name is Maria Skłodowska." The next morning I talked about it in class, as if I'd known that book all my life, but I took great care not to share that passage.

WHEN I GOT BACK to Rome, I told Lorenza about my discussions with Fernanda and Marina, about my sense of uneasiness. Long past dinnertime, we were still in the living room, she sitting in an armchair and I lying on the sofa. Since Eugenio had left for the States, we'd won back that portion of the day for ourselves, and often we just hung out there, reading or tickling our smartphones, and we'd wind up eating late or not bothering even to sit down to dinner at all. They were moments of great intimacy, but it could also be somewhat worrisome in its extreme vacuity.

Lorenza took in my account without comment, almost reluctantly. Then, out of nowhere, she asked me: Do you think I'm too much of a feminist?

I wasn't sure whether that was a naïve question or a trick question, so I answered her question with a question of my own: Why do you ask?

I don't know. Because of what's going on, I guess. It makes me doubt myself.

What was going on, roughly: the anomalous wave kicked up by the Harvey Weinstein case, the redefinition—once and for all, perhaps—of relations between the sexes, the diffuse irritation that was in the air in practically every workplace, and more in general, a new spirit of the times (whatever that means) making its way into the world, making everyone feel secretly guilty.

I said: You're a feminist after your own fashion.

Lorenza got up and went into the kitchen. I heard her peel an apple and chew on the slices. Then she came back and we started talking about other things. Whether or not there was a shortage of feminism in her, and therefore in our marriage, was probably better not to examine too closely. That was the kind of discussion that left even the closest, calmest, and healthiest relationships in tatters, and lately the two of us were decidedly calm, no doubt about it, but there wasn't much left of our relationship's closeness and health.

I fantasized frequently about leaving. My inner life amounted basically to that, the picture of me abandoning Lorenza, Eugenio, and our apartment. In a split second, I would turn my back on everything and walk off without baggage toward a now-unpredictable existence. What would I find out there in the world? Was there something different awaiting me, an alternative that was more exciting than mere self-control? After years of conjugal life, I felt that I didn't know much anymore about the outside world. I pictured it as frantic and competitive, with brutal practices of "matching" on Tinder and informal, trivial bouts of sex. Who could say if these days sexual encounters demanded a rating, like meals at restaurants? Who could say whether there was any such thing as intimacy, anymore, in any absolute way? Whatever the case, getting back up to speed would surely be impossible.

Then I would tell myself that these were just so many excuses to keep myself safe, and that I really ought to just take the plunge: if everyone else could do it, I could do it too. But that's accepting the hypothesis that everyone else was doing it. I mean, take a look at Giulio, to name one example. I wasn't too sure: Did he still have a sex life, or had he turned into a sort of latter-day ascetic?

There was a fundamental decision to be made, and it needed to be made in a hurry, if possible before age forty and the development of serious pathologies: either accept that what Lorenza and I had created—with our fragmentary discussions about feminism, our slices of apple bolted down instead of dinner, our sterility—was the rest of life that awaited me, or else decide that as long as there was life, you must leave no path unexplored.

The matter needed to be examined from a professional point of view as well: How much longer could I go on as a writer, telling stories of nothing but failed ambitions and missed opportunities? If you were going to write, shouldn't you, first and foremost, live, and live madly? But that was where I always ground to a halt. I made sure that other thoughts poisoned my reasoning, distracting me as much as possible from the actual answer.

NOVELLI'S COLUMN, "The Man of the Clouds," lasted six months in all, to be exact from November 2017 until April 2018, when it was canceled due to the author's intemperate outbursts. While it lasted, it gave him some prominence. By now, he was being regularly invited to appear on certain afternoon talk shows, where he was billed as speaking "live from Paris."

In order to recount the second part of the story (the part where everything falls apart), I reread the articles he published in his column from January onward, combing through them in search of signals denoting some change of mood, any detectable alarm bell, but it was pointless. Novelli just talked about the usual topics—climate change, unbridled consumerism, the crisis of reason—but what he was actually feeling deep inside proved indecipherable, as if when he wrote he was taking the utmost care to conceal it, or as if he was first and foremost deeply unaware of it himself.

I'd fallen out of touch with him. Or else he'd shaken me off, eluded my pursuit. I really couldn't say anymore. Adult friendships often seem to wobble and sway in this manner, and most of the time it doesn't really mean a thing.

I knew that at the beginning of the year he'd been in Genoa for a competition for a tenured position that would finally have allowed him to move back to Italy. The interview was supposed to be little more than a formality, especially given the fact that before leaving, he'd described the purpose of it with a peculiar piece of imagery: They really just want to take a look at the eye of the fish. Huh? They want to make sure it hasn't started to rot.

In Genoa he'd taught a seminar on his latest research, with an audience of colleagues he'd all known for twenty years, experts on environmental physics and climatologists, many of whom had had him as their doctoral adviser. He'd enjoyed his round of applause, and during the question time what he'd mostly talked about was the European Union funding that he'd be able to bring to the university. Only the outside commissioner had betrayed a strange attitude: a woman, a professor from Cagliari in Sardinia, who hadn't said a word the whole time, except for the very end. That's when—again, according to Novelli's version of events— she'd suddenly come up with a critique of something he'd said in a television interview, something about ice core samples from Antarctica that just didn't add up for her. Novelli couldn't even remember the interview in any specific detail, but the commissioner had insisted on this point with a mulish determination that had seemed entirely out of place. It had gone on until he lost his temper and had retorted with a tone of voice that was (by his own admission) "a bit too patronizing."

The other members of the review commission said nothing. They'd seemed embarrassed for their colleague and his behavior. Whatever the case, they'd all moved past that impasse, and everything had wound up as planned. Novelli had decided not to go with them to dinner, just to maintain appearances. He'd returned to Paris and a few days later the results of the review commission's deliberations were made public: Novelli's name was in second place.

I KNOW NOW that I'd underestimated the impact of that failure. That said, in the text messages he sent summing up the way things had gone, he'd been laconic (Somebody torpedoed me), and that concise dismissal of the outcome might easily have been taken for a sporting attitude of nonchalance.

Still, when we met again in Rome, two months later, his disappointment was palpable, so much so that he started talking about the competition without even so much as the standard greetings and salutations, as if his train of thought had been chuffing along for weeks on that one and only track. This woman they gave that tenured position to, he said, but then he stopped short immediately. Let's forget about it. Do you know what my h-index is?

Actually, I barely even knew what an h-index was, just that it was some sort of metric of an academic's research activity, and that it was calculated according to the number of citations each article received.

Ninety-eight, son. My h-index is nine-ty-eight. He emphasized each syllable.

I pretended that the number had suitably impressed me, even though I had nothing to compare it to.

The woman they chose has an h-index of thirty-four. Now let me be clear, that's nothing to be ashamed of. Unless you go and carefully unpack the citations given to her papers, because if you do it's obvious that there's a whole system of logrolling and favor-trading behind it. She and a little band of colleagues, always the same names, cite each other's work reciprocally like crazy, making sure they drive up each other's h-indexes. Outside of that group, though, practically nobody even notices their work. Anyway, there you have it: me, ninety-eight, and she, thirty-four.

So how do you explain what happened?

Novelli ran his cloth napkin over his beard, then carefully set it down on the table. They needed to choose a woman. All for gender balance, am I right? Gen-der bal-ance, he said, again punctuating each syllable of the non-Italian word. That's what things have come to.

Are you going to appeal?

He dismissed the idea with a brusque wave of the hand.

He seemed weary. He was dressed as impeccably as ever, and yet he looked a little down at the heels, as if he'd been up and about for too many hours. I got the idea that he'd been sweating under the layers of fabric. But maybe my own state of mind was influencing my perceptions. Novelli had only alerted me to the fact that he'd be passing through town at the last minute, as if he wasn't really sure he wanted to, and that reticence had annoyed me.

You seem pretty disappointed, I said, making a bit of an effort.

He shrugged. He kept spinning the coaster on the tabletop. Well, shall we order something to eat? Without waiting for my reply, he gestured in the waiter's direction.

We ordered a couple of pasta dishes, then sat in silence for a long time, sipping water. Our food arrived and we both ate every bite, though unenthusiastically. When the sunlight dimmed for a moment, I pointed at the sky: What's the name for that, O Man of the Clouds?

I said it to bring the conversation back onto friendly terrain, but Novelli didn't so much as look up. He just shrugged his shoulders, rejecting that offer of playful interaction. He must have doubted I meant it.

We talked about politics for a few minutes, egging each other on about the election results. Novelli asked me if I'd read the platform of the Five Star Movement.

I had to confess that I hadn't, that the thought hadn't even occurred to me. Wallowing in topics that had nothing to do with the two of us made me feel even sadder. So when he finally did ask me how Lorenza was doing, I chose to dismiss the topic entirely: Lorenza's fine.

WE BOTH WANTED to get out of there as quickly as possible, so we agreed to go get an espresso somewhere else. After a stop at a café, we walked to the bridge and then turned down the Lungotevere, the riverfront boulevard. The roots of the plane trees were upheaving the asphalt, forcing us to walk in single file. Behind me, Novelli had returned to his tirade: Carolina had decided to move back to Genoa nevertheless, whether he had a chair in Italy or not. They'd already given notice on their rental, fixed up the other house, and enrolled the kids at the new school. So he was going to have to find another, smaller apartment in Paris, a one-room rental, and he would commute to Genoa on weekends. Or else maybe he'd just ask for a divorce and become one of those part-time fathers. Like Giulio, he'd thrown in.

He asked me to stop for a moment. He rested his weight against the stone parapet and breathed heavily. Are you all right? I asked him.

Yes, I'm fine. It must be the pollen. There's pollen everywhere. The flowers are blooming earlier every year.

We stood there, watching the murky-brown water flow past many yards beneath us. Then Novelli said: You know, I've been involved in dozens of academic job searches in my life. Plenty as a candidate, even more as a member of the review board. I nailed some of those positions, missed out on others. That's normal. I've always taken it as a fair process, just an ordinary part of any scientist's life. But maybe there's a cutoff age past which you can't accept being rejected, and maybe I've aged out of it. Everyone constantly judging you. It never ends. And this time... I don't know. It's affected me differently.

This was the right moment to give him some sign of support, of solidarity. All I'd have had to do was throw my arm around his neck, or even just touch the sleeve of his heavy jacket: anything might have been enough to change things, not just for that day, but for the future to come. Or maybe it wouldn't have changed a thing, maybe it would have just sheltered me against any lingering feelings of guilt. But since we'd said hello that day, Novelli had talked about nothing but himself. I told him that I needed to get back, to let me know if there was any news about Genoa, and to let me know if he came back through Rome again, this time with some advance notice, if possible. We crossed the street and then headed off in opposite directions.

I'D SET A GOOGLE ALERT for Novelli's name. I'm ashamed to admit it, a bit, in part because I never told him about it, but at the time I justified doing it with the idea that it might help me be more in touch with how things were going for him: he almost never let me know when he was going to make a television appearance, and he frequently forgot even to announce them on Twitter. I was sorry to miss them. Without the Google Alert I wouldn't have known about the conference. Instead, one Saturday morning in late March, a couple of weeks after our lunch in Rome, I received an alert: Novelli was going to speak at a conference titled "Women's Empowerment and Climate Change."

I wrote him, very casually, as if I'd just stumbled across the announcement by chance. Sure, he wrote back, confirming that he'd be speaking, it was a sort of TEDx, it'll be streaming if you feel like logging in. The tone of his response was very neutral, difficult to interpret, or it would have been if a few seconds later he hadn't thrown in: It'll be worth your time.

It had been an unproductive day, just one of many. I hadn't done anything but mess around on the internet, caroming from one link to another in search of ideas. The book on the bomb had run aground: the suspicion was looming ever larger that there really was nothing new left to say, and that there was nothing new that *I* could say. *The Making of the Atomic Bomb*, the book by Richard Rhodes that by then I'd read from cover to cover a couple of times and underlined ferociously, already contained everything leading up to the first blast. It had won a Pulitzer Prize. John Hersey's *Hiroshima* contained everything that followed the blast, and it was considered a classic. So where was there any room for me to write anything?

All the same, I continued. There are projects that bring with them a sense of ineluctability, that keep you wrapped up in them well beyond all reasonable expectation, for reasons you cannot fathom. Often they're mirages, and you know it, but you can't help but creep closer, trying to approach them until the minute they vanish before your eyes. That's what the bomb was for me. I was writing more and more slowly, with some sort of lucid desperation, waiting for the moment when I'd find myself empty-handed.

More out of boredom than for any other reason, I logged in to the conference. I wasted a few minutes in the registration process, only to discover that I still had valid credentials dating back to the Paris COP 21. Years later, in fact, I was still receiving email with subject lines like "Resilience" and "Adaptation," emails that I immediately trashed without even opening them.

There was a woman on stage hurling furious anathemas against bankers, for what their boundless greed had done to her land and to the world in general. It took me a while to realize that she belonged to a tribe of Native Americans, a tribe I'd never heard of. Her arguments were vague, but she brought them to bear with an incredible impetus that made them captivating.

In all, her speech lasted ten minutes or so, after which it was the turn of a researcher from Cameroon. She presented data on the correlation between the increase in female employment and the reduction in forest fires in her district, but her English was halting at best, and she started using New Age expressions like "our Mother Nature" and the "harmony of the planet." I turned off the sound and started scrolling through the program in the sidebar next to the live feed.

Obviously, given the topic, the scheduled talks were nearly all by women, scientists but especially activists, representatives of a wide array of different communities: the Terena people, the Kanawha Valley people, the Houma people, and the Mapuche people. Each of them discussed a problem bound up with climate change and female participation in society. There was also going to be a focus group on nonbinary farmers and a presentation by the Mujeres que Luchan collective. Ending the day's proceedings would be a talk by no less than the superstar of environmentalism Naomi Klein. Jacopo Novelli was the only Italian among the speakers, and one of very few men.

I texted him again on WhatsApp: It looks like a student political debate, if you ask me.

I could see that he'd read it, but he didn't reply. It was almost his turn to talk.

The chair introduced him with accolades and honors, as one of the world's leading experts on the environmental crisis, as well as a pioneering figure in the study of cloud brightening. He said: Let's give a hearty welcome to the Man of the Clouds, but he kept the expression in Italian, *L'uomo delle nuvole*, and Novelli finally climbed onto the stage.

THE TALK in its entirety would remain available online for a few months, accompanied by a teeming mass of comments, but then, eventually, it was taken down. I don't know who did it, whether it was Novelli himself or the TEDx administrators, just as I don't know why they didn't take it down right away. Maybe they decided to wait until things calmed down a little bit, to try to make sure that the cancellation wouldn't just engender more uproar. Anyway, it no longer exists. So I'm going to have to reconstruct it from memory, which will entail the occasional inaccuracy, but I can be quite sure that I'm remaining faithful to the underlying meaning of the thing, so powerful was its impact.

Novelli started out with the same phrase I had inserted at the beginning of his interview, a detail that would later make me feel distantly like an accomplice in his plan: Data don't lie. Sometimes people do. But data don't. In data, you have nothing less than the truth about the world. And that's where we're going to start today. What I'd like to offer you here is a data-driven analysis of the alleged gender inequalities in the field of scientific research. I say alleged because, as we shall see together, prejudice and rumor dominate. And nothing is really as it appears.

As a lecturer, the man was in a class of his own. He had a very Italian way of moving his hands, shaping concepts in the clear, thin air in front of him, but an Anglo-Saxon attitude in the way he set them forth, rigorous and crystal clear. He knew how to drop in witticisms and jokes, and here and there, in the slides that he would highlight with the bouncing red dot of his laser pointer, he'd even inserted funny cartoons.

Novelli laid out the main critical issues concerning the situation of women in the sciences in the form of statements collected from the mass media and presented as quotes. According to those statements, or as Novelli said, "relying on the prevailing narrative," men dominate everywhere. They supposedly occupy the highest positions in the universities and research groups, and the largest amounts of funding were assigned to men. Alongside that situation, female scientists suffer from harassment and molestation of various levels of gravity. In the final analysis, the practice of abuse is a full-blown culture, an organized system. And there are a variety of other discriminatory and unfair practices, all of them assigned English names: mansplaining, mobbing, gaslighting (there it was again).

I took these observations very seriously, Novelli said. Very, but *very*, seriously. That is why I set out to measure them. Because I'm a scientist, and that's how science proceeds in its quest for the truth: not by slogans, but by measurement. Now, I hope you'll forgive me if I present you with some graphs.

The data had been processed by Novelli himself along with a coworker, a certain M. Ambrosini, whose name I had never heard before. According to the various curves presented, it was clear that there really did exist a differential in power between men and women in the field of scientific research: if not in terms of pay, certainly in terms of representation. For instance, the percentage of men in the roles of main lecturers in international conferences was much higher. With the exception of this one, of course, Novelli added, triggering a relaxing wave of laughter among the audience.

But at last we had entered the era of heightened awareness! Minorities were making progress on all sides, claiming central roles, female scientists among them. Excellent! he said, First-rate! That's fantastic news. In order to make progress in the procurement of knowledge, we need young blood, fresh energies, imagination and determination.

The camera tended to stay on Novelli and not to wander to the audience, but it swung out into the crowd at that moment and that pan shot allowed me to see how raptly the audience was listening. At last, a man, and a world-renowned professor, who was using his own face to highlight those issues, who was taking a clear position! The camera returned to Novelli.

However, Novelli said, after measuring a phenomenon, a scientist naturally asks the next question: Why? Why these particular differences? Where do they originate? Are they pure social constructs, or are there other underlying causes? It's a well-founded question, to my mind. And all well-founded questions, for science, are legitimate questions. In fact, obligatory. Allow me, then, to move on to the second portion of the analysis.

It took him a while to explain the investigative criteria that he'd developed, working with M. Ambrosini, to quantify the performance of researchers, variously male and female. He provided the mathematical definitions of the indicators, with a painstaking attention to detail that was overkill for that setting. The curves intersected in various ways with the number of articles published, the grades in graduate studies, the levels attained in academia, and the h-indexes. In each graph, male and female trend lines were compared, marked in different colors. One slide after another, and then he began to delineate his vision.

According to his data, women entered the scientific world with the exact same opportunities as men, but then quickly fell behind. While they may have passed their university exams with scores showing every bit as much ability as their male colleagues—or in fact even more—their research performance rapidly dropped. From a certain point on, the curves diverged, and the average quality of women's publications inevitably proved inferior to that of men. At the age that scientists typically competed for teaching positions, that is, between thirty and forty years of age, female scientists were already performing significantly worse than their male colleagues.

In short, according to Novelli's and Ambrosini's analysis, power disparities existed, but by no means did they derive from social injustice. There was a logical, intrinsic foundation: female scientists were less successful in scientific fields because, on average, they were less capable.

I WAS A LITTLE BEWILDERED. I had the impression that I must have misunderstood the last thing that Novelli had said, that there was some serious problem with my understanding of his English. Had he actually said that female scientists were "on average less capable than their male colleagues"? Or was it I who had failed to grasp some subtlety?

Whatever the case, he still hadn't finished. In the cavalcade of graphs and charts that followed, he managed to pull off some kind of sleight of hand. The thesis that he managed to set forth, in just ten minutes flat, was actually the diametric opposite of the starting postulate: gender discrimination definitely existed in science, but it was pitted against men! Because the spirit of the times—he actually used that expression—disadvantaged men. The efforts now underway to impose gender parity in academia were to all intents and purposes so many coups d'état designed to undermine the meritocracy.

If he had just stopped there and gone no further, it might still have been possible to fix things. He'd still have been the target of a hailstorm of criticism, of course, but the matter would remain confined to the academic world. A provocative position, the one espoused by Professor Novelli, obnoxious, but all things considered, grist for debate, food for thought. He'd have found someone willing to defend him from within the university world, and the debate would have quickly died down. But that's not what Novelli wanted, or in any case, that wasn't enough for him.

After a very short pause to catch his breath, his voice dropped an octave. I'd like to exemplify all this with a practical case study, based on a brief personal account, he said. Let's just categorize this as anecdotal evidence, if you will. I recently took part in a competition for a tenured teaching position in my hometown of Genoa. You know how it is, I'm growing older, and the siren song of home is hard to ignore.

He was seeking his audience's approval, but this time, at least as seen online, no approval was forthcoming. In fact, nothing but intense tension.

There was a panel search, Novelli went on, and in the end, the search committee produced its final and unchallengeable decision, the position went to a colleague, a woman. He threw both arms wide in the universal gesture of resignation: These things happen. In academic job searches, it's a competition. You win some, you lose some. Still, before we finish up here, I'd like to show you one more slide. The last one, I promise you. It's a side-by-side bibliometric comparison between my own research output and that of my esteemed colleague, who was instead invited to take the position, Professor Gaia Sensi.

That name, Gaia Sensi, resounded in the lecture hall like a straight-armed slap, especially because the whole rest of the talk had been conducted on the impersonal terrain of statistics. As if that weren't enough, on the screen behind Novelli a photograph of the professor now appeared, slightly grainy because excessively enlarged from a low-res format. On the opposite side of the screen was a picture of Novelli himself, in much higher resolution, with a winning smile. At the center was the graph in question. By now we'd all become familiar with the variables along the x- and y-axis and their meaning. Novelli had been very capable in instructing us as to that mechanism. As a result, the gaping disproportion between the two yield curves, at least in the terms that he'd assigned to them, was clearly overwhelming.

I don't really have much more to say, Novelli said. Data, ladies and gentlemen. Data never lie. I've listened to a great many talks here today, filled with inspiration, and many calls for equity. And equity is a wonderful concept, no two ways about it. As long as it applies to everyone. Thank you so much for your attention.

And with that he walked off the stage. A round of applause came from the audience. Tepid and seemingly uncertain, but still, there was applause. Habits are stronger than anything else, and applause for a professor at the end of his talk or lecture, for that roomful of professionals, so polite and civil, was a conditioned reflex.

Even when the chairwoman took the microphone immediately afterward, she lacked the promptness of spirit it would have taken to comment in full. She thanked Novelli, in boilerplate terms, but it felt like that was costing her a special effort. Then she introduced the next speaker, an English expert on ecosystems.

The scientist opened her mouth to begin her presentation, but no words came. She ran her eyes over the crowd in the amphitheater before her, first one way, then the other, very slowly. Finally, she said: Did you all hear what I just heard? Or was I dreaming? Because I feel as if I just woke up from a horrible nightmare.

At that point, a very different round of applause burst forth: thunderous, liberated. The wave of applause that buried Novelli alive.

I REMEMBER an interval of disorientation afterward, though I couldn't say how long it lasted. I know for certain that I stood up from my desk, went into the kitchen, and wandered aimlessly. Maybe I got a bite to eat. Lorenza wasn't home, and I was sorry I didn't have her to talk to.

When I got back to my computer, the conference had resumed its normal progress. My iPhone was sitting next to the screen, but I didn't dare pick it up, as if I could feel something tingling inside of it. I just sat there, doing nothing, until a text came in from Giulio: a link to a tweet, followed by a question mark.

The tweet was from an American sociologist, Fiona McMulligan, who described Novelli's intellectual exploit as "medieval and grotesque." She expressed the devout wish that the Italian scientist be promptly expelled from every university he was affiliated with (every one of them was rigorously tagged in the tweet), as well as every organization he belonged to.

I tapped on her profile: McMulligan had been present on Twitter since 2011, she had the blue checkmark and something like 900,000 followers. Of course, she had tagged Novelli too. Instinctively I clicked on his tag, which took me to his profile, where I saw the follower count increasing in real time by hundreds and hundreds.

In my own feed nobody was talking about anything else. I knew that it was a digital illusion, that it was a feature of the algorithm to highlight anything likely to be of interest to you, but still: it was astonishing to see. Three or four different hashtags had already been coined, but the one that was prevailing was the simplest one of all: #Novelli.

Meanwhile, the video of his talk had been sliced and diced and scattered all over the internet in incendiary fragments. Taken out of context, his statements were even more appalling. Giulio must have been on top of this faster than me, because he texted me: Our friend has livened up everybody's day here at the university. I asked him what he thought was going to happen next, and he sent me a skull emoji.

A phone call from B. S. interrupted our online conversation. Somehow, unconsciously, I'd been expecting it. Normally, I got my article assignments for the *Corriere* through her. I briefly considered the idea of not answering her at all, but that would only mean postponing the issue. Did you see Novelli? she asked me.

I was just watching now.

You did that interview for us, didn't you? You proposed it yourself.

I sat there without speaking. Confirming it wouldn't do any good.

B. S. said: It would be interesting if you could talk to him, get a few comments. It strikes me that there's been a certain... reaction on the part of the scientific community. And it's not limited to them.

B. S. was in charge of supervising everything at the newspaper that had to do with women's conditions in contemporary society, she'd founded a blog on the topic, as well as a festival. I'd contributed to the blog a couple of times, and I'd been a guest at the festival, where I'd uttered a few cautious and reasonable statements about gender equality.

I haven't talked to him in quite a while, I lied. Actually, I doubt I even have his number anymore.

You could write a piece of commentary if you can't manage to get in touch with him. There's going to be a news item, but we could run it alongside.

I can't, I said.

Listen, believe me, it wouldn't take you long. Thirty column lines is all we'd need. Just enough to provide some context for that deranged analysis he just laid out.

I can't, I said again.

I'm sorry, I don't get it, why can't you?

Because Novelli is a friend of mine.

After the phone call (and after absorbing B. S.'s un-stated reaction in her three or four seconds of silence at the end), I went back to Twitter. I picked up on the last few comments I'd missed in the meantime, a little frenetically. By now there were hundreds of comments, in an array of different languages, and I was sure that I could see only a tiny portion of them all. Novelli was being accused, denigrated, insulted, or else cruelly mocked with dry dismissals and memes.

The algorithm highlighted a thread written by Marina, thoroughly reasoned, in sorrow more than anger, where she replied to him directly, as a female scientist to a male scientist, as a female physicist to a male physicist, delving into the merits of his analysis and challenging both its foundations and his inter-pretation. In his demonstration of the way that men's and women's performance curves diverged after earn-ing their degrees (assuming that it was true, which she didn't necessarily admit), Novelli had still failed to take into consideration the key elements of any reasonable study of gender parity: the implicit sexism present in academia, family obligations, social conditioning. Had Professor Novelli even bothered to wonder why young female scientists struggled so palpably to publish around age thirty, after having been first-rate students?

At the end of her thread, in a completely unex-pected manner, Marina confessed something about herself. When she was working on the structure of matter, she'd been offered a research fellowship at ETH

Zürich. She would have led a team at that university. But she was already the mother of twin girls, and they were still very small at the time. Her husband had told her that he was in favor of the move in principle, but the space between what he thought in principle and what he was actually willing to do was the theater of most of the reality of the condition of women. Marina had turned down the offer, and it had instead been assigned to a male colleague. In short order that team had attained important results, publications had followed, her colleague's h-index had soared, while hers had flatlined. In the end, Marina had given up research entirely. Where did all this show up in the professor's curves?

I instinctively clicked the heart at the end of the thread, but then it occurred to me what it would look like on Novelli's screen, where the words "liked by P. G." would be found to appear. I unclicked the heart, even though I wasn't all that certain that those operations could be reversed.

A number of students at the school chimed in at the bottom of Marina's thread, including Fernanda Rucco, who tossed out a series of eloquent graphs and charts, one after another.

I hit refresh again and there I saw, at the top of my feed, a tweet from Curzia, a picture of a man plummeting into the void, as if he'd fallen out of a plane: beneath him lay a blanket of clouds. Curzia wrote: Male Chauvinist of the Clouds #Novelli.

There ensued a feverish exchange of messages. You'd almost think you were taking delight in it, I wrote her. Because of my play on the name? I thought it was funny. But you seem pretty upset...she wrote back. But you know the man, Curzia, you're friends! She replied that she'd been at his apartment once in her life (I must certainly remember the occasion) and that if she thought about things in those terms then she'd have to expand her list of "friends" to include people of Abu Bakr al-Baghdadi's ilk. If I was so broken up on Novelli's behalf, then why wasn't I tweeting out a strenuous defense?

But I did nothing. I made no defense, I offered no accusations. My Twitter profile remained perfectly neutral, as if I hadn't even noticed what was going on.

WHEN LORENZA CAME HOME, she found me sitting on the sofa, staring into the void. She asked why I looked so pale, and I gave her a quick summary of what had happened, showing her a few clips of Novelli's TEDx. That's disgusting, she commented, with a concision that struck me as nothing short of phenomenal. So you're not going to write about it?

How can I?

The way you always do. You write about it. You take a position.

If I take a position, I'd have to take a position against him. Explicitly.

So you'd rather just avoid the matter entirely.

How can I do it? I asked again.

At that exact moment, my phone started ringing again. This time, Curzia's name appeared. My gaze locked with my wife's, right there on the display. The phone stopped ringing, but started up again immediately.

Answer it, Lorenza said.

I'd rather not.

Then a series of text messages came pouring in, one hot on the heels of the last, all of them from Curzia. She had the questionable habit of sending each sentence as a separate text.

Who is she? Lorenza asked, with great calm, as if she were asking out of innocent curiosity.

No one. I mean, she's a freelancer. Maybe she wants to interview me about this whole mess, I don't know.

Then maybe you should answer. She seems pretty insistent.

We're sort of friends too, I said.

You're sort of friends too?

She probably just wants to talk about what's happened, but right now I don't exactly feel like it.

That's strange. You've never mentioned her before.

I definitely must have mentioned her.

Lorenza shook her head, as if trying to reconstruct. Then she repeated what she'd said: No, you definitely never mentioned her.

Meanwhile, texts continued arriving from Curzia. I couldn't imagine what had come over her. If I'd turned the phone face down, as my instincts were telling me to do, or if I'd thrown the phone across the room, it would just have been worse. So I let the notifications proliferate before my wife's increasingly chilly gaze.

Would you prefer that I go in the other room? she asked after a while. That way you can answer in comfortable privacy.

Don't be ridiculous.

I'm going to go in the other room. That'll be better.

She vanished into the bedroom. I heard her put down her bag, take off her shoes, move other objects. I took that opportunity to put my phone into airplane mode and stop the hemorrhaging streams of WhatsApp messages.

Do you really think I should take a stance on Novelli? I asked in a loud voice. But Lorenza didn't answer. I asked again, louder this time: Should I take a stance on Novelli or not?

Once again she strode through the living room, but as if she had no intention of stopping or wasting any more of her time on that situation, or on me.

Why don't you ask Curzia?

AFTER THAT, an interminable night unfolded, one of those nights that perhaps happen in every marriage, I couldn't say, at least I think so, but which had certainly just happened to us.

For hours, Lorenza and I avoided each other and chased after one another in various parts of the apartment, even though, in the end, we always came back to the sofa, as though invincibly attracted to it. After all, the sofa was the center of gravity of our apartment, and therefore of our life together, a sofa we were thrilled with when we first bought it, but which now no longer fully convinced us: too colorful, too full of flair. It had stopped matching our style.

And it was on that sofa—the same one Eugenio had spilled ice cream on one evening, leaving an ineradicable halo—that I told her I could no longer imagine anything at all about us. I don't know how we'd managed to arrive at this juncture, after starting from Novelli and the notifications of Curzia's text messages, I couldn't say what path of exhaustion had led me to extract that sentence from all the infinite number of potential sentences, but the words were exactly: *I can no longer imagine anything at all about us.*

I told Lorenza that if I tried to think about the two of us together in five years, or in ten years, I saw nothing. I couldn't say who we would become. I couldn't even say *where* we would be. Our future had become a blank, like a blindness.

Everything had unfolded both very slowly and very quickly at the same time. Up until that moment, she had been hostile, but after that admission she suddenly changed. I was still sitting on the sofa, as if glued to the backrest, and she came over to me from behind. She took my head in her hands and caressed it with circular movements, as if she could put my thoughts back into some kind of order just by manipulating my muscles, and mechanically coax out of my forehead, my cheekbones, my jaw, that imagining about us that I lacked.

We'd already talked and talked to excess, but none of it had managed to bring us into contact. And so now her touch brought something absolutely new into the picture. Lorenza walked halfway around the sofa and sat down beside me, pressed up against me the way she did at times, her feet pulled up, toes extended. She'd taken her socks off, though I couldn't say when.

Do you know what comes to mind for me, on the other hand? I'm reminded of that place on Lanzarote, that little town where we wound up having lunch that time.

The place with the naked Germans?

Yes, that's right.

Why do you think it is that we always wind up surrounded by naked people, you and I? I asked, even though I was having a hard time expressing myself.

I don't know, but it wasn't the nudism that I was thinking about. I'm thinking about them because they were all so old, do you remember? Married nudist couples who'd fetched up there after who knows what kinds of lives and what kinds of disappointments. So I'm going to say that maybe we might wind up like that ourselves in a few years, not yet, I understand that, but in a few years. Unashamed, with no one looking at us. And all things considered, it doesn't strike me as such a terrible future after all.

Surrounded by Germans with sunburned ass cheeks.

It's stupid, I know.

Listening to golden oldies by Plastic Bertrand.

At that point, she said nothing, she didn't repeat that it was stupid, so it was my turn to say it: No, it didn't strike me as stupid.

But in the meantime? I asked after a couple of seconds.

Lorenza looked up, as if trying to give a physical impetus to what she was about to suggest, but without relaxing her grip on my arm: in the meantime we could move house. She'd been thinking about it for a while. Before long, Eugenio would be attending university, and we'd get a smaller apartment, maybe with some outdoor space, and I'd finally have an office to myself.

So that's how we'll settle things, I said. By real estate.

That aggression caught her off guard, and to a certain extent it caught me off guard too.

Settle what things?

A terrace instead of a child, everything settled, it's brilliant. Okay, let's buy a new place to live.

We'd been very close until a few seconds ago, but after I said those words, she released herself from the braid we two had formed. Still, she lacked the determination to get up, it still hadn't gone that far.

You know, she said, it's true that there are times when you can really feel the age difference between us, I can feel it quite sharply myself. But not for the reasons you might imagine, it's not the bodies, which you're so obsessed with. I feel it because you still treat your desires like a boy. You're only focused on what you lack, and it's constant.

And you're saying that's a mistake?

I don't know if it's a mistake. But it's definitely a pity.

I remember that I was staring straight ahead, at the shelf where we kept the souvenirs from our travels, so many of them that I'm not sure I'd even be able to say where some of them came from. We had devoted a moment of our attention to each of those objects, discussing them among ourselves, haggling over the price. Now when I looked at them I didn't seen anything special about them. Staring at the souvenirs, I said: The last time I was in Paris, I sought her out. Curzia. I went to her place.

Lorenza didn't move, or at least I didn't perceive any movements in the margin of my field of vision. Instead, she waited for a moment, processed that incomplete information, probably analyzing the strangeness of the verb "sought" in that context. Then she asked: How old is she?

I couldn't feel much, except for some sort of burning sensation in my face, as if something really were emanating from my muscles. She's about my age.

I'm not even going to try, just so you know.

What do you mean, you're not even going to try?

I'd be starting out with too big of a disadvantage. I'm not even going to try.

That's when she stood up. And then, when she was already on her feet—gazing at the souvenirs from our many trips which she, too, now certainly saw as a cluster of things, ready to be tossed into a cardboard box—from that position she said: You ought to see what it's like.

See what what's like?

But as a request it was too much, Lorenza wasn't willing to give me *that* instruction too. That was up to me, and me alone. She headed off toward the kitchen, where she had things to do, because there were necessarily things to do in the kitchen, every single day, inevitably.

Later, we talked again, and after that—it must have been two or three in the morning by this point—there was sex, too, as is the case on certain interminable nights in marriages: sex to erect a barrier to all that talking, because the talking simply had to be stopped, and there was no other way to do it.

We performed the rituals that always follow sex with barely a hint more of sadness than usual: each of us, in turn, in the bathroom, the wet washcloth swiped over the mattress cover, the stated intention to change it in the morning.

I took a Songar tablet, but I still got almost no sleep. On the other hand I dreamed a lot, and in one of my dreams Lorenza and I were in a car and, strangely, she was driving. Strangely because, since we'd moved to Rome, she never dared to drive. The GPS seemed to be out of order, it was leading us onto a mountain road. We kept climbing higher and higher. The sun was setting and the view from up there was incredible, such a panorama that Lorenza said it was the most beautiful place she'd ever seen. But at the same time, we were frightened, because we knew there was no way we'd be able to get down from there, distantly frightened, the way it is in dreams. I took the wheel, and after we rounded a curve, the road vanished, our tires lost their grip, and we found ourselves plummeting straight down, hundreds and hundreds of yards, dropping perpendicular, without turning upside down, straight into the sea beneath us.

I wrote down the dream in a note on my phone, ticking away in the darkness, even though it might make Lorenza think that I was texting with someone else in the middle of the night. It was just another habit I didn't know how to break.

WHEN WE WOKE UP again, we found ourselves in the throes of lucidity. It was Palm Sunday and I had promised Karol that we'd attend Mass. He'd been especially insistent, and I'd given in. So Lorenza and I got ready for church, in silence, exchanging bits of logistic information.

Outside, Rome was on a wartime footing: carabinieri wearing bulletproof vests, police officers in squad cars, police officers on foot, police officers on horseback, soldiers leveling submachine guns, special forces, armored personnel carriers, helicopters overhead. An anonymous letter, delivered to the Italian embassy in Tunis, had announced that a certain Atef M. was preparing a terror attack in the city, precisely in the midst of the extraordinary crowds of Holy Week. Identification pictures of him had been distributed, posed facing front and sideways, and sure enough, one glance was all that was needed to peg him as a dangerous individual: hairline straight across the forehead, hoodie brashly open in a V, intense, ferocious glare.

A few days later, the television show *Chi l'ha visto?* managed, through its trademark crowdsourced investigations, to track down that same Atef M. in Mahdia, on the coast south of Tunis, where he lived: the letter had been a vicious vendetta by a coworker, possibly over an unpaid sum of money. All the same, Rome had wound up under siege. Lorenza found our way cut off by a police roadblock. The way around it, considering all the other detours and street closings and traffic jams, would itself require forty minutes, and there was no guarantee of even that delayed arrival. The carabiniere shrugged when we objected. Forget about it, Lorenza told me, let's go home.

Let's try anyway.

The best we can hope for is to get there after Mass is over!

But I promised Karol.

We were still halted before an array of carabinieri troop trucks parked at an angle and the uniformed officer waving for us to get out of the way. Lorenza sat there for a few seconds studying me. Then she said: This loyalty to your friends really baffles me. I'm not kidding.

There was a bottomless array of subtexts in that sentence, so many I couldn't even begin to count them, and perhaps neither could she. We'd slept very little, and only fitfully, and we'd said all those things to each other.

And what's more, it's a very ironic kind of loyalty. You go ahead and see Karol. I'm getting out of here.

She rummaged through her purse, in search of something, making sure she had her house keys or who knows what else, but actually giving me the time to think it over, change my mind and go along with her. I could have interrupted that series of actions by saying, Come on, let's go to the beach, what the hell, forget about Mass, who cares what I promised Karol, it's a gorgeous day, we're together and that's all that matters! But I didn't do it.

I offered to drop her off back at the apartment, but this time she was the one who refused. She got out of the car, and I put it into reverse. The carabiniere had watched the scene unfold through the windshield. I have no idea what he made of the two of us. His gaze suggested nothing more than indifference.

WHEN I WALKED INTO THE CHURCH, Karol was reading the Gospel. There were still a few empty spots in the pews, but I remained standing to make sure he saw me. I made a mental note to make it clear to him, later, just how much effort it had cost me to keep my promise.

In his homily, he spoke in rather cryptic terms about choices, and the opportunities that lurk in every break in continuity. After all, what was the Resurrection of Christ, if not the greatest break in continuity in humankind's history? He seemed to be referring to me, but then *that's the trick of homilies, isn't it*, I thought to myself. Indeed, it's the trick of religion in general: it always gives the impression that it's referring to you. Anyway, I lost the thread before I could complete my line of thought. I was remembering the brief exchange of barbed comments with Lorenza in the car. I wanted to get out of there and call her to mend the breach as quickly as possible. I always wanted to mend any and all breaches as quickly as possible. My relationship with breaks in continuity could hardly be described as a good one.

Once the liturgy was over, at the bottom of the front steps, I typed in the text message I'd composed and edited in my head, a combination of nonchalance and contrition, and then I waited for her reply.

A feminine voice made me look up: Is that you?

Standing in front of me was a young woman, maybe twenty, or a little older, her chestnut hair pulled back by a headband. It took me less than a second to understand that this was *that* young woman.

You're his friend, aren't you?

Yes, I think that's me. Ciao, Elisa.

I extended my hand and for some reason, as I shook hers, I felt the impulse to lead her away from prying eyes. But Elisa wasn't worried. She looked at me closely and with great and almost greedy intensity, as if she wished to study in detail a person she'd spent so much time imagining.

Would you come with me to a place I know? she asked. I'd like to talk.

Instinctively, I turned to look back at the portal of the church, where Karol was greeting the faithful one at a time.

He'll join us later, we've already worked it out.

I went with her, not that I had much say in the matter. When we got to the parking lot, she asked if we could go in my car, because she'd had to take a bus to get there. We got in, and as she was giving me directions, I glimpsed the scene through Lorenza's eyes, as if she were sitting silently at the center of the back seat.

We said nothing more for the rest of the drive. Elisa pointed to the sign on a pizzeria: There.

We took seats at a table set for four, with a reservation in her name.

Your wife couldn't make it?

Something came up at the last minute.

Too bad, I would have liked to meet her. Still, maybe it's better this way. This will give us a chance to talk undisturbed.

A waiter brought us water and breadsticks in individual packets, we opened one each and sat there chomping away at them.

Is this where you see each other? I asked without quite meaning to. She was really very young. I felt a little embarrassed to be sitting face-to-face with her, so I looked around, eyeing the trompe l'oeil paintings on the walls and the tablecloth already sprinkled with crumbs.

It's nothing special, I know that, and yet we're fond of it. Also, the pizza is good. They make it super thin.

I hear that you're studying biology.

Yes, but I'm not as excited about it as I thought I would be. I probably should have chosen something more in the humanities. I care a lot more about that kind of thing, but it's too late to change now.

Too late? I doubt that. You have all the time you need to try out anything that interests you, see what it's like.

I'd been a little more aggressive than I meant to be, and by the strange contagion that sometimes happens between words, I'd happened to choose that exact same expression, "see what it's like," that Lorenza had employed against me in the middle of the night. I felt slightly conned: by Karol, for the way he'd involved me in what was unmistakably a plan of his, and by Elisa herself, because I saw no reason I should even be there, listening to her vent her bad mood about the university, at the very same time my own marriage was going to pieces.

She said: I know that it was you who gave Karol the iPhone. So in a certain sense, it's thanks to you too. Without the iPhone, we wouldn't have been able to stay in touch so easily.

It was true, I'd given him an iPhone a couple of years before that, a 5S that I'd replaced impatiently the third time that the screen broke.

That's why I feel like you might be the best person for me to confide in. Well, actually, you're pretty much the only one!

She laughed in her discomfort. For a moment her composure slid away and she revealed herself for the youngster that she was after all.

Karol and I are in love. I think he told you that.

I didn't know exactly how to react, so I remained poker-faced.

It happened to me at a very particular point in time. I'd just gotten out of a relationship with a guy my age. And he'd behaved like a bit of an asshole. Actually, like a complete asshole. She sucked her cheeks in, as if biting them from within, as she twisted the shiny wax paper of the breadsticks around her finger. Basically, I live on the opposite side of Rome. You know the Raccordo Anulare, the Rome beltway? I live over here. And now we're right *here*.

Diametrically opposed.

Diametrically opposed, exactly. That's why I chose this parish. I wanted a place of refuge, really, new people who didn't know me, and I said to myself that it needed to be as far away as possible. That's how I met Karol. But maybe he's already told you all this.

Actually, no, he didn't.

Ah, okay.

Clearly, that had come as a small disappointment to Elisa, and she showed it as she pondered the fact for a moment. Anyway, she concluded, that's the very short version of the story. And when I think back on it, it makes me start to have doubts.

Doubts about what, in particular?

It just seems a little too random. I mean, I just picked this place out of a hat, and I just picked this parish church out of a hat. What if I'd picked another, maybe not far from here, would everything have gone the same way? Would I have found someone else? A different priest, even? I don't want to give the impression that I'm superficial, I hope you understand. But couldn't it be that right then and there, I was so determined to fall in love with someone that Karol just walked into it without realizing it?

The waiter came over to ask if we were ready to order. I told him that we were still waiting for someone, and he said that the place was going to fill up soon, and there'd be a longer wait for our food.

When he left, Elisa exhaled the air she'd trapped in her lungs. In July I'm finishing my undergraduate degree, she said. Then I'd like to enroll in the master's program, in Padua. Karol has decided he wants to come with me.

Padua? You mean he wants to transfer?

I think the situation is getting a little bit out of hand!

Suddenly her eyes filled with tears. Childish tears, not so much of sadness as they were brimming over from the tension. I wonder if you can help talk some reason into him.

Just then, Karol came in, wearing a normal shirt and jeans. When the waiter came over to meet him, he nodded his head in our direction. He came toward us, beaming, while I nodded in Elisa's direction, as if to let her know that I'd understood, and of course I'd help her, I'd do whatever I could for her. On her face there was no longer the slightest trace of upset.

LUNCH HAD BEEN EXHAUSTING. We ordered three different pizzas and then cut them into equal thirds so we could try them all. Karol and Elisa had an interminable series of pet jokes and phrases between them, and they expected me to watch, taking it for granted that I'd enjoy them as much as they did, but that would have been impossible. More than once, they showed me the table where they always sat when it was just the two of them. But this one time, they weren't alone, this one time someone else was seeing them, someone else could testify to them as a couple, together.

When the time came for coffee, Karol laid his hand atop Elisa's, with a courage that he must have been digging to find within himself all this time. He held her hand there, barely moving his thumb in a rhythmic caress across her palm, for a good solid quarter of an hour, as if to say to me: Can you see this? Do you see that it's true? Everything I was telling you is true, *she* is real!

Elisa didn't reject that contact, but a moment before we all three stood up, she gave me another intense look, like the one she gave me at the beginning, as if reprising her plea for help. Lorenza still hadn't replied to my message.

IN THE NEXT PICTURE I have in my mind's eye of that weekend, I'm sitting on the edge of a bed, in a hotel room with light-brown walls. Next to me is a travel bag with a shoulder strap, the kind of baggage you might bring for a few days away, or an eternity. As for that hotel, it was one of those places ideal for corporate conventions that line the Via Aurelia in endless procession. I'd driven past this one plenty of times, but I'd never dreamed I might actually someday spend the night there.

At home, we'd had another argument, a much shorter one, with very different tones, especially on Lorenza's side, but that argument, too, seemed shrouded in distance, even though it had just taken place.

Dinnertime had passed long ago, and I wasn't particularly hungry. All the same, I went down to the ground floor. The restaurant was vast and sprawling, a sort of parade grounds that stretched out. Outside the plate glass windows, a fountain was producing synchronized jets of water, displays that featured changes in lighting. I chose a place that offered a good view of the TV screen, just to have something to rest my eyes on. In the end, there had been no terror attack in the city.

As I was standing up, leaving my dinner untouched on its plate, I received a text from a number I hadn't entered into my directory: This is Elisa. Have you already talked to Karol by any chance?

I wrote back that I hadn't had the time to do anything.

Well, that's a relief!!! Because I'm not as sure as I was when we talked. I still need to give it some thought.

Then, immediately following: I don't want to throw away something beautiful. That would make no sense.

And then, right after that: What do you think I should do?

I assured her that I was the last person on earth she should think of asking, especially that evening, but I didn't go into detail and she didn't get the reference. She had asked Karol for my number, with the excuse that she wanted to share some of her poetry with me. In fact, now that we were on the subject, she really would like to have my opinion, if I didn't mind. They were poems she'd written for herself, nothing with any claims to greatness.

If you wrote them for yourself, why would you want me to read them? I wrote back, just to tease her. Then

I added that I really knew nothing about poetry, but sure, she could send it to me if she wanted to.

We went on texting like that for a while, until Elisa sent me a Word document, and I really did start reading her poetry, right there in the restaurant's dining room, without any idea of what to think of it, not that I even bothered to wonder.

I STAYED IN THE HOTEL on the Via Aurelia for five nights. One evening, in that same restaurant, I found myself watching Novelli on TV. He was a guest on a Mediaset broadcast, part of Berlusconi's empire. The whole show was about him, and the episode was titled "A Nobel Laureate Under Attack." I asked the waiter if he'd please turn up the volume.

In the hours leading up to that moment, a series of events had followed, one hard on the heels of the last, and I'd taken part only from a remote distance, as if separated from them by a sheet of soundproof glass. On Monday the faculty council in Paris met on an emergency basis and voted to suspend Novelli from all teaching responsibilities, indefinitely. In a press release issued simultaneously, the French university publicly distanced itself from the abhorrent positions espoused by Professor Novelli, positions that not only profoundly violated the beliefs of the academic community but also served to undermine the dignity and well-being of female scientists everywhere, and specifically of our esteemed colleague Gaia Sensi, to whom we send a collective message of the utmost solidarity.

Like any other professor of his stature, Novelli had working ties with a sizable number of institutes of higher education: in Europe, the United States, China, and Australia. The communiqué from the French university opened the floodgates. In less than twenty-four hours, Novelli had been given the heave-ho by one and all. I watched the falling dominoes of his career on Twitter. Of all the institutions, only the Emerging World Climate Forum even deigned to add to its announcement that, although relieving Novelli of his position on the board, the forum thanked him for the invaluable work he had done over the course of his years there.

On Wednesday, I received an email from Novelli, written in English. Novelli was extending an appeal to us all, colleagues, friends, and acquaintances, asking us to stand behind him in what was not merely a personal battle, but rather a struggle to vindicate the objective right to speak truth. The email went on to review the story of the TEDx conference from his point of view (reiterating, once again, that he had done no more than set forth objective, statistical facts) and the media lynching that he'd undergone as a result. We are heading straight into a world where science is afraid of the things it discovers, he wrote. Is that the kind of progress we're working for? If, then, like him, we aspired to a different future, if we truly cared about independent research, then it was crucial that we sign the accompanying letter in his defense, written spontaneously by his colleague Robert T. Friedman. That letter would be sent at the end of business the following day to various newspapers in an array of different countries. The letter was attached.

I recall that I was reclining, practically lying on my back, and I had my laptop perched on my belly. I'd read the attached letter once, and then again. I'd googled Robert Thomas Friedman and found out that he was embroiled in an alleged harassment case on a university campus in Missouri. He didn't seem to have published scientific papers of any prominence in quite some time. Then I'd examined the email a little more carefully. Novelli hadn't sent it expressly to me. It was addressed to himself, with an unknown number of people no doubt bcc'd. I decided I could afford to waffle until tomorrow.

The next morning a second email arrived, with RE-MINDER as the subject line. I hadn't opened it and I'd let more hours still slip by. Finally, Novelli had reached out to me directly. I was brushing my teeth and I noticed my iPhone vibrating like an insect on my desk. Did you see the letter? he'd written me a few seconds later. So will you sign it? At that point ignoring him had become impossible. I'm sorry, I'd written back. I don't agree with what you said. And sending that letter strikes me as another misstep.

Then I'd gone back into the bathroom and sat down there to wait for the next text message. I understand, Novelli wrote. I waited for him to add something, but he didn't, so I followed up, writing: I know this has been a dark period, J.

I'd used his first initial, for Jacopo, intentionally, in an attempt to show him a crumb of human warmth, in spite of everything else. But he didn't want my warmth: he wanted my signature. You have until seven this evening, in case you change your mind, he wrote back. It had the ring of an ultimatum, and to all intents and purposes, that's exactly what it was. But it wasn't restricted to the letter and my signature. It was far broader, all-encompassing: that was a deadline on my loyalty toward him, our friendship, the two of us.

AND NOW THERE HE WAS, Professor Novelli, on the TV screen mounted too high up on the wall of my new dining room on the Via Aurelia. He was seated with a bit of a slouch in the central chair of the broadcasting studio.

He didn't look especially downcast or dejected: if anything he just seemed annoyed. As if the media circus that had been unleashed around him was nothing but a vast waste of his time, a distraction that was preventing him from focusing on far more serious matters, such as the ever-accelerating melting of the arctic ice.

The conversation must have been progressing in a lively manner for some time, but Google Alert had misfired and I'd missed the beginning. In any case, the general tone of the debate was pretty unmistakable. It was one of those talk shows that preferred to embrace any radical minority position, whether right or wrong, as long as it was at loggerheads with the views of the mainstream media: right then and there, defending Novelli was exactly that type of a position.

The host invariably addressed him as Professor, but whenever he spoke of his absent rival, Gaia Sensi, he simply referred to her as Gaia Sensi. That difference in treatment of course aroused no chorus of protests. After canvassing the guests for their opinions, which swirled confusedly around the concept of freedom of speech, the microphone returned to Novelli. With one of his characteristic paradoxes, he said that he'd prefer to say nothing about freedom of speech. Those were discussions for journalists and intellectuals. He, on the other hand, was a scientist, and in science, freedom of speech wasn't a problem that even came to the surface. In science there were hypotheses, data, experimental testing, and peer review from the community. End of story.

The host prodded him: Was it true that the journal to which he'd submitted his paper on gender equality hadn't even considered it for publication? So it would seem, Novelli replied. At that point, the host spoke directly into the camera: So are we clear on what's happening here? Are we clear about the fact that in the name of political correctness, we've actually come to the point where we're censoring the scientific research of a respected professor? We're not talking about criticizing him: we're talking about dismissing his work entirely, refusing even to take it into consideration! Is this not a new form of the old Fascist regime? Let's not forget that Professor Novelli won the Nobel Prize!

Claiming that Novelli had won the Nobel, stated in those terms, was an overstatement of the fact, but it certainly had its effect on the audience. Novelli didn't bother to correct him.

There was another rapid round of opinions, during which he, the Man of the Clouds, barely nodded along. He seemed increasingly detached. Finally, the host addressed him directly again, this time with a different, more paternal voice: How are you feeling now, Professor?

Perhaps Novelli just hadn't been ready for that sudden switch in approach. He changed his position in his chair, uncrossing his legs and then recrossing them in the opposite direction. He cleared his throat. Then he spoke in a rather muddled fashion, muttering that by now we had all lost the habit of truth, that we lived in a world where facts had been junked, replaced piecemeal by whatever interpretation seemed most convenient. He'd been working on the climate emergency for more than twenty years. No one knew it better than he did.

All right, but how are you feeling *inside*?

At that point Novelli grimaced in a way I knew quite well: compressing his lips into a flat line and staring down at an indeterminate point. A little disappointed, he said. But not by the universities or the journalistic newsrooms, those are nothing more than...institutions. They are abstractions.

Well, in that case, disappointed in *what*, Professor?

In people. I feel disappointed in people.

The dining room had emptied out, but the fountain outside continued to repeat its cycle of aquatic variations. When the broadcast was over, I wrote a text message for Novelli, a wry observation to undercut the drama. I don't remember what I wrote, but I do remember that it really, *really* wasn't funny. I saw the checkmark to show it had been read, and for twenty minutes or so I sat there, stupidly waiting for a reply. I signed the chit, adding my room number, got up, and walked toward the elevators.

A FEW DAYS LATER, I went to Turin. It seemed like a logical choice: retreat, go back to what existed before. By now I'd had it up to here with Rome. I felt like it was in some way bound up with what was happening to me. The filth, the chaos, the dark of the streets after sunset, the hordes of stunned tourists, the streets shut to traffic without warning, the roadblocks: living there had done me harm. Perhaps that's why, because they had understood it long before I did, my parents had regularly sent me postcards from Turin, the whole time I'd been living in Rome. A couple of postcards every year, as if I now lived in Australia.

Before going upstairs to their apartment, I explored the courtyard garden. It hadn't changed since I was a child, but the vegetation had grown denser, especially at certain points. Maybe it was because nobody went down there anymore.

Seeing me arrive without Lorenza caused no surprise. I was almost always alone when I went to see them, like a phantom devoid of human bonds or any existence in the now. My mother took a few seconds to examine me at the threshold. She said that I had bags under my eyes and that I probably needed to take better care of myself. The conventional phrases typically uttered in this context were soon out of the way, and we sat straight down to eat.

Over the years, the brief lectures my father would deliver to accompany our dinners had changed many times, although some topics returned cyclically: the oil crisis, cold fusion, inflation, the theory that if you simply took the last zero off the number of people in the world you'd immediately solve all our problems. The topic of energy was always front and center, as if he lived in constant lurking terror of waking up one morning to a world without force.

That evening, though, he was worried about water. An unusual subject, but not a completely new one (I vaguely remember as a child listening to explanations about the looming end of our world's water resources). Did I know, now, that in the water meant for human consumption tests had revealed extremely high levels of sex hormones, and especially estrogen?

I most certainly did not know that. I almost never knew the things that my father knew. In fact, it was astonishing that he still managed to keep finding new things. I had the suspicion that he worked up specific topics before I came to visit in order to amaze and impress me.

Basically, it means that we drink cocktails of female hormones every day. Do you by any chance drink tap water in Rome?

I explained to him that we had a whole-apartment water filter, more than anything else for ecological reasons.

The water in Rome is terrible.

As far as you're concerned, everything in Rome is terrible, I said, in an attempt to lighten the tone of the conversation, unsuccessfully.

The endocrine disruptors that we all used to consume on a daily basis, he went on—all of us, *including me*—have had disastrous effects, especially on our sexual reproduction. And especially on men. It's clear, isn't it? Evolution never expected us to gobble down large quantities of estradiol. The data on demasculinization were very clear for fish, but there was no reason to expect that things would go any differently for human beings. In fact, the average length of the male member has shrunk by almost an inch in just the past sixty years.

My mother said: You've got a little bit of a twitch in your eyelid, the one on the left.

I laid my forefinger on my eyelid while my father added something else about sperm counts.

I wondered whether that evening's topics had been selected with any specific intent. I'd never made any reference to Lorenza's and my failed attempts, but then our failure to produce offspring was already a well-known issue.

The boiled beef is good, I said.

I didn't get the head, my mother replied. The butcher advised against it.

So much the better, I murmured under my breath. The head had always freaked me out.

That food-related digression brought my father's monologue briefly to a halt. He sat there studying me, as if trying to gauge the exact right time to get started again. In the end, he must have decided to give up entirely, because he said: So what about this guy, Novelli? An odd duck.

We watched him on TV, my mother confirmed. That's the guy you vacationed with.

He seems a little confused, he said.

You were in Sardinia together, my mother pointed out.

All of these were statements, not questions, so I felt no need to express my own opinion. They both seemed to have a pretty clear bead on the situation, though: there was this scientist who had invited me to spend the summer holidays with him, as his guest, and now that same scientist was being asked to appear on talk shows as an advocate of straight up, old-school male chauvinism.

Are you sure that there's such a word as demasculinization? I asked my father.

Of course there is!

It sounds a little odd. Demasculinization. I can't even quite manage to pronounce it.

AFTER DINNER we moved over to the sofas, and for a while, we looked at old slides that my father had had digitized. He'd been doing a lot of that lately. Eventually, he would put together a full-blown archive. Some people prefer to get them printed, he said. The idea of having an entire lifetime in a flash stick is a little frustrating.

There was a picture of the river Po, taken from the balcony of our home on the day that it overflowed its embankments. Our cellar was flooded, and every old issue of *Le Scienze*, which my father had collected and stored, in careful sequence, going back to the very first issue, had been crushed into blocks of muddy newsprint. We'd thrown them away, taking shifts with the wheelbarrow. The whole time he'd been very quiet, probably grieving over that loss.

Do you remember the flood? he asked, noticing that I had focused on that picture in particular.

Of course I remember it, sure.

I decided to ask him, in my turn, whether he remembered all those lost issues of *Le Scienze*, but then changed my mind at the last minute. This is one of the things I've never understood about my father: whether my decision to study physics at the university had satisfied him or not, and whether he knew that part of the reason I'd decided to do so was tied up with his own catastrophizing imprinting and his loss of that collection of *Le Scienze* in the flood. By the time I already had my degree, he frequently quoted one of Einstein's maxims, most likely apocryphal: "A researcher who has not made his great contribution to science before the age of thirty will never do so." When I walked away from the field of research without leaving behind me any significant contribution, he hadn't raised his voice in protest. He hadn't said a word, really, except for once, from the sofa, with his arms crossed: And what about physics? And I had replied, And physics, well, nothing. That was all I had to say: Ah, physics? Nothing.

Maybe he'd interpreted my desertion from science as a personal betrayal. So I was abandoning physics, and to work on...what, exactly? In what field, then, would I be an expert from then on, as a *writer*? He'd never asked me those questions, but if he ever had, my reply would have been that after all my years of study, what I was seeking was exactly that: incompetence. I wanted to finally become an expert in nothing.

I'D PLANNED to stay overnight, but I hadn't told them that in advance and my bag was still in the car. I hugged them both, left the building, and drove through the streets of that neighborhood for half an hour, in search of something that not even I could clearly express: a twinge of deep feeling, a sense of belonging. Then I pulled over to reserve a hotel room. I reviewed the last-minute deals that were available and, finally, chose the Hotel Boston. I'd always been curious about the place, that façade in an eclectic style, and I'd heard that each room was different from the others. At the reception desk I asked if I could have the room with the crocodile hanging from the ceiling. I'd seen a picture of it on TripAdvisor. It was occupied, however.

My room had heavy curtains and a dark parquet floor that creaked when you walked on it. It seemed to call for walking barefoot, so I slipped off my shoes. There was no one on earth at that moment who had any idea where I was, except of course for the desk clerk, to whom, however, I meant nothing.

I undressed, started some music on my iPad, and for a while I danced in my underwear in the space between bed and window. When I was a kid I used to dance all the time, I'd do it with one ear peeled in the direction of the door, lest anyone come in and catch me in the act. The things you do when no one else can see you: Aren't they enough to keep on going? To dance, to feel responsible for nothing, to live for momentary euphoria.

I looked out over the inner courtyard: for the heart of Turin, it was quite luxuriant. There was even a small, dark, rectangular tank where shimmering orange carp swam in disorderly fashion. The sky overhead featured the city's typical cloud cover, low-hanging stratocumulus formations, without shape or outlines. They let me glimpse, though just barely, the diffuse patch of light that was the moon.

IN THE MONTHS THAT FOLLOWED I lived in orbit. Not that I never returned home, in fact I went back often, but I spent as little time there as possible. Then I'd catch another train, another plane, or go by car if the destination allowed, and I'd stay in another hotel, for a week or thereabouts. I'd leave, come home, and leave again, incessantly.

The official story was that I was doing research for my book. Writing has the unquestionable convenience of justifying (nearly) any extravagance. No one save Lorenza and Karol had any idea of the authentic reasons for this frantic activity. That said, Lorenza and I felt we owed no one the truth about what was happening to us, at least not yet; after all, we ourselves would have been stumped if we'd been obliged to name it.

I never toured the cities. I cared nothing about the cities, they were all the same, or in any case, exactly what you'd have thought they'd be. All I was interested in was the hotel rooms, and I was most pleased if they overlooked an interior parking area.

After checking in, I always did the same things in the same sequence: masturbate, linger in the shower under a scalding-hot jet of water, open the minibar, order a grilled ham-and-cheese from room service, phone Lorenza before I was too drunk to carry on a conversation, drink more, and masturbate again, if I had the strength. I couldn't put a number on the amount of time I wasted battling against the evening with light switches, but I do know that the various hotels' electrical systems entertained me to a far greater extent than anyone would reasonably surmise. Around nine o'clock I'd have attained a sort of catharsis, a fleeting condition of pure absence, whereupon I'd fall asleep.

As for my book on the bomb, it had been languishing for a while now. I hauled the same brick of a book on nuclear deterrence everywhere I went, as if its mere presence was a warranty of my commitment. In all those months I doubt I produced more than thirty pages or so, along with a few articles for the newspaper: the basic minimum required to certify to the outside world that I hadn't died. In contrast with what I had supposed, emotional instability offered absolutely no stimulus to creativity, or if it did, it sure wasn't working for me. The conditions of precarity and anxiety might seem romantic, but they were also excellent reasons not to write.

Spending all that time in hotels, though they were hardly five-star destinations, was still expensive. I toyed with the idea of an artist residency somewhere. I even looked into it, but they all seemed intended for foreigners, ideally Americans. And after all, an artist residency would have entailed committing to a project, moments of interaction and evaluation, obligations to teach lessons and interact socially, while all I wanted was anonymous spaces and silence, dimly lit rooms with neatly folded towels, places that freed me of any and all responsibility.

I decided to confront the situation in a systematic manner. From all the emails I'd received in years past, I dredged up invitations that I'd declined, in Italy and around the world: festivals, bookfairs, workshops, seminars. I wrote fifty or so responses, all worded in roughly the same form, trying to negotiate a rain check. Nominating myself as a candidate was certainly unusual, and perhaps embarrassing. Not surprisingly, many of the organizers didn't even bother to write back, but a few did. Once I'd established contact, I explained that due to my needs as a writer, it would be convenient for me to stay longer with them than was strictly necessary.

Utrecht Cosenza Bratislava Hanover Gorizia Frankfurt: Google Maps kept a faithful record of my travels in that period, and the mapping itself shows a welter of lines.

Abu Dhabi Leopolis Jerusalem Lima Cartagena de Indias: the farther the better, as far as I was concerned, but also the more difficult to wangle. On my intercontinental flights I'd scroll through the entertainment program in search of the films in the Lord of the Rings cycle and watch them in order, guzzling cocktail peanuts and prosecco as I did. If those films weren't available, I'd nod off, resting my head against the pull-down blind of the porthole. One night the woman sitting next to me politely asked me to move aside so she could take a picture of the aurora borealis, but I wouldn't budge. I informed her that there was nothing special about it: nothing but charged particles precipitating along a perpendicular line into the Earth's magnetic field.

The idea that I would still communicate with Lorenza, and in fact did so several times a day, might seem paradoxical, and perhaps it was a contradiction in terms. Actually, the inconsistency didn't stop there: while I was spending most of my time in hotels, we started looking for a new place to live. We exchanged links to real estate sites, and we even went to see a number of apartments, discussing how we'd arrange the furniture, getting carried away with all the wrong details, a veranda that wasn't to code, original flooring that would have to be removed in any case, like a couple of rank beginners. We were seriously considering the possibility that as a couple we'd reached the end of the line, and at the same time we were planning our future together.

And so, while it's certainly true that for a period stretching from the last half of 2018 well into 2019 I was basically living in hotels, that captures only part of the truth. In those months and months away, the multitude of things that Lorenza and I were managing together continued to exist: a leak in the bathroom that required us to bathe with a bucket for a couple of weeks, Eugenio's final high school exams, and the day that he laid a hand on my forearm while we were studying together, as if he wanted to keep me from leaving. Even sex still existed, infrequent, apprehensive, but still there. We'd never do it the same night I returned to Rome, first we'd need to process the mistrust we'd built up, but sooner or later, it happened. After all those years, Lorenza and I were more than a love story at a juncture of crisis. We were also an infinite constellation of other inextricable aspects: a system of well-established habits, a network of social relations, a bureaucratic apparatus. We had to continue functioning. And continuing to function cost us little or nothing.

THE PAID TRAVEL entailed a number of social obligations: presentations, panels, events. Toward the end, I'd do whatever I could to avoid dinners and cocktails, but I couldn't always pull it off. On those evenings it might happen that someone else would come up to my room with me, but it was a rare occurrence, and in any case they never stayed until breakfast. I felt no guilt at those chance occurrences, quite the opposite: Wasn't that exactly the reason why I was conducting this new and nomadic existence, wasn't this exactly how I was complying with Lorenza's commandment, to go ahead and see what it's like? The way I interpreted it, seeing what it's like meant, first and foremost, getting into an elevator with someone, anyone, who wasn't her.

On one of those occasions, my iPhone disappeared, along with all the cash in my wallet. I was in Barcelona and it was still the middle of the night, roughly four in the morning. I was already starting to have momentary episodes of dissociation: for a few seconds, after waking up, I wasn't sure where I was. I remember that the hotel room in Barcelona was wallpapered with a pattern of alternating vertical stripes, in two different shades of blue. I got out of bed and picked my trousers up off the floor. I went through the pockets and rummaged in my backpack, but the phone wasn't there either. The wallet was there on the side table, even though I didn't remember having left it there. When I looked inside, I wasn't surprised to find it cleaned out. Actually, my credit cards and IDs were still there. Only the cash was missing.

I went into the bathroom and took a long hard look at myself in the mirror. I had a purple bruise on my left shoulder, a haloed bite mark. I ran my fingers over it, with an impression of utter mystery. My head was spinning, and what I needed was a long drink of water and a hot shower, but instead I went back out to the hotel room, straightened up the bed, and then lay down on what would have been my side of the bed back home, my back straight against the pillows.

I wasn't able to get back to sleep, and actually I didn't even try. I watched the dawn filter in through the gauziest layer of curtains, but it wasn't until eight that morning that I called Lorenza from the hotel phone. She asked me in some alarm why I was calling on that number, and I explained to her that I'd lost my cell phone. She said nothing for a few seconds, drinking in the implicit meaning contained in that detail, then told me that she was on her way out, in fact she was already running late, and she'd see me when I got home. Maybe, before she hung up, I got a chance to whisper I'm sorry.

THOSE EPISODES would remain suspended in midair between us, as impalpable as clouds, just as what had happened in Calais the previous autumn hovered in a state of suspension, an allusion let slip over the course of a night and never mentioned again. But at least now I can dare to tell the story of Calais, here and now, March 16, 2022, because in the meantime many other unimaginable things have happened in the world, and we all look more and more like survivors, and from the point of view of survivors perhaps it is possible to recount everything.

At Orly Airport, after letting the airplane take off without me, I rented a car from Thrifty, an economy model, but one that had a USB port. So I plugged in my phone and listened to *Skeleton Tree* while driving on the highway. Nick Cave put out that album with its black cover after the death of his son Arthur, who fell from a white chalk cliff high above the English Channel. The album had mostly been composed before Arthur's fall, but every line of the lyrics, every harmony in every composition, exuded loss. In that period,

I listened to *Skeleton Tree* on constant rotation and thought frequently about Arthur.

It was a kind of cure. If engendering a child entailed the possibility of such a traumatic separation, then paternity wasn't really the thing for me. I hadn't been deprived of an opportunity: I'd been *spared*. One listening after another, Nick Cave's lament for the untimely and unacceptable death of Arthur would finally rid me of my yearning for a son of my own.

In response to the text I'd sent Curzia—I'll join you in Calais if you tell me where you are—she replied without betraying a hint of emotion, just the link to the hotel. From a rest area on the highway, I'd reserved a hotel room. I knew I'd need it if for no reason other than to leave my luggage there, or maybe to take a shower. In any case, it seemed a more elegant approach.

The place was roughly at the standard of an Ibis economy hotel. The room had a large window and the sunlight streamed in. I sat down on the only chair and remained motionless for a while, my head strangely empty. I'd texted Lorenza to say that I'd missed the flight because of a problem with the bus, delayed due to an accident on the way to the airport. I was going to look for a hotel room to spend the extra night I'd have to stay, I didn't want to go back to Novelli's place. In fact, I hadn't even told him about it. As long as I was there, I'd take advantage of the opportunity to visit the Curie Museum the next day. It might prove useful for the book.

All things considered, the truth of my situation wasn't really all that different. I really had missed my flight, I was in a hotel room, I hadn't told Novelli about it, and there was a concrete possibility of getting back to Paris in time to visit the museum. Aside from all that, nothing else had yet happened. I couldn't have dreamed, before this, that I might feel so calm and determined on the verge of a betrayal. Excitement was just a background sensation, like a copper wire transmitting a weak electric current.

I opened the minibar, pulled out a bag of tortilla chips, and wrote another text to Lorenza: Hotel room out of a horror flick! Luckily just for one night. I had a completely incoherent instinct to call her, but I resisted the impulse. I took off my shoes and continued to wait.

When Curzia returned, it was almost dark. She texted me to join her in the lobby. I was ready, showered and dressed, but I let another fifteen minutes go by to avoid seeming overhasty. I found her sitting in an area dotted with sofas and love seats, a four-seat arrangement at the far end of the room. Scattered across the coffee table was her photographic equipment. One of the seats was piled high with heavy clothing. Sitting with her was a young man. Without getting up, Curzia said: Hey, there you are! I leaned down and kissed her on the cheek. Then I introduced myself to her colleague, a guy named Sasha. They were both wearing mud-caked technical hiking boots and Decathlon fleeces, their cheeks were ruddy from the cold. I said that it was pretty clear that they'd just come from a refugee camp and asked a few polite questions about what they'd seen. Sasha showed me a few of his shots on the screen of his reflex camera, and then asked me what I was doing there. Research for a book. Does it have anything to do with the Second World War? I don't know. He made a face and shot a glance at Curzia. I mean, I guess the war does have something to do with it.

By now it was almost eight o'clock, and I was just hoping that the guy would clear out soon, but Curzia said: I'm hungry, shall we get some dinner? From the way she looked at us, it was clear that the invitation extended to us both. We climbed into their rental car, with Sasha at the wheel and me in the back seat. Curzia turned up the music and started moving to the rhythm of a piece of Arabic music. I asked her if she really liked that music and she told me that she adored it. Do you understand the words, though? No, only *habibi*. What does that mean? Sasha gave me another bewildered look in the rearview mirror. Come on, *habibi* means darling, my love, everyone knows that.

Curzia was flailing her hands in the air, sinuously. I asked: Haven't you had your fill of terror attacks? Are you still really hungry for Arab music? I didn't really know where the hell that comment had come from. Suddenly stopping her accompaniment, she snarled: What the fuck does that have to do with anything?

We went into a pub where they'd been the night before. I would never have chosen a place like that if I'd been with Lorenza, it wouldn't have even made it onto the short list of possible venues. I continued to see things through Lorenza's eyes, at least in part. Maybe such long-term relationships really are a form of sickness. Another form of the premature cataracts that I had developed over the years.

Curzia and Sasha insisted I try the Welsh rarebit, it was the local favorite, and no, I couldn't look at the ingredients first. I had to just order it and see. All right, then.

A pan of melted cheddar cheese in which swam slices of greasy sandwich bread and, atop it all, bobbing on that lake of grease, a fried egg. So that's what Welsh rarebit was. Okay, okay, I'd eat every last bite. Anybody want to make a bet?

Curzia and Sasha went back to talking about their article. They worked out some of the details of delivery while I was already starting to feel lousy from what I'd eaten.

We went back to the hotel. In the parking lot, Sasha rolled a couple of cigarettes and handed them around, then said he wanted to go up to the room to do a little postproduction on his photos. Curzia and I stood there in the depressing parking area, considering what to do next, until she said, Listen, I think I'll go upstairs too. I'm exhausted. She really was too. She'd been outdoors all day long, interviewing young refugees, absorbing chilly wind and human suffering. Okay, I said. I can't feel my feet, she went on. Okay, I said again, but it must have sounded resentful, because there ensued another, longer silence, and then Curzia said: Listen, I don't know what kind of ideas you've gotten into your head, but that's not the way these things work.

She stepped close and hugged me in the middle of that desolate parking lot. With her head resting on my chest, she allowed herself a few seconds of repose. Then she planted a kiss on my cheek and walked into the lobby.

The next morning I went down to breakfast very early to avoid running into her. But Sasha was there, we nodded hello. Then I sat down at a separate table. I checked out of the room and got back in my car.

After his son's accident, Nick Cave didn't play another concert for months. How can you go back to singing and performing after that kind of a crushing loss? But then, recently, he'd started performing again. When he greeted his audience for the first time, he said: We've been in a strange place... I'm coming out and blinking into the light... and I've seen Tasmanians.

For his first return performance, he'd chosen a concert hall in Hobart, Tasmania. The same island where Novelli thought there might exist a shot at salvation for us all.

As I was driving back, leaving the north coast of France, away from the cliff where Arthur fell, and as I was hurrying away from my first and unsuccessful attempt at cheating on my wife, I made a resolution to take Eugenio to a Nick Cave concert. I resolved to do it the first chance I got, as soon as he came back from the United States. And maybe, if he wanted, I'd invite his taciturn young friend, the girl who preferred trap as a musical genre. I even texted him, and he'd responded with a GIF of a baby dancing for joy. I normally couldn't make heads or tails of the GIFs he sent, but I understood that one clearly.

AFTER MY PHONE WAS STOLEN in Barcelona, I chose to stay away from home for a while. In spring 2019, I wound up living at Curzia's house for a while. I mean, it wasn't as if I was hanging up my clothing in her closet or anything like that. I was just sleeping on her couch, with my suitcase lying open on the living room floor. The events of Calais, or to be exact the nonevents, had swept the field clear of a fantasy about the two of us that had been hovering in the realm of possibility for months, without any real intention of consummation, most likely in my mind more than hers. They'd gone down in our own private joke parlance as the "Great French Miscue," or GFM. Once we got past that, we were free to inaugurate an unfettered friendship based on a solid foundation of cutting sarcasm.

Monte Sacro was an unfamiliar neighborhood to me, which made it relatively easy to pretend that I was in some faraway city and not just a few metro stops from the life I was preserving in a state of suspended animation. Every morning I'd go for long walks along the river. It gave me time to think, but more importantly got me out from underfoot for a few hours. Curzia worked at home, just like me, but we didn't have the minimum quotient of familiarity required to spend all that time in the same room.

One day I found myself in a local food market and I went a little wild with my grocery shopping. When Curzia saw me deposit my bags and bags of food on the kitchen counter, she looked up briefly from her computer: Oh, sweet Jesus! You're not going to start cooking dinners for us, are you, my little homemaker?

The apartment was always a mess. People would show up without warning and then hang around until late at night. Smoking was allowed inside, and the trash was taken out only when it became absolutely necessary. I suppose that the very fact that I noticed certain aspects of Curzia's way of life really did make me the petty bourgeois that she accused me of being. But I'd never lived like that, not even when I was a university student, back when Giulio and I were roommates. Giulio and I were good, well-behaved students, always bent over our books, holed up in our respective rooms. We had scheduled chores and cleaning routines, assigned at the start of each month. It would never have occurred to either of us to ignore those rules and regulations.

After my initial grocery-shopping misstep, I gave up on the idea of cooking. We relied to an unhealthy extent on takeout meals and food delivery, even though I had always been opposed to that because of the recurrent urban imagery of delivery scooters hit by cars on their way to bring people like us sushi. Curzia scolded me for that attitude, explaining that it was the kind of thing that from my privileged vantage point counted as sheer hypocrisy. Plus, having a home-delivered dinner was just plain handy.

Leaving aside her relentless, understated mockery, she was happy to have me there. She was going through a pretty grim period. Freelance journalists live a precarious life whatever the larger situation, and the end of terror attacks in Europe meant a decline in demand for her services. The news agency she wrote for had considered her their go-to for Islamic terrorism for so many years that now they hardly knew how to repurpose her. The rest of reality had been split up into beats among her fellow reporters: one covered migrants, another wrote about European elections, and a third tended to parliamentary feuds and maneuvers. They all defended their own territory aggressively, to say the least. Curzia cursed them for it, even though she knew she'd have done the same in their place. Every morning I watched as she prowled the internet in search of story ideas, and then got on the phone in the hope of wangling even just a few minutes of consideration from the managing editor. If the day was a good one, she'd sit down to write in the afternoon, but when it came time to turn in her work, they'd tell her to chop ten column lines, and then another ten, and ten more after that. The evening almost always ended in a tirade: *Those fuckers left me with nothing but a sidebar!*

She complained frequently, or maybe the word is obsessively. Did I realize that these days newspapers had dropped their fee per item to forty euros? Forty euros! I could make more money by cleaning houses.

I don't think that's really in your wheelhouse, Curzia.

Sarcasm remained the only acceptable idiom for us to communicate in. If I'd dared to analyze the situation in serious terms, Curzia would have told me I didn't know what I was talking about. After all, I was the one who had it easy.

In my turn, I would tell her all about Lorenza; she'd developed a soft spot for my wife, even though she'd never met her. Actually, she had a soft spot for the way I described her. She liked to torment me on account of an expression I had used once, "taking some time off for myself." I had incautiously told her that I was taking some time off for myself. Practically every evening, Curzia would ask me what extraordinary things I had done that day with the time that I taken off for myself, and I was almost always forced to admit that I'd done practically nothing with it.

We talked about Novelli, too, and frequently wound up expressing sharply contradictory opinions in the space of just a few minutes. For instance, Curzia was equally indignant that I had failed to take a public stance against him and that I had refused to offer him my explicit moral support and solidarity. So what's the right thing to do? I would ask her. How would you have handled it?

Me? she'd retort. I pick my friends carefully *in advance.*

IN THE PAST FEW MONTHS, the climate emergency had become a fashionable cause. For the first mass rally of young people in Rome, Curzia's wire service had already assigned a different journalist, but after hours of nervous prostration she informed me that she would be going nevertheless. I suggested I could come with her: I'll take the photos. I can be your Sasha.

You? You're a pathetic photographer. Sasha is a genius.

We tore down the Via Nomentana at terrifying speed, my arms around her waist as she wove in and out of traffic on her scooter, and in minutes we were in the middle of a river of young people. I felt a little out of place, like a tourist of some kind. When I was in high school, I'd attended only a very few protest marches. Those were the years of the No Global movement, and I tried to palm off my apathy as intellectual superiority. I wondered what I would have done today if I were seventeen years old now. Would I have gone to school like a good boy, along with three other classmates and a teacher who was industriously coming up with things for us to do, even though deep down she was looking at us with utter contempt?

I lost track of Curzia and for a while I just walked along, keeping up with the procession. A featherlight papier-mâché globe was being tossed from one group to another through the air. And as I was following its trajectory, I noted Eugenio on the sidewalk. Of course he was there. Why shouldn't he be? The globe caught him off guard, hitting him lightly in the back of the head. But Eugenio whipped around in some alarm. He was always on the alert, nerves wire-taut since he was little. I never could figure out why, or how I could teach him to relax.

He hit the globe lightly, launching it back up into the air. He was with a small group of young people, and among them was Sara. From their gestures I realized that they were insisting that he allow them to write something on his arm. Finally, he gave in. He rolled up the sleeve of his jacket with a certain theatricality and patiently waited for Sara to write something in Magic Marker, or maybe she was finishing a drawing.

The official version—that I was on the road frequently doing research for my book—was what he knew as well. Actually, I suspected that he and Lorenza talked a lot. They exchanged a lot more information than I knew or guessed, and lately they'd been eating dinner together, just the two of them. If so, though, Eugenio gave no sign of it. When I was away, thinking about him gave me an ever so slightly sharper sense of guilt than normal. So I thought about him as little as possible. I had never allowed myself to miss him.

At the protest march, too, I kept my distance. While he was standing there letting himself be decorated, he let his gaze wander, in my direction as well as elsewhere. I was afraid he might spot me, but his eyes ran over me without recognition. When he walked off with his fellow students, I followed them for a while and then turned off into a side street.

WHEN I GOT TO PIAZZA VENEZIA, I ran into Curzia. I think I've got what I need, she said. Let's head home.

When we got back, she went into her room and shut the door so she could concentrate. I remained alone in the living room. I sat down on the sofa and texted Eugenio: Did you go to the protest march?

Naturally. Where are you?

I dropped by, but just to take a look.

Sorry I missed you. Was it for an article?

Since I didn't answer, he went ahead and wrote me again: Are you coming over this evening?

I have to leave again.

He sent me a sad-face emoji.

I called B. S. at the *Corriere della Sera*. I told her that I'd wound up in the middle of the student strike for climate in Rome, pretty much by accident. Of course, they had all their news pages overflowing with Greta Thunberg, but considering that I'd reported for them on COP 21, I don't know, maybe there could be a reasonable link between the two subjects. She gave me seventy column lines.

When Curzia came back out into the living room, I was still finishing my article. She plopped down on the sofa and sat there for a few seconds without moving.

They took the piece, it's all good, she said. Wanna go out? I feel like a pizza.

Just give me half an hour.

I saw her cast a sideways glance at the screen of my laptop. What are you writing?

Something for my newspaper.

About what?

The protest march.

Did they ask you to write it?

As long as I was there.

She straightened her back against her chair. After a moment she said: I have to say, you're unbelievable.

I'd pulled my headphones off just one ear, but at that point I took them off entirely.

You insisted on coming along, and now you steal my coverage.

Hey, it's nothing, just a piece of commentary.

Right, one of *your* pieces of commentary. Is it going to be a front-page commentary?

We don't write for the same paper. What do you care?

Are they going to put it on the front page, yes or no? How would I know?!

She leaped to her feet with a jerk and gathered up her things. Listen, I'm going to get something to eat. I'm hungry. When you're done, you can give me a call, or do whatever you feel like. A second later, she'd gone out the front door.

I turned in the article, which was nothing special, or at least it didn't strike me as much at all. Even after stripping it of adjectives, it still sounded verbose and a bit saccharine. Maybe seeing Eugenio in the procession had influenced me.

I took a shower, and then devoted myself to Twitter for a while. By ten, Curzia still hadn't sent any messages at all. Even though it seemed a bit sentimental as a gesture, I took a Post-it off her desk and wrote her a message. I hardly thought I owed her an apology, not really, so I didn't add one, but I did say that I was sorry if there had been a misunderstanding on both our parts, and I meant it. We were both going through too much craziness right now to be of much help to each other. Still, it had been a pleasure to torture Amazon Alexa with her for all those days.

I caught a taxi. Once aboard, and with the destination not yet finalized, I texted Lorenza to ask if she minded my returning home at that hour of the night, and without advance warning. She wrote back saying it would be no bother. On the other hand, she said that it struck her as quite strange for me to ask permission to come back to my own home.

SOME TIME LATER, Giulio came to Rome. He had to pick up his passport with a work visa for South Africa. We met outside the embassy. Since the university allowed him to do it, he had decided to take a half sabbatical. Regulations allowed him to undertake activities elsewhere that would prove useful to his academic development, and so, officially at least, he was going to teach a cycle of seminars at the University of Cape Town Graduate School of Business.

Whereas, in reality?

Whereas, in reality I've enrolled in a course to become a park ranger. In Kruger National Park.

In Kruger National Park, I echoed him. There must be lions, I'm guessing.

Plenty of them. As well as hyenas, hippopotamuses, and Cape buffaloes.

Snakes?

Aplenty.

Giulio knew about my incontrollable fear of snakes from a mountain hike we'd taken together back at university.

Assuming high-handedly that the subject might be of any interest to me, he started telling me about spitting cobras. According to certain ethologists, spitting cobras had developed that talent specifically to target humans. Our ancestors attacked these cobras with spears, in other words, from a distance, and they had found a form of self-defense. There was a channel inside their fangs that was curved at a right angle. That meant that when the venom passed through, it was sharply accelerated.

Basically, natural selection shaped them to kill us, Giulio summarized. They've done tests, with researchers as targets. At ten feet, they were hit dead center in the face ten times out of ten. Would you care to see a video?

I'd rather not.

Anyway, most of the time spitting cobras can only blind their victims. But not black mambas, those are seriously dangerous. They're fast and they're very aggressive. We're going to take a course to learn to handle them.

To handle them, I repeated under my breath, got it.

He was euphoric, and every so often I'd notice that he'd slip his hand into his jacket pocket to touch his passport, as if checking to make sure it was still there.

He'd let his hair grow out. I asked him if this was the beginning of a general transformation he was undertaking for his future in the wilderness. He was going to be gone for months. What about Adriano? I asked him, with an unintentional hint of reproof.

Giulio had put his phone back in his pocket. I don't think it will do us any harm to be apart for a while. After a moment he added: I don't remember when I last updated you.

I think you and Cobalt had come to a written understanding.

Right, there's an understanding, he confirmed. But let's just say that it only works on paper.

The document established the exact division of expenses and time, but one Friday, when Giulio arrived half an hour late because of a delay in the metro—half an hour, no more—Cobalt had refused to let him take Adriano. It had ruined the whole weekend. If the boy had so much as a hint of a cold, that was a sufficient excuse not to let him take Adriano. And any time there was a meeting at school, Cobalt took great care not to let him know, so she could accuse him later of failing to attend. That sort of situation is a constant, Giulio said. It's pretty unnerving.

At Christmas he had organized a trip to Norway, but two hours before they were scheduled to leave, Adriano's passport had mysteriously vanished. Very mysteriously, he reiterated. He showed me a series of screenshots of the merciless exchange of text messages with Cobalt.

Do you save all your chats?

Only the very worst ones. At first I did it on my lawyer's advice. But then I just kept it up on my own.

After a pause, he went on to confess: I kind of lost it about the passport going missing. But he didn't say in what manner.

For a number of weekends, he'd been able to see Adriano only in the presence of a social worker, who sat with them in utter silence, monitoring them. In the room set aside for that process, there were plastic toys that looked vaguely carcinogenic, and Adriano refused even to touch them. Therefore, father and son sat there without speaking, getting increasingly irritated with each other. Knowing Giulio's extreme sensitivity, the idea of him being put in that kind of a situation with Adriano for hours, under observation by a woman he'd never met in his life, struck me as a latter-day form of medieval torture. Finally, at a certain point, Adriano refused to go to those meetings, which meant they no longer saw each other.

I had to leave his birthday present in the elevator, Giulio said. At that point, Cobalt must have realized that things were spinning out of control. She asked if she and I could meet privately, after I don't know how many years. It was very strange. We were supposed to be there to talk about Adriano, but instead we found ourselves talking about us, things that had happened a thousand years ago, before Adriano was even born. People get obsessed about unbelievable things. It seemed to be going well. We were almost... civil. But then Cobalt must have felt guilty. All that talk about us must have caught her off guard. She started bringing up her boyfriend, Luc. Suddenly it was all Luc, Luc, Luc. Luc says this, Luc thinks that. To hear her tell it, Luc has very clear ideas about anything and everything, from the big bang onward. I made fun of her a little, because Luc really had nothing to do with what we were talking about, I assure you. And that's when she lost it. "Don't you dare judge him!"—you know, that kind of thing. Okay, okay, whatever. Even though, from the way she turned on the waterworks, it doesn't seem to me that Luc is making her all that happy.

What about you? Are you seeing anybody? I asked him point-blank.

Not exactly.

After a moment of silence, Giulio asked, What about you?

No. Not exactly.

My surprise at that question must have been obvious, because he added: You may not be aware of this, but Lorenza and Cobalt correspond every so often. They've stayed in touch over the years. Or maybe they just got back in touch recently, I couldn't say.

We had lunch together, in a café on Piazza Fiume. Then Giulio asked me if I still had time to go downtown with him to buy a backpack. The one he owned was too big. We walked up Via Venti Settembre. Along the way, he talked practically the whole time, even though he kept checking in with me: Let me know if I'm boring you.

About a month before that he'd received a phone call from a stranger. Are you Giulio? Yes, that's me, who's calling. I just wanted to inform you that a number of your personal documents are scattered across the street all over Rue Keller. They seem to be pretty personal, by the way. In fact, I found this phone number. If you want, I'm glad to send you some pictures.

The stranger wasn't French and had terrible pronunciation. In fact, Giulio's first thought was that this might be a phishing expedition or a con game: Personal documents of his scattered in the street? How could that be? But the street that the guy had mentioned was exactly where his lawyer's office was located, so the report possessed a strange credibility.

A few seconds later, a text came in on his phone: a photograph of a page from his divorce decree. Giulio cut off a meeting with one of his students midway through and rushed out of his office and headed to Rue Keller. Once he got there, sure enough, the papers were scattered all over the place. It had been a windy period in Paris and a gust had scattered the contents of his file all over the place, on the sidewalk and in the traffic lanes.

My whole life was lying there, he said. Just scattered in every direction. Copies of my personal documents and IDs, personal emails, pictures of Adriano, bank account numbers. All sorts of sensitive information, anything you could think of. Once the case had been settled, the law firm had decided to get rid of his file and had simply tossed it in the trash can on the street.

Not even a dumpster: just an ordinary trash can. It was so absurd that at first I didn't want to believe they'd done it. I managed to talk myself into the idea that the file had just been blown out the window, I don't know how. I collected everything, and in the meantime I had finally realized what had actually happened. So when I was done collecting it all, I went upstairs to the lawyer's office, and I made quite a scene, first with the secretary and then with the lawyer herself. She had refused even to see me. I was so furious she must have thought that Cobalt might have a point after all. Anyway, butter wouldn't melt in her mouth. A complete deadpan. She told me that it's standard practice for them to throw away their files. What else are they supposed to do with them?

At least sort the different types of paper for recycling, I joked to cut the tension.

At least sort the different types of paper for recycling. Exactly.

We were standing in front of the sports equipment store, but we didn't seem ready to go in.

Outside of the lawyer's office, I wandered around for a while, Giulio said, sounding stunned.

You should have called me.

You haven't seemed particularly available lately.

He didn't say it with any resentment. It was a simple observation of fact, as if that was the sort of thing that happened to everyone at times: they become unavailable.

In the end, he'd decided that he couldn't just let matters run their course. He'd gone to the nearest police station and filed a criminal complaint. The police officer at the desk didn't seem to understand what the issue was, or at least pretended not to get it. But Giulio had made up his mind. He'd had to wait four hours or so to file his official complaint. And as he sat there, in the police station waiting room, surrounded by a menagerie of human types, at one of the lowest points in his life, if not the absolute lowest, after seeing everything that he had once been, as he put it, literally trodden underfoot, well, at that very moment he had felt... he didn't know exactly how to put it. But pretty good, really.

Free?

I don't know if free is the right word. But what came to mind was the Kruger National Park, a place I'd been many years ago. In my mind's eye, I glimpsed one landscape in particular, a clearing that opens out suddenly at the end of a road, and I said to myself, "I'd like to be there." Very simply. Why couldn't I be *there*, instead of in that police station trying to persuade a policeman that taking a person's whole life and scattering it across a city street must necessarily constitute a crime of some kind? The next day I signed up for the park ranger training course and applied for the sabbatical.

And now you need a new backpack, I said.

We entered the store. After a first exploration, we had lined up three models. We examined the capacity of the various pockets, the stitching, the zipper covers, the ventilation spacers. Giulio didn't care about the colors, but he knew that the really vivid hues would set animals' nerves on edge. In the end, he chose a gray Arc'teryx, compact and stern in appearance. He just put it on his back and we walked out the door.

We walked all the way to Via del Corso. With his backpack, Giulio really looked as if he was about to set off, on foot, from the center of Rome to South Africa.

Why don't you come with me? We'd have fun.

Too many snakes.

Oh, right, the snakes. I was forgetting.

Okay, I said, so now you're going to become a park ranger. If a cobra doesn't spit in your eye first, that is. And then what? Are you going to move to Africa and work as a safari guide?

For a few seconds, Giulio turned his face up to the sun. Well, for now I'm going to become a park ranger, and then we'll see. The way things are going in the world these days, if you ask me, everybody needs a plan B. I have South Africa. But what about you? Have you thought of what your plan B should be?

FOR STARTERS, I could move to his apartment in Paris. The fact that I would be living there while he was gone freed Giulio of the moral burden of knowing he was leaving it empty for months. You can take care of the various utilities, he told me, but don't dream of trying to kick in on the rent. All right then, I agreed. I'd just have to make that sacrifice to keep from turning him into the world's greediest capitalist.

He left instructions on how to take care of the plants and how to get the water heater to restart when it turned off. He reprised his invitation to go with him several times, so frequently that we turned it into a game: each time I had to come up with an ever more ridiculous excuse for turning down the invitation. If we'd both gone, it really would have made him happy, but I wasn't equipped with the same level of internal autonomy, nor did I share his contempt for danger. I'd always admired those qualities in Giulio, especially his lack of fear, whether it regarded ferocious beasts, impossibly challenging calculations related to general relativity, or leading protest marches, but as a way of life, it also struck me as downright exhausting.

The day he left, I went with him to Charles de Gaulle Airport. I watched him head off through security, then I took the train back to the city. The sky looked like one you'd see arching over a continental plain somewhere farther inland, and I realized I felt nothing: nothing about that instant, and nothing about the empty weeks that stretched ahead of me.

My stay in Paris created less mistrust in other people than when I'd been changing cities continuously, and in fact they accepted it willingly: friends and acquaintances, the newspaper, my parents, Eugenio. Perhaps they thought that living alone in that sort of a capital city I must be having a high old time, but my routine was very different from that: I'd wake up pretty late, spend my mornings writing or reading, my afternoons taking very long walks in competition with the Health app to take more steps than I had the day before, and sometimes, at night, I'd go see a movie in the Montparnasse multiplex. Most of the time, though, I'd just stay home. I'd look out the window, watching the hustle and bustle down in Rue de la Gaîté. I found it hypnotic, and would watch until the wee hours as people entered and exited the so-called commercial theaters, or watched sports matches on TVs in bistros, until the street suddenly emptied out at a certain hour of the morning. In any case, I never had anything alcoholic to drink before six in the evening, I'd only buy red meat twice a week, and every evening I'd reflect for at least half an hour about whether to reach out to Novelli, and then I never would.

One afternoon, as I was returning from a walk, I ran into Cobalt and Adriano standing in front of the street door. Adriano had dug his heels in concerning a Lego game that he'd left at his father's apartment. Cobalt felt the need to justify their presence: He wouldn't give me a moment's peace.

I invited them to come upstairs, and it was a bit strange to walk up two flights with the three of us in single file. When I unlocked the door, Adriano ran inside while Cobalt stood uncertainly on the landing. Come on in, I told her. She shook her head: No, I'd better not.

Please, come in, I insisted, even though the doubt had occurred to me that Giulio might actually not be too happy about it.

Cobalt looked around with a perplexed expression, as if she'd imagined that room many times before, and now the details weren't lining up with what she'd expected. She set her son's backpack down against the wall and took a seat in the armchair without removing her jacket. I said that I'd put some coffee on. Adriano was taking his time in the other room. I could hear him rummaging around in the toy box.

If you ask me, it was just an excuse, she said.

It's his home, he can come here whenever he wants.

Her eyes came to rest on something, and I followed the line of her steady gaze, fetching up against a primitive statuette, possibly carved out of ebony, with a head of frizzy hair. We bought it together in Papua, she explained, pronouncing Papua with a French accent, and stressing the final *a*. Giulio said that it was a fake. I had no idea he'd kept it.

For a few seconds she gazed at it raptly. Then she asked me if I was still working on physics, at least in my free time, and I replied with a confession: I doubted that I'd be able to solve even the most basic kind of mechanical calculation now. *Pas vrai*, she said. If you tried, it would all come back immediately.

I restrained myself from adding that maybe I had a different idea of how to spend my leisure time than she did. Cobalt's vocation for physics was unbroken, invincible. The rest of the world's knowledge might stir some curiosity, but it was clear that it had a completely different standing for her.

We haven't had much of an opportunity to talk, you and I, she said.

No, I guess we really haven't.

You may have formed an idea of me that's, umm, a little strange.

I assured her that I had no particular idea about her, and Cobalt shrugged: We used to have a good time with Lorenza when it was all four of us. Too bad that it turned out like it did.

She left her coffee half-finished and called Adriano. She said something to him that I didn't understand.

When she spoke in French she changed, losing any trace of insecurity and regaining the peremptory quality that I had noticed in her from the very first day of that summer school session. Compared to those days, though, she seemed a little duller, more lackluster. I assured her that she could bring Adriano whenever she liked, but I had the distinct impression that wasn't going to happen. And in fact it didn't.

BECAUSE I STILL HADN'T VISITED the Curie Museum, I decided to take advantage of the opportunity now. It had fairly limited visiting hours, only in the early afternoon. The building was located on the university campus, on a quiet street in the Fifth Arrondissement. Not that there was much to see inside. I took a look at the explanatory labels on the walls and the instruments in the vitrines, but without much enthusiasm. The unmistakable intention of the curators had been to present the discovery of radioactivity only in terms of its positive outcomes: medical applications and the production of energy. No reference to radiation's carcinogenic potential, and certainly nothing about the atom bomb.

You couldn't even go into the laboratory proper. There was a rope to keep visitors out, and you could only peer inside. I examined the working table, covered with white tiling, the glass bells, beakers, and retorts, the sink against the wall, the ceramic bobbins, two switches with oversized handles, like the ones you see used for electroshock therapy: though none of the objects were original (the real ones were contaminated with radiation and would continue to be for centuries); the place as a whole emanated an aura of sanctity. There was a mannequin dressed in a black outfit, the austere lab coat worn by Maria Skłodowska, as if her phantom were still guarding the room. I thought back to what Giulio had said about his visit to Karabash, where the level of radiation remained extremely high, and the fact that the sense of danger had made the place seem *attractive*. I took a very slow panoramic video of the lab with my phone, hoping to capture that disturbing quality so that I could use it later.

Before leaving, I purchased a postcard of an already-aged Marie Curie, leaning on the railing that overlooked the courtyard, as well as a book of her lifelong correspondence with her daughters Irène and Ève. I still didn't want to go home, though, so I took a seat on a campus bench. There was a steady stream of students coming and going. In a corner stood a collection of tall, slender tanks, chained together: argon, carbon dioxide. I remembered when I was in university, the first time I used liquid nitrogen to refrigerate a circuit, the sense of responsibility that filled me when I poured a smoking stream of the incredibly cold fluid out of the dewar, under the supervision of the laboratory technician. That was a time when Giulio and I were still cherishing the illusion that we'd be able to harness the forces of nature, govern the whole universe, if only we could discern the exact formulas to do so.

In the days that followed I read Maria Skłodowska's letters and her daughters' responses. I've never been interested in epistolary collections, I'd found them boring and obsolete, but that's exactly why they were well suited to this new routine. My limited French kept me from speeding through the book, and that, too, was useful. The preface quoted from a note that Marie had written to a childhood friend, telling her about the aftermath of her husband Pierre's sudden death: "My life is devastated." I guessed that that might be a good translation, even though the verb was stronger still in French, *saccagée*, looted or plundered: "My life has been plundered."

Marie knew that her love for her daughters would never take the place of what she felt for her late husband. It was an impossible attempt to compensate. Perhaps well aware of her own coldness, or the enormity of her grief, she had decided to personally teach Irène algebra and trigonometry, as if her love could be transmitted in that form as well. She ended one of her letters by sending her daughter a method for constructing an ellipse that she might not have known. A burst of tender mother love encoded in mathematical formulas.

I'M READING Marie Curie's letters, I wrote to Curzia. They're very interesting.

They are? she wrote back. I doubt that.

At this distance, in the terse format of text messages, we'd resumed functioning in a way. She told me that she was capable of visualizing me exactly in the state I was tipping into, within the context of my obsessive new routine, and that the image filled her with disgust. More than once she had threatened to board the next plane and show up at my doorstep, but we both knew that it was a false threat, a way of harmlessly evoking the Great French Miscue and rekindling that minimal residue of mutual attraction.

When her friend the correspondent organized a cocktail party at her home, she arranged for me to receive an invitation. A cocktail party? I wrote back. You must be joking.

Just shut up and go. And dress properly.

Inexplicably, as the party drew nearer, my nervousness grew. The day of the cocktail party, I was actually seized with an uncontrollable agitation, which took the form of an excess of aesthetic zeal: I went to get a haircut at Franck Provost and I purchased a pair of new trousers, because all the ones I had seemed too casual. Lorenza was guiding me remotely with her yeses and noes.

As I expected, there was no one I knew at the cocktail party. The first person I wound up talking to was a young man my age, who began by politely inquiring as to what I did for a living, and then telling me that he worked in investments. I asked him which bank in particular he worked for, which struck me as the obvious next question, but he replied with a smile: no bank, perhaps he hadn't made it clear. He owned an investment fund. He showed me a picture of the airport he was financing in a rural part of India, more or less as you might do with pictures of a home renovation.

I lingered by the buffet table for a while, then screwed up my nerves and took a second scouting excursion through the party. In one of the little groups, the conversation was being monopolized by a rather elderly woman, Luisa T., whose name I had already heard elsewhere. Of course, she'd worked as a culture correspondent from Paris for nearly thirty years, she'd known *those* writers, frequented *those* salons, the usual twentieth-century stories that made the present seem so feeble and superficial. It seemed like she'd barely deigned to notice my presence and I was already turning to leave when she suddenly zeroed in on me: And you, sir, why are you rolling your eyes like that?

Why, I wouldn't dream of rolling my eyes. I have problems with cataracts and sometimes I find myself moving my eyes as a result.

Cataracts at your age?

She stepped closer, as if she wanted to test my claim by examining my pupils. Everyone else took advantage of this opportunity to flee, and there we were, all alone. Who are you? Luisa asked. Then, holding on to my hand a moment longer than necessary: And exactly what are you doing here in Paris?

I replied that I wasn't exactly sure, and she nodded, as if it showed.

I managed to elude her pursuit, but then I ran into her again on the landing. She gestured imperiously for me to help her with her overcoat. I googled you in the meantime, she told me. I hope you'll forgive me, but I no longer read contemporary writers. Fiction in general bores me. Indeed, it alienates me. But I know that my son loves your work. Are we leaving?

Outside, I asked if she needed a taxi, but she lived near the Solférino metro station, it was an easy walk: And stop being so damned ceremonious!

But tell me, she added after a bit, eloquently touching her left ring finger, where is your wife? In Rome. Are you divorced? No, no we're not. Separated? No, not separated either. Sweet Jesus, who do I have to kill to get the story?!

After that last exchange we walked along in a different sort of tension, or at least I did, until Luisa stopped in front of a street door and punched in her access code. Come in, let me offer you a cup of tea. Don't ask me for anything alcoholic because there's nothing of the sort in the house, she said.

She lived on the ground floor of a historic building, in the apartment that had once been occupied by the concierge. You reached it by going through a tiny courtyard, then opening a door located under a staircase. It looks like the entrance to a speakeasy, I said.

True, but don't get your hopes up. Everyone's thrilled at the beginning, but believe me, the wonders cease pretty quickly.

And in fact the apartment consisted of a single bedroom, a bathroom without windows, and a galley kitchen that hardly lived up to the name. But there were two large windows overlooking the garden. The rest of the building belonged to a Swiss businessman who was never there. In fact, the lights were all off. I can fantasize that the whole place is mine, Luisa said.

I sat down while she made the tea. The room had a very high ceiling, so impressive that I felt called upon to comment. She looked up and then said that to take the curtains down you'd have to call the fire brigade, so she'd decided not to try. They were covered with dust, and thus they were bound to remain.

She gave me a quick rundown of her love life: two ex-husbands, four children, eight grandchildren, in a perfect geometric progression. Luckily, they all lived far away. As was inevitable at that juncture, she asked if I had children of my own and I supplied the standard answer, namely that my wife had a son from a previous relationship. She's older than me, I pointed out.

I understand. Does that make you feel like a bit of a hero?

I don't know. Maybe so, I confessed.

I focused on my tea as I tried to think how to get the conversation back onto the subject of the curtains, but Luisa beat me to the punch: I don't miss either of my two husbands, not a bit. But sometimes I miss the things I knew about them. Because I knew *everything* about them. Years and years of work to collect that information. And then . . . nothing. A huge waste of time. Tell me what you're working on now.

I told her about my book on the bomb, and how I was trying to reconcile the archival material and the eyewitness testimonies, the difficulties with accessing firsthand documentation because so much was in Japanese. Luisa listened impassively.

When I finished talking she stood up and took the teacup out of my hands, as if our happenstance encounter had come to an end.

I can't claim to have a thorough knowledge of you, she said, as you know I only just googled you a few minutes ago. But from what little I've been able to guess, you're going through some kind of…crisis. Can we call it that? At the same time, you're working on a book about things that happened in Japan seventy years ago that are no longer of any interest to anyone. I'm curious: What's your criterion for choosing the topics you write about?

HAVING SUCCESSFULLY SURVIVED, for better or worse, that ordeal of social interaction, I went back to my solitary biorhythm. One day in Paris now resembled the next, and so they all seemed shorter. I could go on living this way ad infinitum, I thought to myself, keeping everything steady, avoiding any interference.

But other people still existed. One day I received a phone call from Marina. It wasn't like her to reach out to me, and in fact she hastened to ask if she'd caught me at a bad time. I replied with total sincerity that she wasn't catching me at any particular sort of time.

She thought that it was important to give me the news directly: that student for whom I'd served as a coadviser, Christian…Christian, of course. Well, this time he was successful.

At Giulio's place there was a cube-shaped footrest. Adriano always climbed on top of it on all fours. As she told me the news, I sat down on it.

I asked Marina just how Christian succeeded—I felt more comfortable continuing with the euphemism—and she replied: The most classic variant, with a rope in the garage. This time, it had been a lucid, premeditated act, or at least that's what Christian's sister had told her.

So you and he were still in touch, I said. It was a neutral comment, but it sounded like a criticism, and in fact she retorted: I know that it's odd, but for some reason I'd become fond of him.

Marina was one of the most self-controlled people I'd ever met, but at that point she gave way to a muffled sob. She only wept for a few seconds, then she cleared her throat and added: We're going to buy a wreath of flowers as a group, the school faculty. We're all atheists, so of course we don't love flower arrangements, but nothing else occurred to us. Nico suggested we write the school's motto on the ribbon, the one about virtue and knowledge. I find it terribly impersonal, but that hardly matters. If you'd like to chip in, it would be twenty-five euros. You can pay me when you come back for the course.

MY EMPTY DAYS in Paris made me think much more intently about Christian than I would have done back in Rome, in more normal circumstances. On the strength of the scanty information provided by Marina (with a rope, in a garage) I constructed a detailed fantasy about his last few minutes. Perhaps the objective of his suicide, if there was an objective, was exactly that: to become a recurring thought for those who had outlived him.

I also had a more specific reason for remorse. The day after his hospitalization, I said nothing in class about what had happened, I probably never even said his name, as if the event could be safely ignored. But what was even stranger is that his classmates didn't seem to expect me to mention him. They took it for granted that this situation was bigger than me, or perhaps they didn't feel that they could be given any instruction on the subject of suffering by a professor. The only thing that *did* happen was, at a certain point, that one of the female students in the back row had stood up with a jerk and, interrupting me, asked permission to go to the restroom. I had pointed out to her that she hardly needed to ask my permission, whereupon she'd said, again: So, that means I can go? She'd said with an aggressive edge that seemed to allude to something very different.

If I hadn't done it back then, now there was even less of a reason for me to spend time on Christian. After all, I'd barely even known him: just a few hours in class, one night out and about with him in Trieste, and a Skype call a few months later, in which I'd listened to him lay out the paltry amount of work he had done on his thesis. Marina, after consulting with the rest of the faculty, had agreed to award him his diploma all the same, even though he'd stopped attending classes before the middle of the academic year. Christian had prepared a report on the work he was doing at the Modena planetarium, which involved guiding groups of elementary school pupils while talking to them in hypersimplified language about a subject he'd studied in considerable detail for years: the birth of the cosmos, stellar nucleosynthesis, galaxy clusters, black holes. For his dissertation, they need a coadviser and at the last minute, Marina had asked me.

I'd given him the highest possible score. In his email thanking me, Christian invited me to come see him, he'd be happy to organize a private tour of the planetarium just for me. I hadn't even given the idea a second's consideration. When I opened the email again months later, I realized that I hadn't even written back.

THEN ONE DAY the vision in my left eye got much worse. I stepped into the shower seeing the world as I always had, and when I stepped out, everything was a blur. Even now, I'm skeptical about attributing any kind of cause-and-effect relationship between the two events, and yet that's the order in which they occurred: Marina called to tell me about Christian's suicide, and a few days later I saw the world around me through a film, as if someone had punched me in the face.

My oculist, who had seen me at the mysterious onset of the disease twenty years earlier, and then its subliminal progress, gave me the address of a specialist in Paris who could see me urgently. When I went to see that doctor, she confirmed that my vision had deteriorated by two diopters, a serious drop in visual acuity. She asked me whether I'd had German measles as a child, and whether I'd been involved in any particularly intense physical activity lately, or been subjected to any notable stress.

My vision might still deteriorate from one minute to the next, because critical severity was typical of that disease. If that happened, the prescribed cure, which was actually pretty simple, would become far more challenging. I talked it over with Lorenza, and she said, Come home immediately, and even though she uttered those words in an impersonal tone of voice, as a recommendation prompted by straightforward health concerns, I was immediately swept with an unexpected wave of tenderness. I bought an easyJet ticket for the next day. Then, almost without thinking about it, I texted Novelli on WhatsApp: I'm just passing through Paris, but I'm leaving tomorrow. If you're in the city and you feel like it, we could get together for a drink.

HE WROTE saying we could meet at the Select after dinner, but forty minutes past the agreed-upon time, he still hadn't showed up. The waiter was starting to show signs of impatience, he'd tossed a coaster on the table as an unmistakable invitation to order, but I ignored him, repeating every time he strolled past the table that I was waiting for someone.

The air was very clear. I looked at the lights on the signs across the way, the sheer sumptuousness of that stretch of boulevard, a sumptuousness undimmed by the years of terrorism. I squeezed my eyes shut alternately: the crystalline world of my right eye, the flat and blurry world of my left eye, as if on the verge of vanishing entirely.

A taxi pulled over to the sidewalk and remained there for a few seconds. Novelli opened the door on the street side and his head appeared above the roof of the taxi. He walked around the gleaming sedan, finally acknowledging my presence with a contraction of his eyebrows.

He wore a black jacket open to reveal his shirt beneath. Maybe it was the cut of the jacket, but his chest seemed more substantial. His trousers, black like the jacket, were creased in front, and his feet were shod in white running shoes, so clean they naturally caught your eye. He was carrying a light-brown trench coat, unlined, which he then carelessly draped over the back of his chair.

I waited for you before ordering, I said.

I'd stood up, like a fool, as if we were about to hug, but we didn't. We just shook hands, barely gripping, more brushing fingers. The waiter reappeared immediately with a smile for Novelli as if they were old friends. Novelli asked for a glass of Sancerre. Same for you? All right, make that two.

He sat down, facing the street. Well, then, he murmured, without offering a clue as to what meaning I should attribute to the phrase.

You've changed your style a bit, I said.

By which you mean what?

I gestured at his clothing and then at the glittering interior of the bistro: There was a time when we both settled for the lower-end standards of the hardworking people.

The Select, you mean? But it's a classic.

The waiter set down the two glasses of wine along with two metal bowls, one full of stuffed olives, the other of cocktail peanuts. Novelli ignored the one full of olives, but pulled the other one toward him, digging in for a series of small but frantic handfuls. His phone vibrated in his inside jacket pocket and he informed someone as to his location, in Italian. The person on the other end of the line must have responded with a wisecrack, because Novelli broke into laughter. Oh, definitely, he said, definitely!

After ending the call, as the last traces of amusement died out on his face, he said: Ambrosini will be joining us. Did you ever meet him?

No. I don't think so.

One of my postdocs. Knows what he's doing. He was at Caltech, I had to fight to rip him out of their claws. But he's been worth it.

So you're still teaching at the university.

Novelli seemed baffled by the question. Of course I am. Why do you ask?

He clapped his hands together to get rid of the salt, then picked up his phone again: Look at what extraordinary photography. He's self-taught, would you believe it?

He showed me a landscape in the evening: a line of squared-off buildings atop which rose a blue sky crisscrossed with lighter-hued lines.

This is Ecuador. Just think, it was taken in the middle of the night. He had to use a very long exposure, but he didn't have a tripod, what's it called in Italian? The word slips my mind. Anyway, he stood there, motionless, practically holding his breath the whole time. There's practically no blurring at all, you see? You take a look at this photograph and you just assume: it's a filter, or maybe it's photoshopped. But no, it's not.

He pinched the photo out. These up here are noctilucent clouds, and that's the name we chose for the book, because it's so very poetic, but the publisher doesn't want to use it. He says that people won't know how to pronounce it, and they'll butcher it six ways from Sunday.

Noctilucent, I repeated, because it did in fact have a melodious sound.

Novelli set down his phone. They're clouds that form at unusual altitudes, he said. We're talking about elevations of eighty kilometers. Since this is very close to the equator, the sun is so low that its rays come from below the line of the horizon. At that angle, they reach the lower stratosphere and the only portion of the light that remains is the blue component. The resulting effect is a cloud that emits a light all its own. It's extraordinary. In reality, and here he aimed his forefinger straight up, as if warning me against leaping to conclusions, the fact that we've been seeing this more frequently is an ominous indicator. In fact, a terribly grim one. Because at that altitude there's practically no water vapor. So you understand, right? Those very high clouds are only forming due to the elevated concentration of other garbage, filth like methane, especially. So, really, the increase in noctilucent clouds, magnificent though it may be to behold, is a direct metric for the level of global warming.

He leaned back in his chair, shaken by his own explanation. He plunged his fingers back into the peanut bowl, he set it aside and started to work on the olive bowl instead.

That's the insight that Ambrosini and I started from. More me than him, truth be told. He's still too young to be able to extrapolate as well as I can.

So you two are writing a book, I said.

It was the publisher who contacted us.

He sighed and suddenly seemed to relax.

The question of the book had put me into a bit of an uncomfortable position. I tried to dodge the issue by asking after Carolina.

Carolina is very busy. Very, very busy indeed.

Is she here in Paris?

Novelli shook his head: Genoa. Since the bridge collapsed, she's been in a frenzy of judicial activism. She's been gathering signatures, commissioning expert studies, and appearing on local television news shows. You'll remember that she studied law, as the saying goes, in her youth.

He kept shoving olives down his craw, so fast and furious that one went down the wrong way, causing him to cough for a few seconds.

So now I find out that I married my own Pasion-aria. Who'd have thought it? A crusading activist. She's convinced that she'll be able to dig up and enforce the truth. Too bad that she can't see that we live in a time where nobody cares about the truth anymore.

After a pause, he added: Of course, if in the meantime she could find a little more time for the children, that might be best for everyone.

In the end, his children had stayed with him in Paris, so his mother had moved there to help out. From certain stories he'd told me in the past, I'd gotten the idea that the two of them had a difficult relationship, but I hardly felt I had the right to ask him about it.

We went back to the topic of his book project, or actually he went back to the topic. They were planning a six-stage trip, including a stage in Patagonia, where they hoped to capture a few especially rare atmospheric formations. I felt a completely irrational surge of jealousy, and Novelli must have picked up on that, because for the first time he stopped looking down and raised his eyes, deliberately locking onto my gaze and holding it for a significant span of time.

What about you? he asked me. What have you done all this time in Paris?

I haven't actually been here all that much.

I heard you were at Claudia's cocktail party. The guy you talked to, with the ginger beard, he's a friend of mine.

The one who owns an investment fund?

He's financing our research for the book. He's doing it, so to speak, indirectly.

Indirectly how?

He wants us to find him a place where he can build a sort of... retreat. While we're looking for it, we can also do our research.

Is he a survivalist?

Let's just say that there are two or three aspects of the time we live in that he finds unsettling. And who's to blame him? He has plenty of money, so he'd just as soon be ready for it if it comes.

And he asked you to look into it for him.

Do you find that so surprising? I do still have four articles published in *Nature*.

He pointed it out with a hint of aggression, and I instinctively recoiled: No, it doesn't surprise me. But I thought you were opposed to that sort of thing.

Just then a young man on a scooter headed toward us. He was stylishly dressed, very similar to Novelli. Here he is now! Novelli exclaimed, getting to his feet.

There was no need for introductions, but he went ahead all the same: Matteo Ambrosini, my partner in crime.

The postdoc took a chair from the table next to us and sat down between me and Novelli. Novelli laid his hand on Ambrosini's shoulder and left it there. His mood had suddenly brightened. For a while the two of them started talking together in low voices about a project they'd left unfinished that afternoon. When the waiter came over for the next round of orders, Ambrosini glanced at us both, quizzically, and asked: Do you want to stay here a little longer, or should we go?

Novelli looked at his watch and said he'd rather go. Are you coming with us?

Where?

To Castel. We're going dancing.

I didn't think that place existed anymore, I said. But more than anything else, it was a way to express my amazement that Novelli, at midnight, was about to head to a dance club with his postdoc.

Oh, you'd better believe it exists.

On Saturday we danced until four in the morning, Ambrosini added. There was no stopping him.

I've been told that I have a sort of old-school way of dancing. I move my feet too much. Apparently, you're not supposed to move your feet anymore.

That's right, people these days don't move their feet when they dance, Ambrosini confirmed. But for Castel, it's fine.

Novelli grabbed him by the shoulders again and gave him a shake. He was emanating joy in all directions. Your wife abandons you and your children and you rediscover how much you love to dance, he said. Well, are you coming or aren't you?

THE NEXT DAY, I was on a plane, and a few weeks after that I was in an operating room at the Umberto I Hospital in Rome. The surgeon hadn't bothered to describe the operation to me in advance, he was only interested in knowing whether I'd rather be able to focus on distant things or things up close, and I—as if this meant something profound about me—said that I'd rather see things at a distance.

In any case, I'd studied up on the procedure on my own from the videos I found online, so I knew where he was going to make his incisions, which scalpels he was going to use, how he was going to remove my crystalline lens and insert the artificial lens in its place, folding it in half to get it to pass through an opening narrower than its diameter. All the same, while I was witnessing the operation from under the light-blue bandaging, I wasn't capable of reconstructing the various phases of it. I was awake but stunned by something they'd injected into my hand, and I had the strangest impression that they were operating on someone else, who was lying on top of me. At a certain point a song by Julio Iglesias started up, and the doctor begged them please to put on something else. I started to laugh, but he sternly told me to keep still.

After which I found myself in a room with four other patients, all male, all under observation. Three of them, as you might expect, were elderly, but the fourth one was young, very young: not even in his twenties yet. Both of us were bandaged, our backs against two walls that ran perpendicular to each other, and for a few seconds we talked together as best we could, our words slurred by the anesthetic.

Suddenly, in that dreamy period of waiting, a hand came to rest on the half of my face that was still intact. I recognized Lorenza's touch. In a whisper, she asked me if I was all right. I said that I was, yes, but very tired, and then she said: Rest, I'm right outside waiting for you. Then she kissed me very delicately on the forehead and vanished once again.

AT HOME, I could neither read nor write; even music was too intrusive. All I wanted to do was sit in the darkened bedroom. The pain arrived in waves and then ebbed away. Lorenza, too, came into the bedroom intermittently, but toward evening she lay down next to me, taking a break from her day. She was tapping rapidly on her phone, while I rolled the locks of her hair around my forefinger. This would have been the perfect opportunity to talk about us, but instead we found ourselves talking about others.

I told her about the evening I went out with Novelli, how we had nothing meaningful to say to each other, and how he managed to drag me out to Castel. That place still exists? Lorenza asked. That's exactly what I said at the time.

Novelli and Ambrosini had made friends with some girls, just for the hell of it. Well after three in the morning, Ambrosini wanted to leave and so did I, but Novelli wanted to stay. So there we were, me and the postdoc, walking all alone through the streets of Paris, deserted the way they had been during the time of the terrorist attacks. We'd pissed in the Saint-Sulpice fountain because, considering our urgent need, it had seemed like the most respectful way to deal with the situation, and then and there, while we were peeing, I'd worked up the nerve to ask him what the hell they were both thinking when they decided to put together that study on gender equality and present it at a conference. Ambrosini swore that it was Novelli who'd dragged him into it. It was just supposed to be a game at first. What kind of a game was that? I'd asked. Anyway, the last thing he expected was for Novelli to actually present the results. Novelli hadn't clawed Ambrosini away from Caltech. Hell, Caltech had practically kicked him out. Of course, he'd been angry at Novelli, who wouldn't have been? But it was water under the bridge. Novelli was still a luminary, a genius, whatever else people might think. And most of all, Novelli was a friend of his.

Neither of us could really walk straight, and as we staggered along, with the seemingly endless fence around the park on our left, I told him that being friends isn't enough in certain situations, and Ambrosini took that opportunity to drive the dagger into my heart: It really hurt Novelli's feelings when you abandoned him.

In the rest of that evening's excursion I had also discovered that the job search in Genoa had by no means been crafted for Novelli's benefit. If they had wanted him so badly, wouldn't they have just picked up the phone and called him? Ambrosini had pointed out to me, as if it were the most obvious thing in the world. They'd issued a standard call for applications because he wasn't the designated candidate, obviously enough. But Novelli had done his best to impose himself, with the sheer weight of his many credentials and titles, because he wanted to get back home to Genoa so badly. On account of Carolina, I had murmured. Yes, that's right, on account of Carolina, he had replied, and that was the moment when the two of us implicitly faced off as to which of us could claim the distinction of knowing the professor better. I'd said once again, How in the fuck did you two think it was a good idea to do that study? and then he'd headed one way and I'd headed the other.

I'm not surprised, Lorenza said after a moment's silence.

What in particular doesn't surprise you?

That Novelli has found a new audience.

Is that what you think? That I was an audience for him?

I'd talked too much, and though I'd talked slowly, I felt strangely exhausted now.

Do you remember that time in Sardinia, when he took me for a ride in the kayak?

Yes, and? I asked with a hint of terror.

Don't start churning up ridiculous ideas. But in a way it's even worse than that. When we got to the other side of the cliffs, he started asking me questions about your work. I was evasive, because it wasn't clear what he was driving at, until he finally asked me the question directly: *How much does he earn anyway?*

Lorenza bent her head back to look me in my un-bandaged eye: Sometimes you misjudge other people.

Tears were still seeping out abundantly beneath my bandage, and though the tearing was just a post-op re-action and had nothing to do with genuine weeping, for hours it kept me in a state of strong but latent emo-tion. Suddenly that weakness was transformed into something different, a sense of extreme vulnerability. Lorenza noticed it. What's wrong?

Nothing. I mean, I don't know.

She stood up to take a hard look at me from a dis-tance, then said: It's the anesthesia.

But it was only local!

Calm down and breathe. Do you want me to open the window?

No, the sunlight is too strong.

It's the anesthesia, Lorenza said again, but she was a little scared.

She knelt on the mattress and took my head in her hands with the special gentleness she was using with me in those hours. I told her that I was sorry, that I was so sorry, and that I was ashamed.

Ashamed of what?

The prematrimonial course, I said.

What about the prematrimonial course?

She didn't even remember it anymore, but I did, because I couldn't stop thinking about it: during the course Karol had asked us to do that exercise in which we were supposed to give up four of our five senses, and I'd been willing to give up my sense of sight.

Well?

Well, I made a mistake. It wasn't true, the answer I gave. Because I missed looking at her, being able to see her completely and continuously was something I really missed.

You're only going to have to keep the bandages on for twenty-four hours, you know. You haven't gone blind!

But that's not what I was talking about, I said, I was talking more generally, I was talking about the last year and even before that. I was ashamed of the time I wasted by myself, of the way I misunderstood other people, true enough, but also myself, because what I misunderstood was first and foremost myself and my desires. I hadn't understood the first thing about my desires, and that wasn't a normal thing at age forty, was it?

It's just the anesthesia, Lorenza said again, and I responded, No, the anesthesia has nothing to do with it, you have to listen to me. I was ashamed of the phone someone had stolen, that night in Barcelona and yet other nights, I was ashamed of Guadeloupe, especially of Guadeloupe, even if we'd never admitted it to each other.

At that point, she stood up and for a few seconds kept her back to me. We had old shutters and blinds on the windows, and even though they were shut tight, light still filtered in through the gaps and cracks. I thought Lorenza was about to leave me. I thought that this was the end.

Instead, she came around the bed and sat down on my side, right on a line with me. She leaned over me. Now her lips were almost touching my ears, and what she said after that she said in a whisper, even though we were alone at home: But I'm the one who took you there, don't you understand? It was me.

I tried to focus on her with my unbandaged eye, through the veil of saline secretions, without success. But why?

Because it was necessary. Only that we had to be far away, very far away, among people who knew nothing about us. We were together and I held your hand the whole time, you remember that, don't you?

Yes, but *why*?

To show you that with me beside you, you could let yourself go. And that afterward you'd still be alive, and in fact we'd both be alive. And truth be told, here we are, together. Now do you understand?

My head was starting to spin and I could feel the gauze, drenched, over my eyes. I was afraid it was going to come loose. I don't know, I said, maybe it really is the anesthesia.

Lorenza leaned in and spoke to me again, very close: You never need to be ashamed when you're with me. Never. Because there is nothing, absolutely nothing, that you are that can arouse my disapproval.

THE DOCTOR had told me that with the new lens I would see a festival of colors. That expression—a festival of colors—had struck me as a bit much, but it turned out to be quite accurate: once the bandages had been removed, the apartment looked gaudier than ever. Especially the living room credenza (which had been sold to us as an antique, though it was very possibly a piece of fraud): it was an extraordinarily vivid purple hue. I wondered if this was how Lorenza and Eugenio and everybody else had always seen the world, or whether credit really was due to the artificial lens. In any case, I hoped that this exciting sense of novelty would last for a long time.

On my third day of convalescence, Karol came to see me. I went downstairs to meet him on the street. Before leaning in for the hug, I took a few seconds to

observe him: Either they've implanted a trick lens in
my eye, I finally told him, or you have really bulked up.

I've been working out some, lifting weights, he
admitted.

And how are people taking that at church?

He distractedly brushed his hand over his abs:
Everybody likes a fit priest.

We went for a walk through the neighborhood. I
was being cautious to a fault, but he tolerated that. He
asked me how my vision was working, and I replied: A
little watery, a little glittery. Otherwise fine.

The last time we'd seen each other had been on the
Palm Sunday of the year before, but we'd been in touch
by phone and at least up to a certain point, I had also
been keeping tabs on the latest developments of his love
story.

In October, Karol showed up without any advance
warning in Padua, at Elisa's doorstep, with the very
serious intention of moving in with her. Elisa didn't
know her new roommates very well, because classes
in her master's program had just begun. So the priest's
arrival—Karol hadn't understood the potential dip-
lomatic benefit of leaving that detail unstated—had
thrown the apartment into some confusion. He had
called me up to ask my advice about the rather chilly
welcome Elisa had given him, at least in his opinion.
I'd told him to get out of there immediately, find an
Airbnb or whatever else he could think of. He paid no
mind to my advice.

He'd stayed at Elisa's for three days and three nights, in what must have been a crescendo of exasperation, and was in any case certainly a crescendo of phone calls to me: first Elisa begged him to leave, then told him she wanted to break up with him, then told him in no uncertain terms never to come looking for her again. Finally, she'd gone so far as to tell him that his presence there was a source of embarrassment.

Karol had returned to Rome, but that didn't stop him from pestering us both. His obstinate persistence had started to wear on me. After all, I was in some godforsaken place, in a room of some random hotel, where the echo of his suffering only reached me in a muffled form. My comments grew increasingly riddled with a cold and heartless logic, until I stopped answering and he stopped calling.

I apologized now, months later, and Karol forgave me instantly with an almost imperceptible shrug. I came very close to going over the edge, he said, practically a breakdown, but I'll only tell you about it if you're interested. I don't want to tire you.

Of course I'm interested.

When I went back to Padua, I wasn't really myself.

This is what I remember.

I could feel myself suffocating. And when I say suffocating, I mean that literally, even though I was breathing. I kept telling myself, Wait and see, it'll be better tomorrow. But then each morning I'd wake up and things would be worse. It never seemed to end. The

Passion of Christ may have been horrible, but at least it only lasted three days. Mine went on for months.

He made that comparison without a hint of irony, as if he considered it perfectly fair, and I said nothing: after all, this was his field of expertise.

I saw doctors, but there seemed to be nothing wrong with me. The doctor told me that it was an ordinary shortness of breath. Shortness of breath: it makes it sound so ridiculous. He told me to start taking tranquilizers, but you know how I feel about medicine. Then one day I saw a picture of Elisa on social media, and she was with a young man. There was nothing compromising about it, actually, but something snapped inside me. I had various appointments, but I simply ignored them. I caught a train back to Padua. By the time I reached her apartment house it was already evening. I hadn't told her I was coming. Still, before ringing the doorbell I looked up for a moment at her floor. The lights were on and one of her roommates walked past the window. She let out a shout, not of fear but of joy, like a *woo-hoo!* It seemed like a very carefree evening was underway. I realized then and there that I had to listen to that sound as a warning bell. I couldn't just walk into that carefree joy and ruin it all. I needed to stop.

We'd reached the front steps of Santa Maria Maggiore and Karol hesitated as he pondered which direction to go. It didn't really matter. We were just walking for the sake of it.

I just wandered around Padua all night long, he continued, because there were no trains back. In the square outside the train station I met a young man from Colombia named Winston. We struck up a conversation. In the summer, he worked on the lakefront beaches and put aside as much money as he could, but then the rest of the year, he lived on the street. He did ink drawings, not especially sophisticated ones but not bad either, figures of women, and he managed to sell a few here and there. I bought one from him. The way he lived was his own free choice, one hundred percent. And that encounter reminded me of myself, at the start of my calling. I decided that what I should try to do is regain that missionary spirit, go back to the idea of a pilgrimage and a vow of poverty. When I got back to Rome, I reread all of Saint Francis and, I swear to you, I came that close to reaching out to Winston and becoming a homeless person with him. *That* close.

But you changed your mind?

Karol gesticulated, miming a general dispersion with both hands: Nothing happened. You know how these things are.

Do you still talk to her?

To Elisa? Not as often as I'd like. But we write almost every day. She's changed. Studying biology has made her, and here he paused, as he tried to choose the best expression, very rational. I try to fight against that tendency in her. I'm convincing her to devote more of her time to poetry, and to provide her with inspiration I send her songs. Just look.

He showed me the screen of his phone and scrolled down with his finger: a miles-long playlist. Though I wasn't close enough to read the titles, I recognized the album covers. I had listened to many of them during my endless treks through Paris. That was no coincidence: when I gave Karol my iPhone, I'd left my Spotify subscription active, so his library was synced with mine.

In fact, if you have any suggestions, he said. The last few things you added were awful. Especially this one.

Aphex Twin?

I tried listening to it over and over, but I don't get it. It just sounds like noise to me. I'll admit, I started worrying about you.

I deliberately ignored that reference to his worries. I said: Well, I'm glad you're better now.

Karol stopped. He scratched his chin with the edge of his iPhone, distractedly. I'm not sure I would describe it as getting better. Because I was never sick. Aside from being short of breath.

Maybe I misspoke.

It would be very ungracious toward Elisa.

All I was trying to say is that I'm happy you got over her. It wasn't a particularly good match, the two of you.

At the point, he grabbed my forearm and forced me to look him in the eye. Elisa and I are in love.

He had a different expression now, as if he'd suddenly recognized where the misunderstanding lay between us. I cautiously freed myself from that grip, while searching for the right words to say: I thought I'd heard that she was seeing a guy. That she'd got back together with that ex-boyfriend of hers. You told me so, on the phone.

Karol said nothing for a few seconds as he stared down the street, both hands stuck in his pockets again. Then he spoke, his voice very calm: He doesn't matter. Our union belongs to a different category. But I know that's not easy to understand.

Suddenly I couldn't tell whether he was frighteningly fragile or, quite the contrary, solid as never before.

Elisa needs to be a girl her age, to experience what that means, and he forms part of that passage. But the two of us transcend time, so waiting has no importance. The outcome of our path won't change.

And the outcome will involve the two of you together?

Karol shot me a glance of faint astonishment. Of course.

After another moment of rapt focus, he suggested we call her. Now? Well, at least that way you can say hello to her. It'll make her happy. He started FaceTime and we both looked at the display.

Elisa didn't answer. She must be at class, Karol said, dismissively. Anyway, she's supposed to come visit next month. Maybe we can all go back to that restaurant where we ate last time, all four of us, Lorenza too.

The fact that Elisa hadn't answered left us with a sense of incompleteness that we dragged along behind us for the next few minutes, as we walked down Via Cavour. I looked at his back and said, You really are lifting a lot of iron.

I can bench-press 290 pounds.

That seems like an enormous weight.

You have to build up to it.

I walked him to the metro stop. A question had been spinning in my head for some time now. I asked him if he minded my asking a very personal question, but then I changed my mind. Maybe it's just too personal.

Karol urged me to go on with a gesture. So I asked him whether his own personal Passion—and I used the word nonironically, only because he'd done it before me—whether, after everything he'd been through with Elisa, he still believed in God.

There wasn't a second's hesitation in his response: For me, God has no importance. But Jesus does. In fact, it was only after I stopped worrying about God that I truly began to believe in Christ. To understand Christ. Body and blood. Those are words I repeated for years, without any right to speak them. But now I know exactly what they mean.

CLIMATIC INDICATORS confirmed that 2019 had been, on average, the second-hottest year in the past two millennia. Not in the last two decades or centuries: in the past two millennia. That summer eighty-four weather stations scattered across Europe had recorded the absolute highest temperature ever, the thawing season began a month earlier than normal in Greenland, and the *acqua alta* in Venice had hit the highest watermark in the last half century. In its usual unruffled tone, the IPCC's report presented a problematic situation for the entire terrestrial cryosphere, which wasn't limited to the polar ice caps, but extended to all glaciers and permafrost as well. At this rate, it was reasonable to expect a sea level rise of at least fifty centimeters by 2100, and to see it continue for centuries.

Of course, global warming wasn't the only issue: a whale had been found dead on a beach in the Davao Gulf, in the Philippines, with a hundred kilograms of plastic in its belly; the line to take selfies at the summit of Mount Everest had caused the deaths of two mountaineers, and Yemen had been swept by an unprecedented plague of locusts. The mechanism responsible for that insect invasion was emblematic: exceptionally heavy rains (probably due in their turn to climate change) had created a proliferation of locust eggs in areas that were otherwise arid deserts, and the new locusts had developed anomalous characteristics—they were larger, stronger, and capable of flying longer distances—and as they gathered in monstrous swarms, they had laid vast numbers of eggs, triggering further exponential growth in their numbers.

Many believed that at this point, the only thing left was to flee. Therefore, Elon Musk had proposed setting off nuclear warheads at the poles of Mars, unleashing a chain reaction that would (maybe) equip the planet with a virgin atmosphere. On certain social media, especially Twitter, the idea was given serious discussion. But the pictures of Mars sent back to Earth by the rover *Curiosity* weren't encouraging: there was nothing to be seen but a dusty and monotonous surface, aggressively inhospitable. We were going to remain on the same planet for the foreseeable future, and we'd keep doing the same things we'd always done. After all, the reports of cataclysms that kept pouring in did little or nothing to change the way we lived, or at least they didn't change the way I lived and the people I knew lived. If anything, we just dully expected that next year was going to be worse, and the year after that worse still, and so on. If I think back now to the end of 2019, I remember a weary sense of inevitability, as if disillusionment had fully impregnated the cerebral tissues of everyone on earth.

FOR THE ENTIRE MONTH of December, the highs in Rome were well above fifty degrees. Even on the last day of the year, the temperature was mild, an anomaly that no one, not even I, dared complain about. Lorenza and I were looking for new people to spend time with, without baggage or history, lightheartedly. We asked our upstairs neighbors down to dinner: a couple who had just moved in.

After showing them our place and painstakingly comparing the floor plans (almost identical), we got seated in the living room and found we had nothing left to say. Whether he was serious or just kidding around, the man, who was an engineer, took an interest in our record player: he wanted to know if I was a vinyl collector. Actually, I'm not, I replied. But did I use it? I explained that I'd bought it on a whim, but it always had a hum, so it was just a piece of useless furniture now. He really wanted to hear that hum. In order to avoid seeming rude, I went over and leaned under the cabinet to connect the cables. We need to dismantle it, he announced. Now? Why not?

So we spent most of the evening like that, with our neighbor cross-legged on the floor, watching YouTube tutorials. At first, Lorenza had been opposed to the idea of moving our dinner into the living room, balancing our plates on our knees, but in the end she'd given in. Our neighbor cleaned every component, lubricated the whole mechanism, and then reassembled the record player perfectly. Though no one really cared, when he lowered the needle onto the LP, we were all filled with anticipation, despite ourselves. The song started up, but the hum was still there, exactly like before.

Midnight rolled around, and it came as a relief to us all. Most likely, from the next day on it was going to be embarrassing to run into our neighbors on the stairs, but for the moment we didn't much care.

When they left, Lorenza and I raised a glass once again to the newly dawned 2020, this time with greater intimacy. Then we drifted apart for a while, each of us on our phone, tapping out Happy New Year wishes. I'd already felt a strange sense of melancholy wash over me during dinner, as I thought about Giulio, Karol, and even Novelli. I felt as if I had some kind of debt with each of them, though it was hard to pin it down. All of them wrote back, with Happy New Years of their own.

Around 6:00 a.m., a phone call from Eugenio awakened us. He was on his way home and he knew what time it was, but I needed to go meet him immediately, and no, nothing bad had happened to him. I'll wait for you at the beginning of the Via Nazionale.

I put on a tracksuit and my heavy jacket and headed out.

You couldn't miss them, he told me when we met in the street. He pointed down at the pavement. The entire length of the Via Nazionale was scattered with dead doves. I'd already noticed a few here and there on my way to meet him, but on the Via Nazionale in particular, there were hundreds of them, possibly thousands.

What happened to them?

It was the fireworks. At least, that's my best guess.

But why? Eugenio persisted.

Because it's New Year's Eve.

Then they should be against the law!

Tears were welling up in his eyes. I tried to minimize: Given all the endangered species there are in this world, I wouldn't worry too much for the pigeons of Rome. Quite the opposite.

Eugenio glared at me with all the childish indignation he could muster.

Okay, okay. Sorry! I protested.

We headed off, downhill. We walked alone through that small-scale hecatomb of bird corpses, taking care not to tread on the tiny dead. I could have interpreted that moment as a bellwether to something, but I don't think I did, I most probably didn't, and to describe it as such now would be pretty meaningless.

Well, was it a nice party, at least?

Eh, it was so-so.

Did you have a lot to drink?

Normal amount.

In spite of himself, he'd already gotten used to the sight of dead doves, though he'd never have admitted it. In the next couple of hours, the street cleaners would eliminate all traces of what had happened, and he'd never give it another thought.

I know that this isn't very sensitive on my part, I ventured, but at this point we might as well grab some breakfast.

He considered what must have struck him as a gross breach of tact, then asked: Where?

Well, you're the night owl.

He took a look around. That way, he pointed. But we'd have to go all the way to San Lorenzo. You up for it?

I followed him as he reversed course toward the station, telling him as we walked just how unexciting Lorenza's and my night in had been. His jacket was open, and underneath he wore a T-shirt, but I managed to keep myself from telling him to zip up to keep warm. I couldn't quite say what we looked like at that moment, two brothers born a great number of years apart, two odd friends, or parent and child. To all intents and purposes, though, it looked like we were both coming home from the same night out.

Do you really want to go through the tunnel?

It's a shortcut. Why, does it scare you?

Not in the slightest.

Actually, though, it did scare me a little. I said: Well, I'd rather you not go through there alone. He magnanimously allowed that piece of advice, years out of date, to drop.

When he was a child, I had really wished Eugenio would develop a passionate love of camping and chess, because that would make it so much easier to spend time with him. But as it turned out, he showed no inclination for either activity. Then I hoped he'd take an interest in mathematics, but he lacked the gift. For a long time, I'd believed that those differences were the chief obstacle to our relationship, along with the fact that we shared no genes. One day, a few years earlier, I had quizzed him on the "notable products," because the next day he was going to be tested in math class. I listened as he declaimed, head pressed against the window: a plus b squared equals a squared plus b squared plus 2 ab, a plus b cubed equals... When he got something wrong, I'd correct him, in a whisper to keep from bothering the other passengers, and he'd seem mortified, though I couldn't understand why.

Do you remember the formula for squaring a binomial? I asked him.

He barely turned in my direction: Of course I do. But what makes you think of that now?

I don't know. It just occurred to me, that's all.

You're nuts.

When we got to San Lorenzo he headed for a pizzeria. We each ordered a slice, and then a second round of the same, while idly running through our resolutions for the new year. Eugenio was taking it more seriously than I'd expected. To keep from disappointing him, I tried to come up with a couple of resolutions of my own. When he realized that my heart wasn't really in it, he asked what I was thinking about. I responded: Nothing, I'm listening to you.

If for once, entirely hypothetically, I had been sincere and straightforward with him, I'd have told him that I was thinking about the notable products. I was thinking about that time on the train, and not just that time: also all the bowls of pasta I'd cooked for him, all the times I'd waited in the car outside of a party, all the forms I'd filled out, and the pointless advice and warnings I'd proffered, and the humidifier with the shimmering light display that he always had going in the corner of his bedroom as a child, and now I had no idea what had become of it. And I was thinking that all those things, as well as the unscheduled slices of pizza that we were eating for breakfast on January first, 2020, *all* those things put together—I wasn't sure of it, I was just considering it now for the first time—maybe they added up to fatherhood.

GIULIO WAS SENDING me pictures from Kruger National Park. He only had internet access from base camp, so we always exchanged messages at the same time of day, after dinner. The pictures that he sent me were so perfect in terms of lighting and subject that they seemed copied and pasted from the *National Geographic* website. Giraffes, hippopotamuses surfacing, a couple of jackals around a zebra carcass, antelopes on the run, magnificent sunsets.

Sometimes they were film clips caught at night by an infrared camera trap: a leopard would cross the frame, solitary and hypnotic, and its white eyes would light up for a moment as it glanced, unsuspecting, into the lens.

There's something different here, he wrote me. It's a deep feeling of belonging. The animals recognize you, and you recognize them. We've lived together for millennia, we've eaten each other. But now we only allow ourselves to be eaten by lawyers and psychologists.

Or perhaps he'd spent the hours before our exchanges following a honeyguide, the bird that leads human beings to beehives. It summons you, he said, barely able to contain his enthusiasm and attaching a voice message with the bird's strange call. Once you've walked toward it, the honeyguide moves to another tree and summons you there. Step by step, it leads you to the honey. We must have signed some sort of ancestral contract, Giulio wrote me, but we humans have forgotten about it.

So when all was said and done, was the honey really there?

Of course it was.

But even Kruger National Park, he explained immediately afterward, was an illusion: the illusion that human beings could form part of the ecosystem just like all the other species, that nature there was nature in its primordial state. Not so, not at all. Parks were carefully regulated systems, managed invisibly by humans for other humans: every so often fires would be set to beat down the vegetation and ensure sight lines on the animals for paying tourists, the lion population was kept under control with the introduction of new male specimens (who would quickly devour the cubs of other males), while in some wildlife reserves the elephants were subjected to forms of contraception.

In other words, there was just no escape from anthropization. Giulio used that exact word, *anthrop-*

ization, but it struck me that he was referring to something much larger than the national park: there was no escaping human beings, there was no salvation from the all-devouring present.

He'd tell me about his training. He was learning to track animals and calibrate his reactions in case of threat. On the savanna, almost anything that instinct prompted you to do turned out to be the wrong thing. For instance, when confronted with a lion, instinct told you to take to your heels and get out of there as fast as you could. But running away would never work, because showing weakness would make the lion attack. So what do you do? I asked. So you need to negotiate. But what if the negotiations don't turn out as you expect? Then you need to scream as loud as you can.

It works more or less like this: the lion charges, a face charge, just for show, and you have to be cool and collected enough to stand your ground and rise to the same level of aggressiveness yelling at the lion or banging on your rifle. If you're sufficiently convincing, the lion will stop and retreat. In that case, you can take a step back yourself. Then it all starts over again: another fake charge, then you yell back, the lion gives ground, and you make another yard or so of distance away. It can go on for hours.

It seems very metaphorical, I wrote back.

Metaphorical how?

But I decided to forgo any further exploration of the matter. Perhaps it really made no sense to start seeing metaphors everywhere.

In a burst of fantasy, I imagined Giulio with his new colleagues, all aspiring park rangers, as they practiced shouting. I pictured them at the outskirts of their encampment, standing and roaring with all the breath in their bodies into the emptiness of the veld. It must have been the exact type of liberation he'd gone there in search of, or at least I hoped it was: for his sake.

PART THREE

RADIATION

WE'RE SITTING ON THE RIM of a stone tank, Giulio and I, stark naked because that's what regulations require, and look out at the city. The background of an Asahi sign assembles and disassembles rhythmically atop a skyscraper, creating the only movement in the cityscape, along with the car traffic, far, far below. Otherwise: buildings on a color scale of grays and browns, the hills, the cloudy sky. As the crow flies, Little Boy's hypocenter was about a kilometer away, which means that here we are well within the radius of total destruction. On that August sixth of seventy-seven years ago, the portion of Hiroshima that we can survey from here was transformed in a split second into a flat blaze of rubble. And with the exception of the hills, none of what we're now looking at existed at the time.

It was only after we arrived that we discovered that the hotel had a communal bath on the fourteenth floor. The young woman at the reception desk asked shyly whether we had tattoos to show off, pointing on an illustration at the arms, legs, and finally genitalia of a male figure: No? In that case, the bath was at our disposal. Aside from washing stations, the bath area included two hot-water tubs, a very intense sauna, and an ice-water pool in which to enjoy a salubrious thermal shock. In normal times, the place was probably full of tourists, some of them Europeans, but not this year: with us there was only a blind Japanese man, who moved with unexpected agility between the baths and the dressing room, feeling his way with a cane. On account of the health risk, Japan was still closed to visitors, unless it was for urgent work purposes, like ours. That is, if you could consider "urgent" the vague curiosity of wanting to witness historical commemorations and the need, even more evanescent, to close a circle of understanding that was opened many years ago and still remained incomplete. To the German passenger whom we met on the flight, and who sells Japanese farmers chicken-slaughtering machines, Giulio replied unhesitatingly: No, we're here for the bombs.

Getting here was exhausting. Not just because of the physical travel—Russian airspace is closed, or in any case Air France had decided to avoid it: there are missiles being launched constantly down below there, so you could never know. Instead, we veered south, flying over Georgia, Kazakhstan, and the Gobi Desert—but also because of all the months of preparation prior to departure: procuring the visa, begging for letters of invitation, the repeated and categorical rejections of my requests to take part in the ceremonies in Hiroshima and Nagasaki. And all that after having postponed the journey a year earlier, in the summer of 2020, and then again in 2021. In any case, here we were, Giulio and I, looking out at Hiroshima as we sat dripping at the edge of the tank. We hadn't seen each other in quite some time, the tuft of chest hair just above his sternum had turned white, a change that hardly bothers me because the same thing has happened to me. We sit in silence until I finally ask: All right, then, are you ready? Shall we go?

Roughly an hour later we emerge from a pedestrian underpass and find ourselves gazing up at the Genbaku Dome, the only structure that remained standing at ground zero after the atomic bomb blast. The shock wave hit it at a perpendicular angle, which at least partly spared its walls and its steel dome. Both Giulio and I had seen the A-Bomb Dome countless times, in books and on television, but that did nothing to lessen its solemn majesty. We walk around the ruins a couple of times, studying the building. There's someone jogging along the river, so accustomed to the presence of that monument that they don't even bother to give it a glance. The trees in the park are full of cicadas that chirp at a higher frequency than the ones back home, or at least so it seems to me (and Giulio has the same impression). From photographs, I've always had a

different idea of the dome, a sense of austerity and des-
olation, but it actually stands in a setting of tranquility,
right in the city's heart. I look up: the sky is clear now,
save for a few low clouds, lemon yellow in the direction
of the setting sun. I have no reliable way of estimating
an altitude of 600 meters (roughly 2,000 feet), but I'd
bet that on a clear day like this I'd be able to make out
the elongated shape of Little Boy as it falls, just a second
before the flash. Giulio guesses my thoughts, and with
a simplicity that's wholly uncommon for him, says: In
any case, what they did was sheer madness.

We take a few pictures, or really, he takes them.
Somewhat surreptitiously, we've managed to get Giulio
invited to Japan with the qualification of news photographer. Giulio thinks of himself as a dilettante and
is ashamed of the equipment that he owns, but deep
down he's taking his job seriously. In the dark, though,
he has to stop taking pictures, so we decide to go find a
place to eat. I insist on going to a place recommended
by our guidebook, but he's terrified of winding up in a
tourist trap, behaving like any ordinary traveler, as if
such a thing might consign him to eternal hellfire and
damnation. Can't you see that we're the only visitors
here? I retort. We're the only foreigners in all of Japan!

He takes my point. In the end he is satisfied by the
roasted spits of heart and chicken skin, and the setting
seems reasonably authentic. As we eat, we first talk
about an article that he pointed out to me a few days before we left. The piece advocated eliminating once and
for all our taboos against discussing the extinction of

the human race. We should have the courage to discuss that possibility openly, because it's a perfectly plausible scenario, given the development of the climate. To take extinction into consideration, scientists say (and Giulio agrees), would have the positive effect of upsetting people and forcing them to act, as was the case with all the talk about nuclear winter in the 1980s, talk that led to bilateral disarmament.

And do you seriously believe it? I ask.

Giulio seems caught off guard: Why, don't you?

No, I mean, do you seriously believe that, when brought face-to-face with the possibility of our extinction as a species, we'd actually change our behavior?

His face darkens momentarily, as if I'd forced him to confront some gross naïveté on his part. Then he regains his confidence and begins to wax rhetorical about how each of us should become activists immediately instead of abandoning ourselves to defeatism. He tells me of studies he's read about volcanic islands newly risen from the sea, and how quickly they are populated with plants—first pioneer species, which don't need much to live, then plants that batten down the substrate. In short, he talks to me about rebirth, in scientific terms, admittedly, the only way he feels comfortable discussing it, but rebirth nonetheless. I listen to him the whole way through. Then I point out to him that he has a far more solid structure of hope than anything I can bring to bear, because he studies, evaluates, and acts, while I just let myself go, and that's all. That's what I've done ever since university. I don't know why I've chosen that expression, "structure of hope," it hardly even seems that precise, but Giulio grasps it instantly. I have a son, he replies, once again disarmed. What else am I supposed to do?

We get back into the communal bath on the fourteenth floor to look out at the brightly lit city. Later, in our room, we don the hotel pajamas—they make us look like twins. Giulio stays awake much later than me. His phone calls with Adriano are scheduled by the judge's order at specific moments of the week, and though the time difference makes them fall in the middle of the night, there can be no variations. He does not intend to miss even one.

On August sixth, we awaken early. Registration for the ceremony is expected no later than seven, and the ceremony itself begins shortly thereafter, to coincide with the time of the explosion, at eight fifteen. We are directed toward separate areas, me among the international audience (extremely limited), and Giulio with the photographers. At the opening of the ceremony, the public is asked not to sing the Hiroshima Peace Song in an attempt to restrict the spread of the virus. That aside, at least judging from the way the ceremony unfolds, I imagine that the sequence of events repeats itself unchanged every year: there is an offering of water for the victims of the bomb, because on the day of the *pikadon* the burned citizens were pleading for it; there is an offering of flowers and the singing of hymns with heartbreaking lyrics; the Japanese prime minister delivers an address, followed by the governor of the Hiroshima prefecture and the secretary of the United Nations, and for the prayer we all stand and listen to the chiming of a bell; doves are freed. In general, though, the ceremony leaves me cold. It's all too carefully studied and composed, or maybe it's the interpreter speaking English in my earphones, which keeps me separate instead of drawing me in. Giulio is waiting for me at the exit. They wouldn't let me take a single photograph, he complains. Why not? I don't know, he replies grimly. I haven't the slightest idea.

It's just past nine o'clock, and we have a lot of time to kill, the rest of the day: an expanse that lies before us somewhat menacingly. That evening, also here at ground zero, there is going to be a lantern ceremony, which promises to be more moving than the one that just ended, but we've already checked out of our hotel, and so we're forced to wander for hours in the overheated city, without a comfortable refuge. We decide to go see Miyajima, an island in the inland sea, even though it does instinctively promise to be a somewhat conventional destination. Did you notice? Giulio asks me during our ferryboat ride over. During the ceremony there was no mention of the Americans. Never once. They act as if the bomb came out of the clear blue sky, like some atmospheric catastrophe.

Or some divine punishment.

Or some divine punishment, that's right.

On Miyajima, we eat eel and some squishy green-tea desserts. We landed with a horde of Japanese tourists, but after lunch an unexpected rainstorm hits, emptying the island. That means that we have the Shinto temple all to ourselves in the pouring rain. Even after the rain stops, the sky still looks starkly dramatic. There is a very particular type of cloud, an enormous cumulonimbus that in Japan they call a *nyūdōgumo*, from *nyūdō*, "giant," and *kumo*, "cloud": it tends to form in this season, so much so that in some haiku it is used as a synonym for summer. I wonder whether that's the kind of cloud I'm now seeing lowering over terra firma. I briefly wish Novelli were here.

We head back to Hiroshima. It's almost sunset, and throngs are already lining the riverbanks and the bridges. Young women have come with portable fans that they hold up with great elegance before their faces and necks. Giulio and I sit down with our feet dangling over the stone embankment, the same embankment that features in so many survivors' stories. Gradually, as daylight wanes, the first paper lanterns are pushed out onto the water's surface, from moored boats and from the steps. Each paper lantern has a candle at its center and floats on little X-shaped wooden crosspieces. Even if the paper peels off or sags, the wooden crosspieces sail on, bare now, like moving targets. The lanterns are messages of peace, they're the souls of the dead traveling on into the afterlife, or perhaps they're simply a striking piece of choreography—I couldn't say. Still, they communicate something heartbreaking by the simple fact of being here, on this stretch of river, today. Giulio takes pictures furiously, railing angrily at his lens, which got sand in it at the Kruger National

Park, and at himself, for failing to have it cleaned. In fact, all of us are taking pictures, phones held high to improve the perspective. I send my better pictures to the group chat I have with Lorenza and Eugenio. In the meantime, the police have surrounded a man who is having some kind of breakdown, screaming at the top of his lungs as he crouches on the asphalt.

We arrive at Fukuoka station with the last train. It's very late, and I have the impression of having sweated uninterruptedly, so much so that it strikes me as a form of purification, but Giulio absolutely must and will try the local street food. And so, after dropping off our luggage, we drag ourselves down to the riverbank, another river in another prefecture. It's past two in the morning when we finally get to bed, mumbling goodnight because we both wear mouth guards to keep from grinding our teeth. When Giulio starts snoring, I put in my earbuds with the noise-canceling app and the emergency playlist: nature sounds designed to encourage sleep, waterfalls, gusts of falling rain, downpours. In those carpets of white noise I envision the flickering candles moving away into the dark, and now I have no doubt whatsoever that those are souls, the souls of the dead carried by the slow, slow, slow-moving current to the sea.

I REMEMBER that in August 2020 there was a debate about the fact that the current Japanese prime minister, Shinzo Abe, had repurposed the speech he'd given a few days earlier at Hiroshima for the ceremony commemorating the victims of the bomb at Nagasaki. According to an app designed to detect plagiarism, the two speeches showed a 93 percent match. One month ago, Shinzo Abe was assassinated during an election rally in Nara. The man who shot him twice at point-blank range, Tetsuya Yamagami, had fabricated a crude, handmade short-barreled pistol using rubber and duct tape. He knew how to do it, and in any case he fine-tuned it for a year and a half. Perhaps it was stupid of me, but before getting there, I expected to find Japan in a state of shock, with widespread grieving and a heightened state of alert. That was not the case. There was no trace of Shinzo Abe, or at least if there was any commemoration, I missed it. At the commemorative ceremony in Hiroshima, there was talk of Ukraine and even of climate change, but not a word about him. The only person I dared to ask directly, a woman in her early fifties, told me: Very sad, I cried. But that was it.

In Fukuoka, Giulio and I got up too late for breakfast, so we went out to a café where the menu had no illustrations. Luckily Giulio had installed an app on his phone that translated the Japanese characters into English when you focused on them with your camera. We use it to order, and later to translate the fortunes that we got yesterday at the temple on the island of Miyajima. Its translations of my fortunes are crude but comprehensible. One: *Correct your mind and happiness will come soon.* Two: *Marriage is difficult, but if we work together, later good.* Three: *Now flowers didn't bring fruit, but flowers are still ready.* Ready for what? I wonder. Whereas it's impossible to understand a thing about Giulio's fortune, except, at a certain point, the word bitterness.

At the Hakata train station, we rent a Toyota. By linking Giulio's phone to the onboard computer, I discover that it only has one song in its music library, "The Lion Sleeps Tonight." You only have one single, solitary song, I tell him in some disbelief. Oh, right, that's true, he replies. But why? I ask. Oh, because it's a pretty song.

For two days we drive almost without stopping, though Giulio is the driver while I serve as navigator. The interior of the island of Kyushu is verdant, pine forests cover the slopes, their tops all the same height. We spend long periods in silent contemplation, but the hours in the car and the distance from Europe also push us into brief, reciprocal confessions. Giulio asks me what things were like at first with Eugenio, even though what he really wants to ask me is why I should have chosen such a complicated situation when we were both so young. For a while we talk about blood relations and how important they are, in spite of everything. The instrumentation on the steering column is reversed with respect to mainland Europe, turn indicators where you'd expect windshield wipers, and so Giulio starts the wipers constantly, by accident.

In Yufuin we indulge in a walk to a lake that turns out to be something more like a muddy pond. Along the path we run into dragonflies with black wings and shimmering, colorful bodies. Giulio tells me that the shimmering hues are due to layers of chitin, though he's not a hundred percent sure of it. When I point out the color of the maple leaves, once again he provides me with a chemical explanation of that phenomenon. Giulio has answers for everything, as if he couldn't risk falling under the control of something without understanding it. If he has no answers, he fills the void with questions: he wants to know the meaning of the diamond shapes painted on the roadway, he wants to know what ponzu sauce is made from, he wants to know the species of birds we heard singing this morning and, if they really were swallows, where they migrate when it's winter in Japan. He wants to know everything about everything, while I want to know nothing about anything. You just have no curiosity, he says in an accusatory tone, and not an entirely friendly one. And with the same lack of empathy, I retort: No, I don't have much, not anymore. The truth is that neither of us is used to spending much time with another person: in my case, anyone who isn't Lorenza, and in Giulio's case, just anyone, period. Increasingly frequently, and alternately, we're overcome by sudden manifestations of intolerance and impatience, even though we do our best to repress them. What's more, I'm on edge. I'm expecting something from these days, but I'm not quite sure what. And what if I don't find it?

On the evening of the eighth, we arrive in Nagasaki later than expected. The hotel is set high on the slopes of Mount Konpira, and the room offers a stunning view of the port and the Hamamachi district. The road we followed to reach the hotel might be the same one that Tanaka-san walked up with his mother three days after the blast, amid corpses and rubble. In fact it almost certainly is. For a moment I'm seized by regret at having failed to arrange a meeting with him. I exchanged a few emails with the association that he runs, but I had the impression that Tanaka-san was very busy with the commemoration events. Our communications in English were exhausting and riddled with misunderstandings. All the same, at the airport I purchased a scented candle to take him as a gift, while Giulio made sure that candles in Japan have no ill-omened or even funereal subtexts. Now, though, seeing me lost in thought, Giulio insists for the umpteenth time: Why don't you write him?!

I don't know. Maybe tomorrow.

Tomorrow? Why wait until tomorrow?

He goes into the bathroom, muttering under his breath. He doesn't understand my reasons for being so reserved, and to tell the truth, neither do I.

Because the bomb was detonated over Nagasaki later than the one over Hiroshima, the start of the commemoration is scheduled for later too. That gives us time in the morning to walk through the Peace Park, where a black monolith marks the hypocenter of the blast, as well as to visit the adjoining museum. In the dimly lit halls, we see vitrines containing displays of materials transformed by the power of the atomic blast, as if in some religious monstrance: roof tiles dotted with blisters after the heat wave literally fried the stone, the shadows of a man and a ladder tattooed onto a wall, a roll of barbed wire melted into a doughnut, crumpled metal, tattered clothing—and of course bodies, one more piece of organic material among all the rest, faces smoothed by burns, eyes sealed shut, mouths melted. Toward the exit, there's a life-sized replica of Fat Man. It's yellow, a bright, vivid yellow, with the joints at the center painted red. I'd had no idea. I'd always assumed that the bomb was gray: can a bomb ever be anything but gray? Near the replica a film clip confirms the fact: a crew of American soldiers, all startlingly young and bare-chested, roll Fat Man out of a hangar, already painted that goofy yellow. They treat it carefully and deferentially, but without any sense of mystery, as if the bomb were some immense, invaluable toy.

After Hiroshima, I don't expect much from the commemoration, especially considering that the program is practically identical: once again, an offering of water and flowers, once again, appeals for peace and disarmament, once again, silent prayer and the release of the doves. I'm more focused on the heat, which is intolerable today, and how inappropriate my gym shoes are to the solemnity of the event. Here, in the front rows, where they've reserved a spot for me (though there was no way to get a ticket for Giulio), all the men are impeccably dressed in black tie. The woman sitting next to me, a journalist from Chicago who has lived in Japan for years, is also elegantly attired, in keeping with the setting. Her curiosity aroused, she asks me what I'm doing here. I explain, though I doubt that I'm very convincing. She informs me that in any normal year, there would be ten times as many people attending. I waylay the young man distributing small frozen wet towels and ask him for two more. Perhaps I shouldn't have. I drain a pint bottle of water at a single gulp because it's important to stay hydrated. Then, almost as a way to kill time, practically without thinking about it, I write to Tanaka-san's association to inform them of my seat number. It's late, of course, I realize, with our surgical masks and a virtual conversation from a long time ago, there is no real chance of recognizing him, so I've already given up on the idea. The email is just a way of keeping from feeling bad later, just so I can say I made a good-faith effort.

By now nearly everyone is seated. The sign language interpreter is rehearsing a text for the last time, sketching out gestures in midair. That's when I see him, just a moment before he sees me. He's wearing a black suit, a white shirt, and a tie, like everyone else, but there's a light-colored fisherman's cap on his head that gives him an affable appearance. Someone is telling him something on the phone, and I realize that he's looking for me. Then, when Terumi Tanaka reaches my seat, counting the rows as he goes, I'm already on my feet.

Paolo-san? he asks.

Yes, it's me.

I don't know why, but when I shake hands with him, I'm deeply moved. I can barely choke back my tears. We have no way to communicate, I should ask the American woman who's watching the scene over my shoulder, but that would be an intrusion upon this moment, so all I do is say over and over to Tanaka-san: Thank you, thank you. He bows his head and smiles, emanating an extreme courtesy. So I reach down and pick up my backpack from the floor, rummage around inside of it, and pull out the gift I brought him, which suddenly seems insufficient, with the duty-free logo stamped on the bag. I hand it to him all the same, with both hands, as I've been told is the courteous way here. I'd at least like a picture of the two of us together, but the ceremony is about to begin. A young staff member urges Tanaka-san to go to his assigned seat.

It's on account of that meeting, I believe, that every detail of the Nagasaki ceremony takes on a deeper meaning, even though there's not even a translation of what's being said. The graceful choreography, with its simultaneous bows and geometric symmetries, the offerings of water and flowers, the choruses and the doves set free—and today it strikes me that there are more of them, far, far more of them. From time to time I spot Tanaka-san a few rows ahead of me. I wonder what he sees, whether it's just a sequence that he knows by heart and from which he is easily distracted, or whether he still envisions before his eyes, as if in some transparent overlay, the minute preceding the blast, himself as a child in the second-story room, moving lazily between bed and window. It's 10:58 a.m., there's just four minutes to go, and I have a lump in my throat that shows no sign of disappearing. I formulate a thought that I jot down on my phone exactly as I think of it and that I'll transcribe here: If it's possible to weep over the destiny of all humankind in the story of a single child, that's what's happened here to me with his story.

One minute before the recurrence of the *pikadon*, we rise for the prayer. Now the only sounds that can be heard are the pealing of the bells and the clicks of the photographers focusing on the *hibakusha*, the survivors: in a few more years, they will all be gone, and then everything will be different. Tanaka-san's face is inscrutable under his fisherman's cap. That's what 11:02 a.m. finds when it reaches us.

GIULIO STAYED at the Peace Park. He's experiencing the first symptoms of heat stroke. I'm sorry you had to wait, I tell him.

No, it was interesting. There was a sort of counterceremony here. Monks, groups of radical pacifists, antinuclear activists. It kind of reminded me of the years of the Social Forum.

Your line of activity, in other words.

Exactly.

We have an appointment with Tsukie Tagami, a second-generation survivor. I was put in touch with her by my Japanese translator, Ryosuke, and a few months ago I interviewed her on Zoom. Tsukie works as a financial consultant in Nagasaki, and both her parents are *hibakusha*. Even though they are still alive, her father has already had three tumors: one in his stomach, one in his large intestine, and one in his colon. As a girl,

Tsukie was very sickly. She attended school only with long periods of absence. In elementary school, two of her teachers were survivors, and one of them moved her head in a strange fashion, bobbing it continuously, as if her neck couldn't support the weight. One day, in first grade, Tsukie and the other children were cleaning the hallway when the other teacher started vomiting blood, and then she collapsed. Tsukie watched her die that day.

She spots us through the crowd (it's not that hard) and anxiously waves to us to follow her to the car. Moon, she says, by way of introduction. Call me Moon. Giulio and I get in the back seat, she slides behind the wheel. She's wearing black gloves that match her ceremonial outfit. The gloves cover her arms up to her elbows. Sitting next to her is a young man. Perhaps Tsukie brought him with her to help with her English, or perhaps they're just friends. In any case, he's very shy. We drive to another part of the city, to the science museum. Another thing I know is that Tsukie married a son of survivors, and that the two of them tried for a long time to have children, but one pregnancy turned out to be extrauterine, and at the end of the other the fetus was stillborn. As she once told her husband: In the end, the bomb still managed to get us, in a way. As she told me, What remains, after everything, is the radiation.

We eat tofu in various dishes, we eat pickled vegetables, we eat seaweed, and the conversation is hypersimplified on account of the language barrier. We are forced to select the questions and rephrase them repeatedly, when necessary. Why Moon? I ask her. I thought it was Tsukie. She holds up the pendant around her neck with a sickle moon and says, Tsukie, Moon: same. Then she reaches into her purse, finds a yellow flyer, and on the back draws a kanji:

$$月$$

Tsukie, she says again. Her father chose that name because she was born on the day of the moon landing.

The lunch lasts a long time, and later she is the one who chooses a question for me. Overcoming her reluctance to seem intrusive, she asks me why I want to write about the bomb over Nagasaki. I tell her that it is complicated to say in English, but that it's an idea that I've had for a long time. I look at Giulio, feeling guilty for some reason, and finally fall silent. Tsukie smiles at me sympathetically.

As she drives us to our hotel, she puts on a CD of bossa nova music. Giulio knows it and together they sing along in Portuguese, as we drive through the deserted city streets. Giulio and I want to get a little rest, but the futons are only laid out at night, so we both lie down directly on the tatami. He falls asleep almost immediately, like always, but I'm still filled with the emotions of that morning. I think back to my meeting with Tanaka-san and the words that Moon said to us: that what remains is the radiation. It seems true to me, because the dead themselves are radiation. The human body is formed of billions and billions of atoms, for the most part hydrogen, oxygen, and carbon, but there are also all sorts of others present in smaller concentrations: potassium, lithium, cesium, even uranium. Even once the bodies have been pulverized, the atoms continue to exist, and the unstable atoms continue to emit radiation: alpha, beta, and gamma rays, neutrinos that sail undisturbed through matter, toward outer space, for thousands and thousands of years. And so the dead are radiation, indeed, and at this exact instant, as I press my hands against the tatami, it almost seems as if I can feel it, the soft pulsation that emanates from the earth below me, the warmth released by the dead.

But, if that's true, I tell myself, could it be that the radiation itself conserves a memory of what it once was? A spectrum of emission that, if analyzed with the right instruments, would give back to us a consistent image of the person's form, and perhaps even their thoughts? Would it be what, in other contexts, we call a "soul"? And is it possible, then, that all our dead still exist in the form of radiation, all the dead of the past and all the dead of the present, Aunt Koto and Aunt Rui, Makoto and Christian, and that even now they are walking along these stretches of sidewalk, through them and through me?

Lying in bed as I am, I imagine a telescope being launched into orbit, a telescope capable of detecting from that great distance the radiation of the dead. The image of the Earth that such a telescope would give us would be very different from what we now know: no longer a dull planet but a sort of star, unleashing waves of light in all directions, the light of the atoms of those no longer with us. For an extended moment I try to imagine myself there, transformed into transparent radiation as I hurtle with all the other dead souls out beyond the limits of our solar system, among the shreds of comets in formation. I am so thrilled with that fantasy that I'm this close to waking Giulio up and telling him about it: The dead are radiation, did you ever think of that, had you ever *realized* it? But then I decide that it would be better to forget about it. I'll keep that notion for myself, in part because I know that he'd certainly have objections to raise concerning its scientific foundations.

Later, evening has fallen and we're drinking cold sake in a bar in Hamamachi, where a man who's missing many of his fingers is trying to interest us in getting some girls, though we don't understand that at first, not at least until Giulio's app translates the words he's been repeating endlessly: *Massage new wife.*

Finally, it's just the two of us, Giulio and me, in the car heading for Fukuoka. After that we take the train to Osaka. Once there, Giulio insists on tasting pufferfish sashimi. I say, No thanks. I'm too scared. I explain the mechanism of tetrodotoxin poisoning, the way that the internal organs are paralyzed, the timing and statistics on death. When I'm done, he announces: Sounds doable.

Later, we board the plane. It's an interminable flight, and later in the airport, we say goodbye without saying when we'll meet again. And it's at some point

on the trip back to Europe, on that tail of our trip together, that the answer occurs to me—simple, so very
simple—to Moon's question, the answer that I was unable to supply in the restaurant, not that many hours
ago: I write about anything that has made me cry.

ACKNOWLEDGMENTS

Many people and organizations contributed with their advice (in some cases, entirely unconsciously) to the composition of this book. I'd like to thank at least some of them here:

The *Corriere della Sera*, Barbara Stefanelli, Antonio Troiano, Venanzio Postiglione, Stefano Montefiori, Marco Castelnuovo, Scuola Internazionale Superiore di Studi Avanzati (SISSA, International School for Advanced Studies), "Franco Prattico" Master's in Science Communications, Nico Pitrelli, Andrea Gambassi, Roberto Trotta, Filippo Giorgi, Davide Crepaldi, Paolo Gambino;

Nihon Hidankyo (Japan Confederation of A- and H-Bomb Sufferers Organizations), Hayakawa Publishing Corporation, the City of Hiroshima, the City of Nagasaki, the *Asahi Shimbun*, Terumi Tanaka, Tsukie

Tagami, Keiko Ogura, and all the *hibakusha* whose testimonials can be found online, Ryosuke Iida;

Einaudi (too many to mention), MalaTesta Literary Agency;

Ludwig Monti, Giovanni Ricco, Francesca Pierantozzi and Eva Giannotti, Lorenzo Ceccotti, Laura Testaverde, Andrea Mosconi, Maurizio Blatto.

—P. G.